PRAISE FOR M.D. LAKE'S

cold
COMFORT

"A solid combination of high-tech crime and low-tech human nature. I'm eagerly looking forward to M.D. Lake's next novel."
Joan Hess, American Mystery Award-winning author of *Madness in Maggody*

"Oh, how I *love* Peggy O'Neill! . . . Great fun— Keep 'em coming!"
Barbara Paul, author of *In-Laws and Outlaws*

AND FOR THE PREVIOUS PEGGY O'NEILL MYSTERY

AMENDS for MURDER

"A dazzler . . . Lake has a way with language that's rarely matched and the protagonist is wonderful."
Drood Review of Books

"Lake gives us an intelligent, independent female sleuth who gets results . . . A welcome addition to the growing corps of female mystery solvers."
Macon Telegraph and News

Other Peggy O'Neill Mysteries by
M.D. Lake
from Avon Books

AMENDS FOR MURDER

cold COMFORT

M.D. LAKE

AVON BOOKS ◆ NEW YORK

AVON BOOKS
A division of
The Hearst Corporation
105 Madison Avenue
New York, New York 10016

Copyright © 1990 by J.A. Simpson
Published by arrangement with the author
Library of Congress Catalog Card Number: 90-93157
ISBN: 0-380-76032-0

First Avon Books Printing: November 1990

AVON TRADEMARK REG. U.S. PAT. OFF. AND IN OTHER COUNTRIES, MARCA REGISTRADA, HECHO EN U.S.A.

Printed in the U.S.A.

RA 10 9 8 7 6 5 4 3 2 1

This book is dedicated to Regan Metcalf, a campus cop. If she hadn't chosen such a nontraditional career, preferred the dog watch, and answered my questions, there woudn't be a Peggy O'Neill. Maybe someday—thanks to women like Regan—Peggy will make lieutenant too.

Acknowledgments

I'm grateful to Brad Johnson who, fueled by pizza and Mountain Dew, spent long hours helping make the computer stuff accurate, easy to understand, and almost fun.

Every author should be lucky enough to have an editor like Nancy Yost, who knows how to mix criticism with encouragement without diluting the strength of either.

One

It was 2 A.M., the first day of November, and winter had come early. We'd had half an inch of snow, not enough to hide the fall leaves, but enough to skitter and swirl down the streets in the wind. I was in a squad car, on a road that winds along the river below the New Campus, looking for signs of break-ins among the storehouses, lovers in cars and the men who prey on them, and suicides. So far, I'd surprised only an occasional rabbit bounding across the nightscape in my headlights.

The police radio crackled with muted messages not meant for me, a welcome kind of music in the loneliness of the car. It was snowing lightly, and I was relaxed and happy and at peace with the world. I liked my job.

"Car 2018, where are you?"

I told the dispatcher where I was and he told me to drive over to the Science Tower. "Somebody's caught a trespasser in an office on the fifteenth floor," he said. "I'll send a foot patrolman to back you up."

"Copy," I replied, because that's what we say when we mean we've understood the message. I don't know why. It took me two minutes to drive up from the river and cross the New Campus. The Science Tower, a tall, harsh building of granite and glass, is the only University building you can see from anywhere on either campus, and that's too bad.

I pulled up at the curb, told the dispatcher I'd arrived. As I got out of the car, the front door of the Tower burst open, and a man started running down the sloping lawn.

"Hold it!" I hollered and started running, too, but, since he apparently didn't see me and was coming almost straight at me, I didn't have far to go. We collided about halfway between the Tower and my car, and he sat down hard. Overbalancing, I tripped over one of his legs and fell on top of him.

There was some confusion. I scrambled to my feet, slapped snow off my uniform while keeping an eye on him, and then he got up.

I recognized him as a professor of Pharmacy named Jason Horn. He was a small man of about fifty, with a full head of white curly hair and a neatly trimmed beard to match. He wasn't wearing an outer coat.

"Let's go back inside," I told him. "You aren't dressed for this weather, Professor Horn."

"I'm in a hurry," he said, and started to walk away, as if he had a classroom of students waiting for him somewhere. While there are a few teachers on campus who might be able to attract students to a classroom at two in the morning, I knew Jason Horn wasn't among them.

I took his arm, turned him around, and led him back the way he'd come. He didn't put up a struggle. The front door was locked. I opened it with my passkey. Once inside, Horn shook off my hand, and neither of us said a word as the elevator took us up to the fifteenth floor.

Light spilled from a doorway down the hall and a man was standing in it. He was holding a paper towel to one side of his face. When he took it away to look at it, blood sprang from a cut on the side of his mouth.

He looked down at Jason Horn—he was a good head taller than Horn, and about twenty years younger—and said, "For such a little man, you pack quite a wallop."

I asked him who he was and he told me his name was Martin Reid and that it was he who'd called the police.

"I was in my office," he said. "It's down the hall, around the corner. I had to go to the men's room. As I passed this door—this is Lucas Calder's office, you know—I heard a noise inside. I thought it was Lucas, even though he never comes in this late anymore, and I was about to knock. But instead, I decided to try to see what was going on through that." He pointed to the grill in the door down by the floor. "At first I couldn't see anything, and then I saw a light moving around. So, not being a hero, I went back to my office, dialed 911 and then came back. A minute or two later, the door opened, and he came out. It must have scared the shit out of him, seeing me standing here. He tried to run around me, I grabbed him, and he took a swing at me. It caught me by surprise, knocked me down. You know the rest. He dropped his coat, too," he added, nodding in the direction of a trench coat lying just inside the door.

I watched him as he spoke. He was very attractive, and looked a little like my friend Al, except that Al was older and not as well-groomed. Reid's hair was dark brown and grizzled at the sides, but so expensively cut that I didn't think he'd appreciate the word "grizzled." "Graying" would be the word. Al's hair is grizzled.

"I thought you were attacking *me*!" Jason Horn protested. "You're right, I did panic. I'm sorry I hit you, but it was a mistake, a misunderstanding."

"Sure," Reid said, and smiled good-naturedly.

Horn turned to me. "I was just out walking. I wasn't able to sleep. I don't live very far from here. It was the first snow of the winter, you see, and I wanted to get out in it—you know, stick my tongue out and catch some snowflakes." He smiled at Reid and me. When neither of us responded, he went on, more awkwardly: "When I got to the Science Tower, I decided—just on an impulse—to come inside and get warm before walking back home, because it was colder than I thought it would be. The door wasn't locked."

He'd stood by the elevator, reading the list of faculty who had offices in that building, and saw Lucas Calder's name. "I was curious," he went on, "to see what the office of a man like Calder looked like, so I took the elevator to fifteen. He must have forgotten to close his door all the way—he's much too busy and important to remember details like that, I suppose—so I saw my chance, and took it. I was only in here a minute. When I came out and saw Professor Reid, I got scared and panicked. So you see, it's just a misunderstanding."

He was a lousy liar, but the material he had to work with wasn't worth much, either.

Reid said, "Lucas wouldn't leave his door open, and the building's always locked after ten o'clock. If you search him, I'll bet you'll find keys that don't belong to him."

I asked Horn if the trench coat on the floor was his. He said it was, started to pick it up, but I beat him to it. As I lifted it, a flashlight fell out of it, hitting the floor with a thud that was remarkably expressive. I picked it up, put it on Lucas Calder's desk, and started going through the pockets of the coat.

I expected Jason Horn to protest, but he didn't. I brought two keys on a cheap coil of wire out of one of the pockets.

"What's going on in here?"

We all turned, but even before I saw who was speaking I knew who it was: Lucas Calder's voice was as striking as he was, and as well-known. He was tall—well over six feet—and heavy in a solid kind of way, wearing a full-length fur coat that did nothing to diminish his size. His mane of black hair, streaked with white, made him look like a caricature of an orchestra conductor. I'd never seen him in person before, but I'd watched him on television a couple of times. He was famous for his talks on astronomy—time and space, the big bang, stuff like that—a born actor who loved to play exactly what he was: a distinguished scientist. He'd once made me feel that I understood black holes, and that they were relevant to my life, until I tried to share my newly acquired knowledge with a friend. I also owned a coffee-table book Calder had put together, in which he took the reader on a guided tour of the Milky Way—a gift from my Aunt Tess, who'd gotten it for joining a book club.

"As I told you on the phone, Lucas," Martin Reid was saying, "I found that man—he's Jason Horn—in your office. And the police officer's just found the keys he used to get in."

"What's your name?" Lucas Calder asked me.

Peggy O'Neill, I told him and he looked at my red hair

and gave me a little smile as if to say he'd registered that and might want to say something jocular about it when he had more time, and then he asked to see the keys and held out his hand.

I showed them to him, but didn't let him take them. "They look like copies of University keys," I said. "There are no serial numbers on them." I tossed them to Jesse Porter, the foot patrolman the dispatcher had sent to back me up, who'd come in with Calder, and he tried them in the lock.

"This one fits, Peggy," he said. "The other's probably the building key."

"You're Jason Horn, are you?" Calder said, turning to Horn, then added, almost without irony, "I don't think we've had the pleasure of meeting before, have we? How do you happen to have those keys?"

Horn obviously didn't know where to begin. He stammered, like a cat scrabbling for a foothold on ice, looking up at the big man, "This is all a terrible mistake. We don't need the police." It was a plea.

Calder laughed at that. "But they're already here. It seems they're Johnny-on-the-spot. And Jeannie." He turned to Reid and said, "And you, too, Marty. It was a good thing you were here to catch Professor Horn in the act."

"I came in to run a program on the Symore," Reid explained. A sudden thought seemed to occur to him. "That's it, isn't it?" he said, turning to Jason Horn. "That's why you broke in here! You were one of the people opposed to the Supercomputer Corporation—you were even in that bunch of protesters who got hauled away by the cops a couple of months ago for trespassing at the Supercomputer Institute. You must have come in here looking for some way to damage Professor Calder's research."

"That's not true!" Horn replied, panic in his voice.

"What's a Symore?" Jesse asked me in a low whisper.

"A supercomputer," I whispered back. To Calder I said, "Can you tell if anything's missing or damaged?"

His office was so starkly white and neat that it looked

like a hi-tech window display, the only human object in it Jason Horn's rather shabby trench coat, which I'd draped over a chair. Calder tried a few of his file drawers, which were locked, and opened his desk drawers, which weren't, and said that he couldn't see anything amiss.

"But most of my research and important documents are in that thing anyway," he said, gesturing at the computer sitting on the table next to his desk. "Since I keep backups of everything I do on floppy disks, even if he'd stolen or damaged the computer, I wouldn't lose anything important."

"I didn't touch anything," Horn said. "I told you," he added, turning to me, "I just came in here out of curiosity."

"With illegally made keys," Reid reminded him, "and a flashlight."

Horn didn't say anything to that. I couldn't blame him.

I felt sorry for him, standing there at a kind of attention to stretch his height a little, but still dwarfed by Lucas Calder. I felt sorry for him because I knew he was in serious trouble. I'd heard of professors who'd kept their jobs after doing worse things than slugging another professor to avoid being caught breaking into an office: academic tenure's a pretty powerful thing. But Jason Horn wasn't an ordinary professor. The University had been trying to get rid of him for years and I suspected that this would be the excuse they were looking for.

It would be hard to find two members of the faculty farther apart in every respect than Calder and Horn: the one a popular scientist with an international reputation, the other a troublemaker, a gadfly who'd lent his name to so many bizarre causes that no respectable cause—even some of the groups that had protested against the Supercomputer Corporation—welcomed his support anymore.

I considered what to do with him. The obvious thing would be to take him downtown and book him for assault and trespassing. But I don't like going through the process of booking people—the county jail is even more brightly lit, hard-edged, and soulless than the Science Tower, and a lot dirtier.

I decided to ask Reid and Horn to write statements, and then we could all go about our business and let the University sort it out later.

Martin Reid gave me a surprised look and asked me why I wasn't going to put Horn in jail. I told him I would, if I thought Horn was going to run, but that didn't seem very likely. I didn't add that I thought the University would be pleased if he ran.

"But I could make a citizen's arrest, couldn't I?" he asked. "He hit me, after all. Then you'd have to take him to jail?"

"Yes."

The cut by Reid's mouth wasn't bleeding anymore. He looked down at Horn, who'd retrieved his trench coat and was putting it on. Horn met his eyes, then looked away. "I guess my revenge can wait," Reid said, after a moment.

"I have that option, too—of making a citizen's arrest?" Lucas Calder asked me.

"Yes," I said, my heart sinking, afraid I'd have to book Horn after all.

"I can see that you don't want to arrest him, Officer O'Neill," Calder said, smiling upon me as he might upon a newly discovered quasar, "and I will trust your judgment in this matter. Marty," he said, turning abruptly to Reid, "write out your statement for the *cop.*" He sounded pleased with himself, that so distinguished a professor could speak real American.

Horn, doing nothing to make my job more pleasant, said he had no intention of putting anything in writing before he'd consulted an attorney. Then he straightened his shoulders, cinched the belt of his trench coat with a swift yank, and waited for me to change my mind and put the cuffs on him.

I told him he could leave, noted the relief mixed with disappointment on his face, and sent Jesse Porter out with him. Lucas Calder gave them a few minutes' head start, and then he left, too.

Martin Reid sat down at Calder's desk and wrote out his statement. I leaned against the wall by the door and watched him, and surprised myself by wondering if I'd ever see him again. Then I wondered why I didn't feel guilty on Al's behalf because of that errant wondering. Lucas Calder had called him Marty. Not my favorite name, but acceptable. It wouldn't take as long to get used to as Al, which I never liked at all until I started liking Al.

Reid looked up and caught me staring, and to cover myself I asked him why he'd been in his office so late.

"I put it in my statement," he answered. "To use the supercomputers. They're cheaper late at night." His answer didn't mean much to me, but it wasn't any of my business either.

We left Calder's office together. "You like being a campus policewoman?" he asked. "A cop?"

I said I did.

"That's hard to believe," he answered, and when I asked him why, he grinned and replied that it was because he'd seen how much I didn't want to throw Jason Horn in jail. "Can you be a successful cop and not live for those magic moments when you get to toss people in jail?"

"I can. Besides, I don't have any trouble at all tossing people in jail—people who belong there."

"And you don't think Jason Horn belongs there?"

"I don't know where he belongs, but he's not the kind of person I enjoy arresting. Besides," I reminded him, "you could have forced me to book him."

"Yeah, why didn't I?" He gently prodded his face where Horn had hit him. "Maybe niceness is catching."

"Maybe."

Two

Niceness wasn't catching for Jason Horn. The University went all out to get him fired, and they might have succeeded this time, tenure or no tenure. However, almost before the process began, Horn handed in his resignation. It was the end of fall quarter, just before the Christmas break, so his department didn't have to find anybody to take over his classes in the middle of a term.

He still hadn't said what he was doing in Lucas Calder's office or how he'd got hold of the keys. He didn't say what he was going to do next either, and I didn't suppose anybody cared enough to ask. And that's how things stood when the Christmas season arrived and the "Hallelujah Chorus" replaced "Ode to Joy" on the department store Muzak.

It's not my favorite holiday, Christmas. I'd made up my mind a long time ago never to spend another one with my mother in Los Angeles. The kind of verbal abuse that passes for conversation when my relatives gather can be appreciated just as well at some other time of year, and Halloween had already come and gone. Instead, I'd decided to spend Christmas with Carol Parrish, a friend, on her parents' farm.

"A Norman Rockwell sort of Christmas," Al, my veterinarian lover, said when I told him. "Take lots of slides." He was disappointed that I wouldn't be spending Christmas with him, but his kids were there—they live with their mother in Arizona the rest of the year—and he's impossible when he's with them.

The farm was a two-hour drive north of the city, mostly freeway, but the last thirty miles or so were on country roads that became less and less well-marked as the flat white landscape began looking more and more the same. I was glad Carol had offered to drive. If I'd had to drive up there alone, I would have had to stop at every intersection to check the map.

I'd met Carol Parrish when we were students at the U. She'd gotten her degree in engineering and found a job she liked that didn't involve making engines of destruction. I'd gone on to become a campus cop. In spite of—or because of—the fact that we were opposites in just about every way, we'd stayed friends.

Her parents were at the door to meet us when we finally arrived. I'd never met them before. Her father was a tall man with a wreath of white hair around a high dome. He covered a shyness that seemed almost painful by being either blunt or silent. Carol's mom, on the other hand, was cheerful and sturdy, and exuded enough of the social graces for both of them.

Carol's brother Mike was there, too. I'd met him a few times down in the city. Like me, he worked at the University—he did something with computers for the Biology Department. He was a few years older than Carol, tall like his father, and quiet. Carol fussed about both men, especially her brother, as if trying to protect them from themselves. I watched it and shuddered.

Mike had brought a friend with him, a woman named Ann-Marie Ekdahl. She was twenty-six, a few years younger than Mike, but she worked hard at acting more experienced, as if she'd been around a lot and wanted everybody to know it, especially people who probably didn't want to, such as Mike's parents. She spoke English with a Swedish accent that sounded mannered to me, like one of those actors who advertise rye crackers on television. She was taller than I am by an inch or so, and I'm five-nine, and she was beautiful, but I thought it was an overdone kind of beauty, better seen from a distance—across footlights, on a stage.

I wondered what she saw in Mike Parrish.

The morning of Christmas Eve, Mike announced that he had to return to town for the day. Something had come up at the University. One of the Biology professors had lost some data in the mainframe—at least I thought that was what he said—and he wanted Mike to come down and help retrieve it.

"Don't they ever take holidays down there?" Mrs. Parrish asked. And her husband asked Mike why somebody couldn't do the job who was already there.

"Mike is a specialist," Ann-Marie said, putting her arm around him.

Mike appeared to pull away from her. Nothing dramatic, just a small, quick movement that nobody seemed to notice but me.

That night, while waiting for his return, we watched a Christmas special on public television that featured Lucas Calder lecturing on the Star of Bethlehem. It was an entertaining and informative talk, a combination of Biblical lore, history, and solid astronomical research.

Ann-Marie, who was on the couch sipping wine and thumbing through a magazine, said, "Mike tells me, Peggy, that you arrested Professor Calder for something. It must have been very difficult to do."

She was teasing, perhaps trying to be friendly. She probably knew I didn't like her much, even though I made some effort to conceal the fact.

"Once I got the cuffs on him," I replied, "the fight went out of him."

Mrs. Parrish asked me what Ann-Marie'd meant, and I described the break-in at Calder's office on November 1.

"And this Jason Horn," Ann-Marie asked, looking at me over her wineglass. "What has happened to him?"

I told her he'd left the University.

Mike returned then and we opened presents.

My Christmas present from the Parrishes was a dish for my microwave oven. Carol was behind that, of course, since she knew that if it couldn't be microwaved, I wouldn't serve it.

Ann-Marie's present to Mike was a framed lithograph

of a Norwegian troll destroying a town. It was both funny and sad, because the troll obviously didn't know what he was doing. He seemed to just want to get where he was going, do what he had to do, like King Kong in New York. Mike tried to look pleased and to say the right things, but he looked tired and edgy—on account of the long day he'd put in, I assumed.

"Is it an original?" Mike's dad asked, with his usual lack of tact.

"No," Ann-Marie replied, "it is a copy, but a good one, I think. It was expensive, anyway. I have a special affinity—is that the word, Michael?—for trolls." That was the word.

Christmas morning, Carol, Mike, Ann-Marie, and I drove to a cabin the family owned on a lake some thirty miles northwest of the farm. My heart skipped a beat as Mike bumped his car down a snow-covered slope and then just kept driving out onto the lake. I haven't lived here long enough to be comfortable with driving on water, even if it's frozen. I asked Carol how they reached the cabin in the summer, and she said there was another road that wound around behind the cabin, through the woods.

The car followed a road across the lake that someone had made by plowing snow off the ice. Little side streets branched off to the left and right to ice-fishing shacks, some of which looked like Swiss chalets perched in the middle of the lake.

We parked on the shore below the cabin, walked up a steep flight of wooden stairs, and Carol unlocked the door. The cabin had a musty smell, although Mike and his dad had used it when they were duck hunting in the fall. We built a fire in the big stone fireplace and made coffee, and when we'd warmed up, Carol and I skied around the lake and into the hills on the other side of it. We asked Mike and Ann-Marie if they wanted to come, too, but Ann-Marie, not waiting for Mike to answer, said they weren't interested.

"Mike is a good skier, but he cannot keep up with me," she said, and shrugged a "so what's the use" shrug that was as heavily accented as her English. "None of my lovers," she added, "has ever been able to keep up with me." She smiled, either to tell us she understood the double meaning of her words, or to try to make us think she didn't. Mike's face darkened and he stared hard into his coffee.

Carol asked, innocently, "On skis?"

"Of course," Ann-Marie replied, just as innocently.

Mike's eyes jumped between the two women as they spoke, but he didn't say anything and he stayed back at the cabin with Ann-Marie. I thought it was because they had something to talk over.

When we'd skied out of earshot, Carol and I agreed that neither of us would have a lover who wouldn't slow down for us on Christmas Day, whatever other flaws he might have. Carol told me that Ann-Marie was Mike's first serious relationship and, like all the rest of us, he had to learn by getting hurt.

"It doesn't look like a match made in heaven, does it?" I asked.

"No. It's funny, but just after she and Mike got together, he told me—he was boasting, I'm afraid—that she'd come on to him like a Mack truck, she made him think he was God's gift to little girls. Heady stuff for a guy like Mike."

"Her enthusiasm seems to have waned," I said. "How long have they been together?"

"Not very long. One day he's a confirmed bachelor, the next day he's in love. But it looked like he's having second thoughts about her, too. I bet it'll be over by spring."

When we got back to the cabin, they were building a snowman in a clearing next to the cabin, although Mike was doing most of the work. There was plenty of snow. Whatever was going on between them seemed to have been resolved, at least for the time being.

"What do you two think," Mike asked us, "should it be a snowman or a snowwoman?" He was panting with the effort of building a snowman so big.

"A man," Carol answered as we were taking off our

skis. "No boobs. You can't make boobs out of snow, it doesn't look right."

"That's two of us to one," Mike said, and gave Ann-Marie a grin. I was surprised to hear that he'd voted against her. "How do you vote, Peggy?"

"With the majority," I said. Ann-Marie pretended to ignore us, went on patting snow into place as Mike shoveled it up. She was wearing a bright red scarf, one she'd brought from Sweden, she'd told us, because she couldn't get anything like it here. It didn't look all that special to me.

Carol and I promised to help as soon as we'd warmed up and eaten some lunch—it looked like it would take at least that long for them to finish. We got back outside in time to help put the final touches on the snowman.

Suddenly Ann-Marie got busy. She brought two good-sized stones and a gnarled piece of driftwood from the cabin porch, stuck the stones into the head for eyes and the driftwood in for a mouth. She shaped the snow above the stones into heavy brows and then molded a large crooked nose that hooked over the mouth.

"It's a troll," she announced, standing back and clapping her mittens together, either to shake off the snow or to applaud her work.

It looked sinister in the fading afternoon light and in that beautiful, snow-flocked place, and Carol said she didn't think snowmen should be ugly.

"Trolls are supposed to be ugly," Ann-Marie retorted.

"Who said it was supposed to be a troll," Carol retorted, not bothering to make it a question.

"Since Mike already has a troll," Ann-Marie said, "this one can be yours, Carol."

I could see that Carol was about to tell Ann-Marie what she could do with her troll, but before she could say anything, Mike went up to his sister and said, "It's okay," and put an arm around her. "I'll bet it'll scare the owls," he added.

"I don't have anything against owls," Carol grumbled, putting the emphasis on owls.

I said I was cold and was going in to sit by the fire and

have some more coffee, and I started trudging through the snow back to the cabin. Carol hung back, looking as if she were thinking about pushing the snow troll's head off, and Ann-Marie stood watching her, waiting to see what she'd do. Finally, Carol turned away with a shrug and came after Mike and me.

We stayed a while longer, then put out the fire, closed up the cabin, and went back down to the lake and the car sitting on it. As we drove off, I looked back at the cabin in the trees heavy with snow.

"You can't see the snowman from here," I said.

"No," Ann-Marie agreed, looking back over her shoulder, "you cannot see the troll from the lake. Carol's troll," she added.

Three

It was the third week of January and I was working the dog watch again. I take it whenever I can. A woman's not supposed to be a night person; we're expected to live our lives under a dawn-to-dusk curfew like the inhabitants of cities under siege. If something preyed upon men at night, they'd probably abolish night itself.

What with one thing and another—paperwork, mostly— I get home around eight in the morning and, after I've slept six hours, which is about average for me, I have the best part of the day to myself until I have to start getting ready for work again.

"What'd you do with Jason Horn?" Paula Henderson asked me when I came into the squad room. She was playing Boggle with Lawrence Fitzpatrick, waiting for roll call.

I got a cup of coffee from the urn in the corner, went over to them, and asked her what that was supposed to mean.

"He's disappeared," Lawrence said, looking up from the Boggle dice and then quickly down again. The sand was running out in the timer and, as usual, Paula's list of words was longer than Lawrence's, and growing. She almost always beats him, in part because she makes words up.

"Where'd you hear this?" I asked.

"From Sergeant Hiller," Paula said, writing as she talked. Counting Ginny Raines, who's a detective, there are three women on the squad now. I'm still the newest. "He got it from the city cops. They've asked us to look into the campus end of it, see if we can find out anything. Ginny's been assigned to it, so she'll probably want to talk to you when she comes in.''

I asked her how they knew Horn had disappeared. She pushed her list of words over to Lawrence and glanced down at his with a sniff of contempt.

''One of Horn's neighbors in his apartment building noticed that he hadn't picked up his newspapers for nearly a week,'' Paula said. Horn had seemed depressed lately, so the neighbor had notified the caretaker, who'd gone in. Horn was gone, although there was no sign that he'd moved out.

''He's dead,'' Lawrence said absently. He was studying Paula's list of words, his high brow furrowed up into his curly blonde hair. ''I don't think *hyze* is a word,'' he added.

We all looked at him. ''How do you know?'' I asked.

''Because I've never heard of it.''

''How do you know Jason Horn's *dead*?'' I demanded.

''He was a spy, and they killed him. What does it mean?''

''What?''

''*Hyze.*''

''I don't know,'' Paula said impatiently. ''Who killed him?''

''The people he was working for, of course,'' Lawrence said. Lawrence is an avid reader of spy novels.

''It's a lot more likely,'' Paula said, ''that he just went out one night and killed himself. Jumped off one of the bridges.''

''Huh-unh,'' Lawrence replied. ''They would've found the body by now. A body wouldn't go through the ice this year. It'd bounce once and lie there.''

He was right about that. The river's usually so polluted that it doesn't freeze solid enough to support someone walking, much less landing on it, but this hadn't been a normal winter.

''His cover was blown,'' Lawrence went on. ''He was of no further use to whoever was running him, and he was going to lose his job. Maybe his masters suspected he was going to make a deal, spill everything in exchange for getting to keep his humble position in the Pharmacy Department. So they killed him.''

"Who'd they kill?'' another cop, Hazard, asked, coming in. He got coffee and took it over to the smoking end of the room, where he sat down, alone.

"Jason Horn,'' Lawrence told him.

"They killed that flake? Who did?''

"Nobody,'' I said. "He's just disappeared. He's probably away somewhere, visiting relatives or friends.''

Strangely, I was worried about Horn. I thought of the last time I'd seen him, leaving Lucas Calder's office, struggling to maintain his dignity. I'd played a part, however innocent, in stripping him of it.

"Maybe he went chasing one ghost too many,'' Hazard said. One of Jason Horn's interests was paranormal phenomena. Much to the University's embarrassment, he was prepared to go out, day or night, to investigate reports of haunted houses, or anything else that nobody'd ever seen before. "He's just a flake,'' Hazard went on. "They're all flakes, the professors, you ask me.'' Nobody'd asked him. Hazard had seen a lot of changes in his fifteen years as a patrolman, among the most significant being his waist size, the hiring of woman and black cops, and his marital status. Ginny, Paula, and I think of him as "The Hazard of Being Male.''

"What happened to him, then?'' Paula asked.

"Who knows?'' Hazard answered. "Maybe he got embarrassed. The University fired his ass—''

"He quit, he wasn't fired,'' I said.

"He quit so he wouldn't be fired,'' Hazard retorted. "Same difference.''

"I'll bet you also know why he broke into Lucas Calder's office,'' I said.

"Who knows why a fucking flake like Horn does anything?'' Hazard said, raising the level of the discussion. "Maybe he thought Calder's doing Star Wars research, because he's an astronomer.'' He liked that one so much, he started chuckling, then began choking on smoke. "If you were a fucking Russian, would you hire

Horn?'' he finally managed to gasp. He jabbed his cigarette out in a crumpled aluminum pie pan. ''Not even the Russians are that desperate,'' he concluded.

''Fucking Russians,'' I amended.

''Yeah,'' he said.

I said to Lawrence, ''It's more likely Horn was snooping around in Calder's office just to see if there was some mischief he could do. Calder was very involved in the efforts to get the Supercomputer Corporation here, and Horn was active in the fight against it.''

There'd been organized protests against the Corporation back when it was being set up, a little property damage done, a little violence, a few arrests made. I recalled Jason Horn standing on the fringes of one of the groups, carrying a sign.

The Hazard said, ''What's this Supercomputer Corporation crap, anyway? I never understood it.'' He lit another cigarette, knowing it would sharpen his intelligence.

''The University can't afford supercomputers without lots of money,'' Lawrence explained, ''and the only way a university gets that kind of money these days is by doing military research. 'Star Wars research,' as you call it. But our university has a policy against doing secret research, and that means no big defense contracts, which means no big bucks.''

The Hazard's attention span had collapsed. He was reading the Surgeon General's warning on his cigarette package. His lips were moving.

''So, they created the Supercomputer Corporation,'' Lawrence went on. ''It's privately run, although it shares office space with the University's Supercomputer Institute, which actually houses the supercomputers. What the Corporation does is, it buys supercomputer time from the University and sells it to the local defense contractors—of which, as you all know, we've got plenty. The University uses the profits from the Corporation to feed and care for its supercomputers and, when necessary, upgrade them. We maintain our status as a major research institution, and still sleep okay at night.''

''Nice!'' Paula said.

"And," Lawrence added, "Peggy was understating things when she said Lucas Calder was 'involved' in the creation of the Supercomputer Corporation. The Corporation was his brainchild, his alone."

Lawrence continued, his voice ominous. "Maybe Horn thought he'd find evidence in Calder's office that Calder was working on something University faculty aren't supposed to work on. Using the supercomputers he'd fought so valiantly for, for his own nefarious purposes."

"But Lawrence, honey," Paula reminded him, "Lucas Calder's an astronomer. Astronomers don't do research related to war. Do they?"

"Who knows?" Lawrence replied airily.

"Besides," I stuck in, "why would Calder take a risk like that? He doesn't need money."

"Doesn't he?" Lawrence asked. "He declared bankruptcy a couple of years ago. It was a very small item in the paper—I'll bet the University was behind that—but my eagle eye spotted it anyway. Bad investments. Not that it cramped his style any, just the style of his creditors. Then again, maybe he got hold of some more money. He still throws those parties that get into the society pages. You know, 'Galileo and Mrs. Galileo, the former Beatrice Fettucini, came early. Mrs. G. was wearing a sheer—' "

"You've been reading too many novels," I interrupted him. "Horn was just in Calder's office out of curiosity."

"You found illegal keys on him, right? You can't get keys like that on the spur of the moment, and just because you're curious. It takes planning. Is Jason Horn a planner? No. Until you caught him in Calder's office, all he ever did was protest and write letters to the editor. Why did his *modus operandi* change all of a sudden—and why has he disappeared?"

He had a point, about the keys anyway.

"But The Hazard's right for once," Paula stuck in. "The Russians wouldn't be dumb enough to hire a notorious loon like Jason Horn as a spy. Breaking into Calder's office had nothing to do with his disappearance."

"Right," Hazard said, surprised to hear something intelligent coming from a woman, a black woman at that.

"And 'hyze' isn't a word," Lawrence retorted, as Sergeant Hiller came in for roll call.

"He'll turn up," I said.

"Yeah," Lawrence replied. "In the spring. Under the snow."

Four

My birthday, a week later, started out sunny. The snow had stopped around midnight and, as I drove home from the University, the air was clean and crisp. I paused before going into my apartment, to listen to the sounds of snow shovels on cement—other people digging out their walkways and their cars so they could go to work. The air sparkled with tiny stars of ice.

I was looking forward to a hot bath and bed, and then Al and I were going out to dinner to celebrate my birthday, with Ginny Raines and a friend of hers.

The light on my answering machine was blinking when I got into the house. I pressed the play button and continued on into the kitchen to microwave a cup of instant coffee to drink in the bathtub.

"Hi, Peggy," the voice said. It was Carol Parrish. There wasn't any real emotion, it's too tinny a sound for that, but I knew something was wrong anyway. "Mike's dead. I'd appreciate it if you'd give me a call." I made the coffee first.

"They say he committed suicide," she told me. "But he didn't. Nothing could make Mike commit suicide."

I told her I'd come over.

"No," she replied. "I'm driving up to the farm in a little while. I just wanted you to know." She started crying.

"I'll come with you."

"No," she said again. "I'll be back next week."

A few days after she returned to town, she asked me

over for dinner. She didn't talk much about what was on both our minds, just answered politely a few questions about how her parents were and how the funeral went. After dinner, as we were sitting in her living room drinking coffee, the lights off so we could watch the snow falling outside, she said, without much warm-up, "Do you want to know how Mike died?"

"Sure." I didn't really, I just wanted to help her get over her loss by letting her talk about it.

"He was killed with one of Dad's target pistols. In the cabin on the lake. Mom and Dad were away all that week, visiting friends in Florida. They didn't know Mike was planning to go up there while they were gone and they still don't know why he did. I thought maybe he had some horrible disease, you know—at least that would've made sense, I could accept that, even if he didn't leave a note. But they say he was in good health." She paused a moment, then went on, her voice neutral, like a police report: "He killed himself on account of Ann-Marie Ekdahl. Because they were breaking up. That's what the police up there think."

"Were they breaking up?"

"Ann-Marie told the police they were," Carol answered. "He begged and pleaded with her, she told them. Begged and pleaded! Mike wasn't there to object, Peggy, to laugh, to tell them he wouldn't beg that blonde bitch for anything."

I didn't say anything to that.

"Do you think he would?" she asked me.

I said I didn't know Mike well enough to answer that. I told her I was sure neither she nor I would ever plead with anybody who wanted to end a relationship with us. And I reminded her that, at Christmas, she'd told me Ann-Marie had apparently come on to Mike pretty hard—like a Mack truck, she'd said—and maybe that set Mike up for a fall he couldn't handle. And as I said all this I watched the expression on Carol's face change from mild interest in what she was hearing to disbelief, then from disbelief to rage. She practically flew from the sofa.

"You're so goddamned rational!" she yelled. "Didn't

you tell me your brother killed himself, too? Maybe he was murdered, and you just settled for suicide—" She stopped abruptly, perhaps hearing what she was saying, and stood there in the middle of the room bewildered. I got up and put my arm around her.

When she was finished crying, we sat down again and she continued the story. "I went over to Ann-Marie's apartment yesterday afternoon. I wanted to ask her about it, hear what she had to say. She just told me what she'd told the police, said she'd decided they were not 'good for each other anymore,' " Carol mimicked Ann-Marie's accent, "that she'd tried to break it off *gently,* but Mike refused to be reasonable. She gave me a sorrowful look and her big, blue eyes started to glitter with tears. She said she felt guilty about it, felt that she was somehow to blame, she felt 'destroyed,' she said." The thought made Carol get up again suddenly. "She felt destroyed," she whispered, still dry-eyed, *"she* felt destroyed. I came close to killing her then, Peggy, and she saw that in my face. She backed away from me. I told her I thought she was lying, that I knew she had something to do with Mike's *murder.* I was wasting my breath. She just shook her head, as if she pitied me, said she was sorry 'poor Mike' killed himself, but there wasn't anything she could do about it. She had a life to live, too, she said." She whispered those words again, Carol did, and then added, "We'll see about that."

I asked her how she knew that Ann-Marie wasn't upset over Mike's death. Maybe she did feel badly about it and maybe she couldn't help talking in an affected voice. I didn't believe what I was saying myself, since I think there's a connection between how you talk and how you feel, but even if Ann-Marie was a phony, that didn't make her a killer.

"She made a lot of mistakes, Peggy, and they're going to cost her! It was a mistake to try to make it look like suicide, because Mike wouldn't do that. But even if he would commit suicide, he wouldn't drive up to the lake to do it. They found him by the fireplace, Peggy. He loved that place, he wouldn't do it there, he wouldn't have done that to Mom and Dad. And he wouldn't have used one of Dad's guns, either—maybe he would've used his own, but not Dad's. Somebody who didn't know whose guns were whose did it. And Mike would have left a note.''

An ice fisherman had found Mike's body, Carol said. He'd heard what he thought was a shot, dithered a while, and finally gone up to the cabin to investigate. He'd seen Mike's body inside, through a window.

"You don't have any idea why Mike was up there?"

"No."

"Do you know of any reason why Ann-Marie would want him dead?"

"I don't know that either," Carol said. "That's what I'm going to find out." And then, suddenly, she asked me, "Will you help me?"

It took me by surprise. I stared at her a moment and then turned and looked out the window at the falling snow.

No, I wasn't going to help her. Maybe everything she'd said was true. Maybe it was strange that Mike had driven, not just up to the farm, but all the way to the lake cabin to kill himself, and maybe it was strange that he'd used one of his father's guns instead of one of his own. But people are strange, and they often do things they'd be sorry about if they'd lived only minutes—seconds—longer.

My brother didn't kill himself, by the way. He just vanished into the drug culture of the '60s and, for all I know, he's still alive somewhere, maybe even doing okay, just not in any hurry to come back home. It was my father who committed suicide, and he didn't leave a note either, although he usually had an explanation for whatever he did. Maybe he finally got tired of explaining, of trying to figure out why, of conning others, conning himself. And he shouldn't have killed himself where he did either—in his study next to my room. He must have known that I'd hear the shot and be the one to find him. He wasn't a cruel man, not intentionally so. If he'd lived, maybe he'd have wondered why he'd behaved like that.

No, I wasn't going to help Carol try to turn a suicide into a murder. I knew too much about suicides.

"Will you?" she said again. "You're a cop, you know

how to look into things like this—you studied it. Didn't you?"

I laughed at that—if you could call so harsh a sound a laugh. *I studied it.* In the school for murder. I guess I had, although I'd never thought about it that way before.

"I have a friend in the city police," I told her, "in Homicide. I'll ask him to try to find out if the police up north are holding anything back on your brother's death."

She helped me dig my car out of the snow and told me I'd be smarter to call a cab to take me to work. She's a lousy driver. She doesn't think people should be out in cars when it's snowing, but I've always liked driving in bad weather.

The next afternoon, I called Buck Hansen, a lieutenant in the Homicide Division of the city police, and told him what I wanted. Buck and I have been friends since an afternoon last year when I discovered a murder victim and threw up. Something about that appealed to something in him that appealed to me.

"What's it for, Peggy?"

I told him Mike's sister was a friend of mine and the family didn't think his death could be suicide.

He asked me why I didn't call the police up north myself. I said there was a good chance they wouldn't tell a campus cop anything, especially if it was a her. "And then they'd call my supervisors, to find out what I was up to, and I'd be in trouble."

"So you're trying to avoid trouble now, are you?" Buck asked, laughing. "That's commendable."

He asked me if I could have dinner with him that night, he'd probably have something to report by then, and I said sure. I hadn't seen him in a while, and I miss him when I don't.

We met at a downtown deli, where a lot of cops eat. The food's hideous, which makes talking with your mouth full almost necessary. When we'd ordered, Buck summarized what Carol had already told me and added that the investigators hadn't found evidence pointing to anything but a verdict of suicide.

"What about fingerprints?"

Mike's were the only ones on the pistol.

"His dad's weren't?"

The report didn't say anything about Mike's dad's prints.

"The family doesn't think Mike would have used his dad's gun," I said. "He would have used his own. Somebody who didn't know which was which might have used Mr. Parrish's."

"Unless," Buck said, "Mike was trying to send his dad a message?" He said it softly, sending me one.

"His dad's fingerprints ought to have been on it, too," I insisted.

"I just got the highlights, Peggy. You want me to find out?"

"Would you? I met Mike at Christmas. He seemed moody, but not depressed. He didn't look like the suicide type to me."

There was a silence rich with possible meanings. Buck's one of the people who knows about my father. "What's your interest in this, Peggy?"

I told him I didn't have any, I'd just promised Mike's sister I'd do this much for her.

Buck said: "There isn't a 'suicide type' and you know it—or if there is, they don't wear it on a bracelet like somebody with heart disease."

I said I knew that, watched him over the rim of my coffee cup.

"The Parrishes are long-time residents up there, Peggy," Buck reminded me, "so I'm sure the police did a thorough job. They even checked out that girlfriend of his—the woman he apparently killed himself over—and she has an alibi for the night he died."

"Oh yeah? What?"

"She was with somebody who confirmed it."

"How convenient," I said.

"I've probably got an alibi, too," Buck answered. "Come on, Peggy, you've done what you promised you'd do: you've looked into it. We've both got more important things to think about. At least I do. A murder. Several, in fact—but Michael Parrish isn't one of them, thank God.''

We left food on our plates in lieu of a tip.

I called Carol and told her what I'd gotten from Buck.

"She was with somebody, was she?" Carol said. "That doesn't mean anything, you know. It just means she got somebody else to kill my brother for her. I didn't think she'd do it herself anyway, she wouldn't have the guts." There was a long pause as Carol geared up to ask me a question she already knew the answer to and didn't want to hear. "Will you look into it some more for me, Peggy? Try to find out something that'll convince those cops up there it wasn't suicide—check on Ann-Marie, find out who her friends are, who might have killed Mike for her, find out who she was with that night?"

No, I said, and said I was sorry.

She started to say something more, but changed her mind. "That's okay," she said finally. "It's not your problem, is it? I'll have to find some other way to make her pay for what she's done."

Five

We were in bed, Al and I, when the phone rang, but after a while it stopped. It started again half an hour later as I was getting out of the shower and Al was sitting on the living room floor, still naked, reading the paper. It was the first week of February and so cold the whole house creaked, but my apartment was warm. It was 6 P.M., already dark, and we had lots of time before I had to leave for work.

"You want me to get that?" he asked, not moving at all.

I said I would and, dripping water on my blue carpet, I walked past him to answer it. It was Carol.

I hadn't heard from her since I'd refused to help her investigate her brother's death.

She asked me to come over, said she had some news about Mike's death that might interest me.

I doubt it, I said to myself, but to her I said, "Can't you tell me over the phone?"

"I'd rather not, Peggy. Please, it won't take long."

I said okay, I'd drop by before going to work that night—around ten. That would give me an excuse not to stay very long.

I fixed something for dinner that was fast and fortifying, and then Al and I hiked down to Lake Eleanor—I live just up the hill from it—and skied around it and the adjoining park, but it wasn't much fun. It was too cold, for one thing, and for another Al was moody and silent. He'd been that way since New Year's Day, when his kids flew back to

29

Arizona and their mother. He's always that way for a while after being with his kids, but it usually blows over fairly quickly. His silence was getting on my nerves and I was almost glad when we returned to my house and he went home.

I hadn't been in Carol's place since she'd asked me to look into her brother's death. It was a mess, more so than usual.

"Excuse the clutter," she said, by way of greeting as she let me go in ahead of her, "I haven't had time to go through it and decide what to keep and what to give to the Salvation Army. It's Mike's stuff," she added unnecessarily.

This was why she'd wanted to tell me her news in person rather than over the phone, so I could see what Mike had left behind. Luckily she was behind me and couldn't see the face I made.

"My friend Lisa helped me move it over here on Saturday," Carol said. Today was Wednesday—she'd left Mike's belongings scattered around for four days. She wasn't that much of a slob.

While she went out to get coffee, I wandered around in the mess. There were a lot of boxes, mostly full of books and the kind of junk you find in desk drawers that even the owner couldn't tell you why he'd saved. Mike's taste in reading ran the narrow gamut from computer science to science fiction. There were also a few fantasy paperbacks that featured semi-nude sorceresses holding horny dragons at bay with swords of light. None of it was my kind of reading. A large framed picture was leaning against, and turned to, one wall. I turned it around and recognized it as the troll print Ann-Marie had given Mike for Christmas.

"I almost put a foot through it," Carol said behind me, coming into the room with two cups of coffee. "Maybe I still will, but probably not. It's too late for that now. Besides, I like it, and it's not the artist's fault that Ann-Marie bought it."

"You're going to keep it?"

"I don't know what I'm going to do with it, I just know

I won't return it to her. She said it was expensive, so I'm surprised she hasn't asked for it back.''

It was an amiable troll, I thought, even though it was creating havoc in the city it was stumbling through. I could see Carol's point—it was hard to hate something that innocent and pathetic.

I remembered the snowman we'd made at the Parrishes' lake place at Christmas. Ann-Marie'd turned it into a troll, too, but one very unlike this one. She'd made it sinister and ugly—evil. She'd told us she had an affinity for trolls. I wondered which kind—this kind or the one up north.

I found a chair that wasn't covered with something that had belonged to Mike, balanced the coffee mug on its arm, and said to Carol, ''All right. You said you've got news. What is it?''

Even her glasses couldn't hide the glitter of excitement in her brown eyes. ''I got a phone call yesterday, Peggy. From Montana, from an old friend of Mike's named Bob Ness. He'd only just heard about Mike's death. And Peggy, listen to me! Bob doesn't think Mike committed suicide either!''

I fought the urge to look at my watch. I wanted to get out of there. ·

Carol saw that. ''You can leave if you want to, Peggy, but wait till you hear the whole story, please! Bob's folks own a resort outside Bozeman. The last two years, Mike's taken a week off from work and gone out there to ski, usually in early spring. But Bob says that Mike called him the night before he died and asked if there was a vacant room for the following week—he wanted to get away from here for a while! Get away from *here* for a while, damn it, Peggy!''

''I heard you the first time,'' I said. ''Did he tell Bob why?''

''He said he had some thinking to do, that's all, and he'd maybe tell Bob about it when he got there,'' Carol replied. ''Bob said he'd make a room available. Mike told him he planned to leave the following Monday and drive out there—this was Friday, Peggy, and Mike was murdered on Saturday.'' Carol, in her excitement, got up and came across the room, as she'd done once before, when she was angry. "Do you still think it was suicide, Peggy?" she asked, looking down at me.

I shrugged uneasily, stared at the wall opposite me, over the boxes of stuff that had once belonged to Mike. I glanced at the troll. He stared back at me over falling buildings and people in flight. He had nothing to tell me.

Carol stooped down, putting herself and her blonde, curly head between me and the troll print. "Then how about this, Peggy?" she said. "We couldn't figure out why Mike went up to the farm before he died. Well, here's why! His *skis* were up there! He didn't go up there to kill himself, damn it, he was planning a vacation, a skiing holiday—to think something over!"

"How come Bob Ness didn't call you or your folks before now?" Mike had been dead over two weeks.

"When Mike didn't show up when he said he would," Carol answered, "Bob called Mike's apartment. He didn't call any of us, he said, because—well, you don't, I guess, do you? Besides, that's just the sort of thing Bob might do himself, change his mind and not bother to tell anybody about it. It's also the sort of thing Mike would have done, too. Say he's coming and then not show, and not call to cancel."

I sat back on Carol's sofa and stared into the story she was telling me and didn't say anything for a long time.

"You've told the police all this?" I said finally.

"You're the police, Peggy."

"The city police, Homicide," I said impatiently.

"Mike was murdered two hundred miles north of here. The police down here don't want to get involved in a murder that took place up there, and the police up there think Mike's death was a suicide."

More silence.

"It was murder, Peggy. You know it was."

I started to say what I thought I wanted to say, but she saw that and her eyes filled with tears. So I didn't say that, I looked at her expectant face as it started to melt into grief again and I said, "Yes," as if I thought it was murder, too.

Six

Mike's murder—or suicide, for that matter—didn't have to be related to Ann-Marie at all. Mike was older than Carol and he'd moved around a lot before coming back here, going to the University, and getting a job. But there was no way for me to find out what kind of troubles or sorrows he might have acquired in his past life, or who from that past might have wanted him dead. So Ann-Marie was the only suspect I had.

She'd told the police that Mike had been upset over their breakup and he'd begged her to change her mind. I didn't believe that, even when I'd tried to tell myself I did. At Christmas, I'd seen that, while he was in love with her and might even have hoped they'd stay together, he was prepared for the worst. Mike had a look on his face that said he was always prepared for the worst.

So it was a good bet that Ann-Marie had lied about why he might have killed himself. That didn't mean she was involved in murdering him, though. She might enjoy letting other people believe a man had killed himself on her account. She might even believe it herself.

The first thing I did the next afternoon was call Buck. I reminded him that he'd been going to ask the police up north about the fingerprints on the pistol that killed Mike. He said "Oh, yeah" without enthusiasm, then said he'd been told Mike's were the only prints on the weapon.

"Wiped clean," I said. "That's odd, isn't it?"

"Mr. Parrish always cleaned his weapons after he used them, Peggy."

"Really? You mean, when he polished the grip, he held the pistol by sticking one finger in the nozzle, so there wouldn't be prints on it?"

"Muzzle, Peggy. I don't know. He could have held it with a cloth. You know him, ask him." Buck was clearly not very enthused about the case.

I know it's muzzle—I'm actually a good shot with both pistol and rifle. But I don't like guns, not even the one on my belt. And it wouldn't matter if I asked Mr. Parrish or not. It wouldn't change my belief that Mike's death was murder, or the belief of the police up north that it wasn't.

I asked Buck for the name of the person Ann-Marie had been with the night Mike died, her alibi, but he couldn't help me with that, or wouldn't, so I had to call the police up north myself.

I got passed up the line from a trooper to a sergeant to a captain of detectives who wanted to know what the University police's interest was and, for that matter, what the University police was. He wondered why the teachers and students couldn't get themselves arrested by regular cops like everybody else. I said I sometimes wished we had the facilities of the city police, especially the cells for working faculty members over with hoses. He guffawed at that and said he'd bet I'd be good at the third degree, being a woman and all, and I said he ought to see me, what teeth I have left are filed to sharp points.

We carried on a bit longer in that mode and finally he liked me so much that he gave me the name I wanted, even threw in an address, and then asked for mine. I told him I couldn't give out that information, since my husband was the jealous type. We rued that together for a few moments, and I hoped we hung up friends, because I didn't want him placing a call to University police headquarters to find out what was going on down here.

Ann-Marie had allegedly spent the night Mike was killed with a man named Terry Rhodes. He lived on Central, a street that runs through what was once a good neighborhood a long time ago. Now most of the buildings, with the exception of the bars and pawn shops, are empty.

I parked in front of a boarded-up Scientology church and sat in my car until a trio of drunks reeled past in elegant slow motion. I checked the address to be sure I'd gotten it right, because it didn't look like Ann-Marie's kind of neighborhood, then got out and went down the street to where Terry Rhodes was supposed to live.

The address was an apartment above a porn shop. I climbed a narrow flight of stairs next to the shop, knocked at the door at the top, waited, and when I heard nothing, knocked again and got the same response.

I went back downstairs. Someone, perhaps the owner, had spray-painted a slogan across the front of the porn shop that said, "Porn is the theory, rape is the practice."

I pushed open the door and went in. Because I was upright and wearing clothes, the customers didn't seem to know what I was, so I walked through them as if invisible.

A display case separated me from the clerk. It was filled with garishly colored plastic penises in a variety of sizes and shapes that ranged from modest to hyperbolic. The bored clerk, his elbows resting on top of the case, appeared suspended above it like a magician over a table full of surprises.

"You're not vice," he told me.

"No." I pushed a crowded ashtray way off to one side. It smelled as much of marijuana as of stale tobacco.

"Just want to look, then, or out gathering impressions to take back to your women's outrage group? Or trying to find a present for your man? Lots of ladies do that, you'd be surprised."

He gave me a grin still containing traces of humor. His teeth had once been nice, but now they were yellow and desperately in need of a dentist. He was about thirty and he'd been born with a good face, but he'd neglected to develop it. It was growing old without maturing, like a vegetable left in the refrigerator too long.

"I'm trying to find the man who lives upstairs," I told him. "Terry Rhodes."

"Why?"

"I want to talk to him."

Without saying anything, he held out his hand. I got out

my shield and showed it to him. Something resembling interest flickered in his eyes. "You're a campus cop, huh? You're a long way from the University," he said. "I'm Terry Rhodes. What do you want to talk about?"

"Ann-Marie Ekdahl," I said. "She says she was with you at the time her boyfriend was killed."

"What do you mean, 'was killed?' I heard he committed suicide. An open and shut case, as they say on television."

"It's better if they leave a note," I told him. "It relieves the police's mind. And his family doesn't believe he killed himself."

He laughed suddenly, a noise probably never heard in this place before. A man standing next to me, staring into the display case as if it were filled with saint's relics, looked up with a start, perhaps to see if Rhodes was laughing at him.

"No shit," Rhodes said. He leaned back against the wall behind him and put his eyes back to sleep. "Well, you go back and tell them he killed himself all right. It was about time some poor sucker killed himself on account of Ann-Marie."

I waited for him to go on. When he didn't I asked him what that was supposed to mean.

"Ann-Marie's a needy lady," he replied. "That's how she comes off to people—to men, at least. Needy. And that kind attracts losers—suckers who can't save themselves, so they decide to save her. Like me," he added, and gave me a grin that was a weird mixture of pride and shame. "Excuse me," he said, addressing the man standing next to me. "You want to fondle something in the case, or you just looking?"

The man didn't seem bothered by the question. He stared at Rhodes for a moment and then asked for change for a five dollar bill. Rhodes gave it to him in quarters and the man sauntered through swinging doors into a back room.

"You make it sound like she was involved with a lot of men," I said.

"Do I? You know what she says to me once? She drapes

her arm around my shoulders and brings her face real close to mine, gives me a deep stare, and says, 'Sex is just an extension of my friendship, Terry.' '' He did a fair imitation of Ann-Marie's Swedish accent. "I was young and stupid at the time. It came as a real shock, you know?''

He was confusing me. "Young and stupid at what time?''

"Oh, yeah.'' He gave me his slow, yellow grin. "I guess I didn't mention that to the hick cop who drove all the way down here to interview me. Maybe he forgot to ask. At the time I married her, married Ann-Marie.''

"You were her husband!''

"Am her husband. We haven't lived together for a while—but we aren't divorced.'' A bleak hope, like the February sun outside, lit up his face briefly. He dug a cigarette out of his jacket pocket and lit it, almost immediately put it in the ashtray and forgot about it.

"How long did you live together?''

"Two years, maybe a little more. We got married in Germany, just before I got out of the Army. A couple of days before Christmas—*Weihnachten*, in German. Two years, the worst two years of my life—and I want them back. I want *her* back. See? I'm crazy. We're all crazy, the men who love Ann-Marie. Like I say, the only surprise is that one of us didn't kill himself long before now.''

He'd met her when he was stationed in Germany, and they got married there. She was working as a secretary for a German company that did a lot of business with Sweden, so they wanted a native Swede. He'd thought she was in love with him, but after they came to the United States and he got out of the Army, he realized he'd only been a fast, easy way for her to get here and become a citizen.

"I thought she came to this country as a child,'' I said, "with her parents.'' According to Carol, that's what she'd told Mike.

"No, she'd never been here before I brought her home with me. The spoils of war,'' he added with a laugh. "Actually,'' he went on, "life with Ann-Marie wasn't so bad, once I got used to her ways. I got so I could spot the next guy she was going to go to bed with—I got so I knew her type. It was almost weird, you know? We'd be at a party or something and I'd see this guy across the room. I'd nudge her and nod in his direction and she'd give me that smile. You ever meet her? She has a smile like a cat when it's really contented.'' I've never thought cats had any expression on their faces at all, just function. But then, I'm allergic to them.

A many-splendored thing, love. "That kind of behavior's gotten a little dangerous, hasn't it?" I said. "You and Ann-Marie might find it safer to go back to the old ways— the kiss on the cheek, the quick hug, the small, secret smile.''

He ignored the sarcasm. "To be honest with you, sex doesn't interest me all that much anymore anyway. After putting in twelve, fourteen hours here every day, it's kind of like a busman's holiday.''

"You said you could always tell if a man was Ann-Marie's type. How about Mike Parrish?" I asked him.

"I never met him," he said, "so I wouldn't know.''

"You know his name.''

He didn't blink. "Wouldn't you know the name of the one lady stupid enough to kill herself over your man?''

He had a point. "You were married two years, and then you split up. Why? It sounds like a match made in heaven.''

"Ha-ha. She got ambitious. I wasn't enough for her.'' He shrugged it off, as if it didn't hurt at all.

"She didn't want to live with a clerk in a porn shop— or do you own the place?''

His lips twisted in disgust. "I was in school then, the Business School at the U. I didn't work here then—I'm just working here till I get my shit together.''

The world was holding its breath, no doubt, in anticipation of that day. "Didn't she want to wait for you to graduate and get a decent job?''

His eyes hopped around the store, as if the answer might be there somewhere. He hollered at two men down one of the aisles not to tear the plastic that covered the magazines.

"I guess not," he said finally. "I guess she didn't.''

He didn't sound convinced. He didn't convince me that that was the answer either.

"Ann-Marie used you to get into this country. But she stayed with you two years. Then all of a sudden she got ambitious. What was she going to do? What did she leave you for? She's still a secretary, isn't she? She was a secretary when she was with you and that's what she is now. How has she improved her situation?"

"I don't know," he said again, annoyed, as if my questions were flies buzzing around his eyes. "Drop it, okay? And lay off Ann-Marie. She hasn't done anything wrong, and you don't have any right to be pumping me like this. She was with me the night the guy killed himself."

"What a coincidence. Do you and Ann-Marie get together often like that?"

"Not often. Once in a while."

"Your place or hers?"

"Hers. She wouldn't want to spend time in a dump like mine," he said, looking up at the ceiling, the underbelly of his place.

"What'd you do that night?"

"Now c'mon, officer!" he said, recovered enough to try a real laugh this time. "This is a lady we're talking about!"

"I mean, were other people around—people who saw you, who could support your statement that she was with you that night?"

"Huh-unh. Sorry about that." He began slowly spinning a display rack of condoms that were decorated like Zulu warriors in *National Geographic*. "You satisfied yet?" he asked. He gave me that slow grin that seemed to be a speciality of his.

"That Mike Parrish committed suicide? No. Maybe Ann-Marie has the kind of power over men you say she does. But I doubt that it was her exotic beauty or sex appeal that killed Mike Parrish."

"Then what was it?" He made it sound like a challenge.

"I'll let you know," I replied, "as soon as I find out."

He got mad then, started around the counter. "You're calling me a liar and my wife a killer, and I don't have to take that. Get out of here!'' I backed toward the door, wondering what was in his system besides pot. "I told you, me and Ann-Marie were together when that dumb shit was killed. You're—"

"Was killed?" I repeated. "Is that what you said, Terry? When that dumb shit was killed?"

He stared at me, confused for a moment, and then recovered. "You know what the fuck I mean. Get out. It's against the law for cops to harass honest businessmen, and you're bad for business."

It wouldn't have been much of a challenge to knock him into a shelf or two of skin magazines, but I wasn't on a crusade at the moment and besides, I'd forced him to say something he didn't mean to say. It wasn't much, but it was something. So I got out of there.

Seven

According to his sister, Mike had worked in the Biology Department, which was where he first met Ann-Marie. Carol didn't know exactly what Mike did in Biology—he didn't have a degree in that field—but it was something to do with computers. Mike had earned a degree in computer science at the U.

I have a friend who works in Personnel. His name's Rick. He's been there a long time and, instead of becoming one with the red tape that surrounds him, he's become one with the scissors you can sometimes use to cut through it. I deal with him whenever I have to try to locate people who work for the University, or once did. We're both redheads, which forms a bond.

I told him what I wanted and he worked his computer.

"Here she is," he said, "warts and all." He scanned the screen. "There aren't any warts though. What do you want to know about her?"

"Does she still work at the U, for one thing."

"Nope. She worked here from February 1987 to April 1988, and that's it. A senior secretary in Biology. No other University jobs. Anything else?"

"Parrish, Michael."

His fingers clacked the computer keys and he watched the screen. "Nothing," he said.

That meant Mike hadn't had a civil service appointment, he'd been faculty of some kind.

"Could I see Ekdahl's file?"

"No." A look of horror appeared on his freckled face.

The office was a large one, crowded with computer terminals, telephones, typewriters, paper, file cabinets, and people busy with all those things. In the middle of it all, Rick's supervisor, Mrs. Beebe, was sitting in her glass cage of an office, looking like Stalin in his tomb, except that she was sitting up straight and her moustache was thinner. She was turning the pages in a thick book labeled "Procedures." Every now and then her tongue would dart out of the side of her mouth, as if she were savoring a particularly well-turned phrase.

Rick sauntered over to a bank of file cabinets directly in front of Mrs. Beebe and pulled out a drawer. He thumbed through it until he found the file he wanted. Mrs. Beebe's eyes rolled up from her book and studied him for a moment and then, lulled, sank back to "Procedures." Rick brought the file to me and said, "I hope this is what you're looking for."

I thanked him and walked away with it. Rick would make a very successful criminal. He'd managed to snatch a file from under the nose of one of the minor priestesses of civil service, brought it to me, and let me walk away with it without doing anything to interest her at all. Perhaps that sort of thing isn't as dramatic as an escape from a prisoner-of-war camp, but it involves the same skills and some of the same risks.

I sat in the coffee shop of the student union and read Ann-Marie's file. It consisted of her job application, a copy of a payroll form, a social security application, and a three-month and nine-month probation report, both signed by her supervisor, a woman named Betty Hall.

Ann-Marie hadn't just passed probation, she'd soared through it with flying colors. On a scale going from "Unsatisfactory" to "Excellent," she'd received all "Very Goods" and "Excellents." Under "Comments" was the sentence, "Conscientious and hardworking, an asset to the office." Six months later, her supervisor was just as enthusiastic.

Under "Reason for leaving," on the termination report, she'd written, "To take a better-paying job."

I turned to her job application form. Under work experience she'd listed a company in Hamburg, in West Germany, called Manfred Stiller AG. I remembered enough of my college German to know that AG stood for "Inc." Ann-Marie'd worked there as a secretary from 1984 to the end of 1986. She'd given "Multilingual Secretary" as her job title and, under "Job Description," put "Typing business letters and forms in German, Swedish, and English." She didn't say what the company did. All that Terry Rhodes had said was that it did business with Sweden. Apparently it did business with England or America, too.

I took out my notebook and wrote down a chronology. According to her application, where she had to show that she was entitled to live and work in this country, she and Terry Rhodes had gotten married in December of 1986—at the time she quit working at Manfred Stiller in Hamburg. She'd kept her maiden name, if that's what Ekdahl was. She and Rhodes returned to this country shortly after that and Ann-Marie had started work for Biology in February of '87. A little over a year later, in April 1988, she left Biology to take another job. Rhodes had told me they'd been together about two years. If he was telling the truth, then she'd left him in late '88, half a year or so after leaving Biology.

I wondered about the better-paying job she'd quit Biology for, and what her life had been like in the year between leaving her husband and suddenly coming on to Mike Parrish like a Mack truck, as he'd described it to Carol.

There didn't have to be anything significant in any of it, I reflected as I walked back to Personnel. It was just a day in the life, the story of a million women, a few of them friends of mine. But Ann-Marie wasn't a friend of mine, she was a possible murderer. Therefore, everything in her file had a potentially rich symbolic meaning—it was just that I didn't have the key to the symbolism.

I gave the file back to Rick. "Hey," he said, "your hair's on fire, you know that?"

"At least I don't attract rabbits," I retorted. Rick looks more like a carrot than I do.

Back outside, the trees and students cast long shadows on the snow. It was 3:30, too late to go over to Biology and talk to Ann-Marie's former supervisor. If she was willing to talk to me at all, I didn't want to be working against the clock. So I went skiing instead, and stayed out until it was nearly time to go to work.

I was assigned the New Campus, on foot. I spent the first couple of hours wandering through the buildings that surround the Science Tower like acolytes around their priest. All the buildings on that side of campus are well-lit, day and night, and kept at a constant temperature because of all the sensitive equipment they house. I don't feel at home anywhere there.

Around two, I crossed to the Science Tower, retracing the route I'd taken last November with Jason Horn in tow. It had been Horn's route, too, when he'd taken the elevator to the fifteenth floor, to Lucas Calder's office—just on an impulse, he'd said, out of curiosity. I was the one who was curious now, but not about Calder or Horn. I was curious to know if I'd find Professor Reid in his office at that hour of the morning. He'd told me he often had to work that late—something to do with using the supercomputers.

Lucas Calder's door was closed. Just for the exercise, I stooped and peered through the transom, as Reid had said he'd done when he'd heard noises inside. No flashlights were moving around in the darkness tonight.

I continued on down the hall, around the corner, to Reid's office. Light spilled through the transom. I hesitated a moment, then knocked.

Half a minute of silence passed. I was about to turn and go when the door opened. Reid was taller than I'd remembered, and leaner. There was a look of surprise on his face, as he took in my uniform hat and coat, before he recognized me.

"What can I do for *you*?" he asked, raising an eyebrow.

"Nothing, I'm just passing through. Part of the job. Thought I'd stop and say hello, if you were in," I added, babbling. "You told me in November that you sometimes work this late."

"That's right," he said, "so I did. You want to come in?"

"Not if I'm disturbing you. I'm Peggy O'Neill, in case you've forgotten, Professor Reid."

"Call me Marty," he said. "No, you're not disturbing me."

His office was considerably more cluttered than Lucas Calder's had been. Like Calder, he had a computer on a table next to his desk and a lot of other equipment scattered around the room that looked expensive and hi-tech. The computer was on, but the screen was blank.

"That's not a supercomputer, is it?" I asked. I didn't really think it was, but a conversation has to start somewhere.

"No," he said with a laugh. "What made you think that?"

"You told me you worked this late sometimes so you could use the supercomputers. I just wondered."

"I am using a supercomputer, but it's not here. It's over in the Supercomputer Institute—I've never even seen one. I access it through a modem. That's a modem," he said, pointing to a small box on his desk. "It lets me go from my desktop computer to the supercomputers via telephone."

"Is 'access' a verb?"

"It is now," he replied, as if I'd really wanted to know. He explained that he'd just fed the supercomputer some data, and was waiting for the result. "When it's ready, a message will flash on my screen, telling me where it's stored—sort of like electronic mail, if you know what that is."

When I'd first heard of electronic mail, from a secretary friend of mine, I'd wondered if it would mean the end of the epistolary novel. I decided not to share that one with Reid—Marty. Instead, I said: "In Calder's office, you told me it's cheaper to use the supercomputers at night. Why's that?"

"It's like calling long distance," he answered. "It doesn't cost as much during off-peak hours. Plus, during the day, you sometimes have to wait a long time to get access to a supercomputer. It's mostly researchers without families who like to work at night—or researchers with small grants who can't afford the daytime rates.''

"Which are you?"

"Both,'' he said. "What about you? You always seem to work nights, so I take it you don't have a family either.'' It was almost a question.

"I don't,'' I answered.

"Any serious men in your life?'' That was a question.

"No.'' He looked at me longer than necessary, maybe on account of the uncertainty in my voice.

"I don't know why,'' I said, thinking I'd like to change the subject, "but I thought there'd be some kind of telescope in here somewhere.''

"I haven't looked through one of those in years,'' he said. "Today we have scanning devices looking at the stars through telescopes—radio telescopes. They feed us data from space that the supercomputers process for us. Nobody could process that much data with a pencil and paper. Even using an ordinary mainframe computer, it would take three days to get the results I'm waiting for. With the supercomputer, I'll have them in about that many hours.''

I wondered what he did with all the extra time that gave him, but didn't ask. I didn't know what a mainframe computer was either, assumed it was something big and plodding—a giant abacus, maybe.

"Doesn't sound as romantic as scanning the sky through a telescope, the old-fashioned way,'' I said.

"It's a different kind of pleasure.''

He glanced at his watch, then asked me if I skied. I said I did—cross-country—and we agreed that we should go skiing together sometime. As he wrote down my home phone number, I realized, with a pleasant sense of shame and a fleeting mental image of Al, that I'd gotten everything I'd come for. So I got up to go.

"Did you read in the *Daily* that Jason Horn's vanished?'' I asked.

"Who?'' He followed me to the door. "Oh, yeah. I don't suppose you've heard anything?''

"Nothing.''

"He's probably in Jamaica, lying on the beach with a beautiful woman."

"I hope so," I said.

I took the elevator back to ground level, retracing again my steps from the beginning of winter. My mind was cluttered with the pale memory of Jason Horn, with a murder that might be a suicide or vice versa, and with Marty Reid, who might be trouble.

Eight

The next afternoon, I went over to the Department of Biology to try to talk to Betty Hall, Ann-Marie's former supervisor, the executive secretary who'd signed the evaluation forms for Ann-Marie. The department was on the Old Campus, in a relatively new building for that campus—beautifully done art deco. Biology occupied the second and third floors.

The sign on the receptionist's desk said "Barbara McKay." The woman sitting behind the sign was about twenty-five, with curly brown hair that emphasized the fact that she had a large round head and was short, plump, and good-natured. Or maybe the dimples told me she was good natured. I told her my name and asked to see Betty Hall.

"You're the campus policewoman," she said. "I probably would've recognized you even if you hadn't told me your name, on account of your hair. A friend of mine once pointed you out to me—said you were a friend of his sister's and a campus cop. It's okay to call you that, isn't it—cop?"

I said sure, that's what we called ourselves. "Mike Parrish?" I asked her.

Her face clouded and she nodded, said yes. Mike had worked in the Biology Department too, she said, he was a nice guy. She couldn't understand how he could've killed himself. He was bitter over the way the department treated him, but still . . . "You just never know, do you?" she said, shaking her head.

I agreed that you didn't and asked her why he was bitter at the department.

"He didn't think the faculty gave him enough credit for what he did. He thought they took him for granted."

"And was that true?"

"I wouldn't know," she answered with a shrug, "I just work here. He liked to come in and gripe about it sometimes."

"Did he want more credit," I asked, "or more money?"

"Well, both, I guess. Mostly, I think he just wanted more recognition; I don't think he was all that interested in money. But I never expected he'd kill himself. He could be pretty funny sometimes, in a 'life sucks' kind of way, but I didn't think he was *despondent*."

I'd finally met somebody besides Mike's family who acted surprised that he'd killed himself. Just to see what her reaction would be, I said, "Not everybody's convinced he did kill himself."

She didn't blink an eye. "Really? I thought he shot himself with a gun or something. You think it might've been an accident?"

"Or murder."

"Murder!"

"That's what his family thinks."

"No! Not everybody liked him like I did, and he didn't like everybody either, but who'd want to murder him?"

A good question. "You knew him," I said. "Maybe you could suggest somebody."

She thought about it a moment, narrowing her eyes to help, carefully pinching a long fingernail she hadn't been born with between two teeth, finally shook her head. "Huh-unh," she said. "Of course, he and I weren't dating or anything—I just knew him in the department. He sometimes stopped in here and had coffee with me on my breaks, we did lunch sometimes, too, but that's just crazy, murder, though maybe not any crazier than him wanting to kill himself. I don't know." Then a look that was more startled than frightened spread over her face and she said, "You don't suspect *me?*"

I said I didn't have any suspects at all.

"But you're sure it was murder?"

I shook my head. "No, I'm not sure it was murder." Listening to this woman talk, who'd known Mike, made me doubt even more what I was doing. She was a normal human being. Murder was something she watched on television; it was the evening news, entertainment.

"Not sure what was murder?" a woman's voice behind me asked.

I turned. She was tall and angular with a firm jaw and a long thin mouth, and her steel-blue eyes matched her hair and the expression on her face.

Barbara McKay didn't miss a beat, said, "Betty, this is Officer O'Neill. She's from the University Police."

Betty Hall gave me a quick up-and-down and said again, "Not sure what was murder?"

"We were talking about a mutual friend," I explained. "I was saying I wasn't sure his death was murder."

"Who?" Her eyes didn't blink, didn't move from my face. There'd been a nun in the grade school I'd attended who would stare at me like that, all too often. I'm still working to overcome a tendency to wither under it, or want to pee.

"Michael Parrish," I said. "He used to work here." She seemed to relax when I told her who we'd been talking about.

"Parrish," she said. She shrugged, started toward the partially open door behind Barbara. Then she turned and gave me a puzzled look. "He committed suicide, didn't he?"

"His family doesn't think so."

"And so you're here, to look into the matter?"

"Yes," I said, and plunged in with both feet. "I was hoping you'd be able to give me some information that would help."

"So." She thought about it a moment. "From what I knew of Parrish, he could very well have committed suicide. But as long as it doesn't take very much of my time . . . come in."

I followed her into her office. It was larger and more

richly appointed than even the chief's office at headquarters. I looked around and said, with genuine admiration, "This is very nice."

"I couldn't run this department from a phone booth, could I?" she retorted with no trace of humor. "Now what can I do for you?"

Walking over to see Betty Hall, I'd considered possible ways to approach her. I wasn't making an official inquiry, after all. If I told her it was official, and she checked my story, I'd be in trouble. That wouldn't be so bad, I've been in trouble before, but I also wouldn't get anything out of her if she had anything to give. I finally decided to throw myself on her mercy, stick as closely to the truth as I could, and tell her that I was doing a personal favor for a family devastated by their son's and brother's death. I've found that the truth sometimes works, too.

I did that, and tried to suggest that I didn't share the family's suspicions, I was just humoring them. She listened, sitting up straight in her chair, her eyes never leaving my face, and I was glad I wasn't trying to tell any kind of elaborate lie under that steady gaze. When I'd finished, she relaxed, settled back into her chair, and folded her long fingers. She had beautiful hands.

"You are doing this on your own time, then?"

"Yes."

"Then we shouldn't waste it." She pressed a button on her intercom and asked Barbara McKay if they still had the file on Michael Parrish. Barbara squawked that they did, and Betty Hall told her to bring it in. While we waited, she asked me a little about police work, and found it interesting, as lots of people do, that I like patrolling at night. She nodded, indicated that she approved, and on account of that, I decided I liked her. She took the file from Barbara, scanned it quickly, then asked me what I wanted to know.

I asked her when Mike had started working in the department and what his job was.

"He started here in January 1988," she said, looking up from the file. "He'd been here just two years when he died. His official title was Computing Coordinator. He was a research specialist, a position that's somewhere between civil service and faculty, but it isn't either.''

I asked her what a computing coordinator did.

"Increasingly less and less. Michael Parrish was hired to help the Biology faculty and graduate students in their research, show them how to adapt their projects to the computer—for example, set up programs for analyzing data, create models, simulations. But as our faculty and students have become more and more familiar with the computer, the existence of someone like Mike Parrish becomes less important. Some of our faculty now even have Masters and PhD degrees in Computer Science in addition to their degrees in Biology, whereas he had only a B.A. in Computer Science. At the time of his death, he was in charge of the programmers we have working for us. He also ran introductory workshops for our new faculty and students, and he did some advanced programming for a few of the older faculty members whose skills aren't at that level.''

"So he did know a good deal about computers.''

"Oh, yes. He was very good. But we didn't need him any longer as much as he thought we ought to. That was the problem, or one of them. He grew resentful.''

"And you think that would be a motive for his suicide?''

"I'm not qualified to make judgments like that, Miss O'Neill.''

"Was he in danger of having his job cut out from under him?''

She shrugged. "He would not have been fired, if that's what you mean. He had a kind of tenure.'' She added: "And *he* hadn't done anything to incur the wrath of central administration.''

She said that with such bitterness that I was taken aback. I asked her what she'd meant by it and she replied that she'd meant nothing.

I thought: I wonder why you're lying?

"At the time of his death,'' she went on, "we hadn't yet decided what to do with him. We were working on redefining his position. He had his uses. Perhaps he would have ended up being shared among a number of departments. But whatever we decided, he would not have liked it. I don't suppose he described his career to his family in quite the way I have, Officer O'Neill, so his suicide must have come upon them unexpectedly. What else can I do for you?" She wasn't even breathing hard after all that.

I couldn't think of anything else to ask her about Mike. Everything she'd told me could be interpreted as a motive for suicide.

"Did he have problems with any particular member of the department?" I asked.

She smiled. "Do you mean, can I think of a member of the department who had a motive for killing him? No. He had a chip on his shoulder, he could be sullen, but he was not important enough to anybody for them to want him dead. I feel quite sure of that."

"What about friends in the department?"

"I don't believe he had any. But Barbara"—she nodded at the door—"seems to have considered him a friend, according to what I heard her telling you. That was the first I knew of it, although I do recall having seen him in her office on several occasions."

"What about a woman who used to work here?" I asked and, before I could finish the question, saw her face start the interesting process of becoming stone. "Ann-Marie Ekdahl?"

She sat up straight again, caught herself, then pretended she was just looking for a more comfortable position in her chair. But that's all it was, pretending.

"Ekdahl?" she said, as if hearing the name for the first time. "What's *she* got to do with Michael Parrish?"

"At the time of Mike's death," I told her, "they were going together."

"No," she said flatly, "that's quite impossible." The words escaped from her mouth before she had any time to think about it. It startled her as much as it did me.

"Why do you say that?"

"Because—" She stopped, giving her brain a few moments to catch up. She started over, from the beginning. "I wasn't aware they even knew each other," she said.

Much better. Then, picking up a red ballpoint pen and bending it between her fingers, she added, "Yes, I suppose she could still have been here when we hired Parrish. I don't remember. I didn't know they knew each other and I certainly wouldn't have thought he was her type."

"What was her type?"

"I wouldn't know." Her hands were slowly bending the pen between them, back and forth. "A much stronger man, I would imagine, a more *successful* man. Michael Parrish was neither strong nor successful." She waited a moment, then asked, "Why are you interested in her? Do you think she might have had something to do with his death?"

"The police think he killed himself on account of her."

Again she had trouble knowing how to react. She just stared. And then she gave a laugh and said, "People don't do that anymore!" She added, "But maybe . . . a weak man . . . I don't know. She certainly had a way about her."

I looked at her and she looked at me and we both knew she'd just slogged her way through a mine field, and we both knew that I'd lose on the deal if I pointed it out to her.

I decided to move onto some touchy ground myself. I'd already told her that my investigation wasn't official, so it would be hard to slip past her the knowledge I'd gained about Ann-Marie from reading her personnel file without her wanting to know how I'd acquired that knowledge. It takes a court order for a campus cop to get official access to somebody's personnel file.

"What did you think of Ann-Marie?" I asked her.

"I don't see—" she began, and then she shrugged and said: "I recall that her performance was satisfactory. Senior secretaries have a tendency to come and go, so I can hardly say more than that. It's been—what?—two years, I believe."

"You were her supervisor, weren't you?"

"Technically, of course, yes," she answered. "But she worked directly for one of the professors on a project he was engaged in, and I didn't see her often. That happens frequently, you know. A professor gets a large grant for a project, there's a lot of paperwork and coordination, and one of our secretaries is assigned to work for him until the project is completed.''

"I'd like to talk to the professor then," I said.

"You're very persistent, aren't you? I'm sorry, but Professor Lock has left the University. He was lured away by Yale, unfortunately—and he took his project with him.''

"Did you fill out her evaluation forms, or did Professor Lock?" Betty Hall had at least signed them, I knew.

"Professor Lock," she replied, without any hesitation at all. "I have no memory of what he put on them.''

On paper, at least, Ann-Marie hadn't been just a run-of-the-mill secretary, since her evaluations were full of superlatives. Maybe that's the sort of thing a professor who considered himself too important to expend any thought on evaluating his secretary would do, but I'd be surprised if a supervisor like Betty Hall would forget it.

"I know I've taken up too much of your time already," I said. "But I wonder if you could get Miss Ekdahl's file and—just in general terms—tell me how long she worked here and what Professor Lock's opinion of her was. I'd also like to know where she went, if you have that information." I was hoping to get her reaction to the evaluations she'd signed, but mostly I wanted the name of the company she'd left Biology for. Departmental files sometimes have that information. The file Rick had showed me in Personnel didn't.

"That would be a breach of confidentiality, Officer O'Neill," Betty Hall said, "as I'm sure you know. I'm going to pretend that you didn't ask me for such a thing." She made it sound as if she were doing me a big job-saving favor. "And I'm sure we have no record of where she went when she left here.''

How could she be so sure of that, I wondered, if she had so little recollection of Ann-Marie?

The pen Betty Hall was playing with got tired of the game and broke softly in two, leaking ink onto her long fingers. She gave the two bleeding halves a disgusted look and dropped them into her wastebasket. They made a loud clunk that, along with her expression, told me the interview was over. I thanked her for her time and help and, firmly closing her door behind me, I left her wiping red ink off her fingertips with a Kleenex.

Barbara McKay looked up at me from her typewriter as I walked past her desk. "Did you get what you wanted?" she asked in her most receptionist-like voice. She also sounded slightly out of breath, as if she'd been running, but you can also sound that way if you've been breathing very shallowly as you eavesdrop at a door. I know that from personal experience.

I gave her a long, stern look. She stared back, and blushed to the roots of her curly brown hair. "Yes, thank you, I did," I replied, "Ms. Hall was very helpful." I bent down to read the number on her telephone's dial, but she put a plump hand over it, shook her head, and quickly wrote a phone number on a piece of notepaper and handed that to me.

"It's Miss Hall," she corrected me, speaking as if she were well aware that the walls were thin and that she was auditioning for a part. "She doesn't like the title Ms. It's a non-word."

"Thank you for telling me that," I said, pursing my lips to get the right tone to compete with hers. "And it was nice talking to you, too," I added as I left her office, knowing I'd be talking to her again.

Nine

I had other things to do before I could call Barbara Mc-Kay. Break up with Al, for instance.

He wanted to get married. That's not how he put it, but that's what he meant. He proposed that, to begin with, we move in together. Maybe it was the "to begin with" that tightened my skin and made the hairs rise on my arms. Being scared makes me angry.

I like Al a lot. He's the kindest man I've ever known. He's a veterinarian, and I've watched him work with animals. He handles them deftly and gently, the way he makes love. I like the way he makes love, too, because it's how I make love.

I like him as much as, but not more than, I like coming home to my apartment and finding that it's just mine. It's my world, and I can decide who I want in it with me, if anybody, and when, and for what, and for how long. I like Al almost as much as I like doing whatever I want to do without having to try to fit it into somebody else's schedule or trimming it to his preferences, stated or implied. I'm pretty sure I'll never want children—millions of women do, so I'm not needed there. I do know that I don't want other people's children—in this case, Al's by his ex-wife.

"Anything else?" he asked, when I'd gone through some of that with him.

"Just one more thing," I answered, ignoring the voice in my head that was telling me to shut up now, I'd made my point. "You don't really want to marry me, you just

57

want a replacement for the wife you feel guilty about having left because you've forgotten why you did."

"You win all the battles, don't you?" he said after a while, and went home hurt.

After he'd left, I stalked barefoot around my beautiful apartment, scuffing the rug where Al had been sitting, and kicking the newspaper he'd left open on the floor. Part of me was full of righteous anger, and another part was smiling a nasty little kid's smile and thinking of Marty Reid, and my eyes were full of tears.

It was time to get ready for work.

The next evening, I called Barbara McKay at the number she'd slipped me when I was in her office. I'd assumed it was her home phone, and to judge from the noise in the background—a childish howling that sounded like a daycare center in an earthquake—it seemed I was right.

"I expected you to call last night," she said, "but I suppose you were busy, out catching felons," and she asked me if sometime she could ride with me in my squad car. She thought maybe she'd like to be a cop, too, if they took women with children. She was divorced.

I said I didn't get the squad car every night, most nights I walked a beat, but if she was serious about it, the next time my turn came around, I'd give her a call. Or she could walk my beat with me, up to her belly button in snow.

"Great! Gimme a couple of days to get a sitter for Shaun. That's my son, he's three, I guess you can hear him. Well, did you get what you wanted from Iron Betty?"

"Not everything," I said, "as you know."

She giggled. "There's a vent in her door near the floor; you probably noticed. If I squat close to it, I can hear everything she says in there. She really clammed up when Ann-Marie's name came up, didn't she?"

"Do you know why?"

"She hates her guts, that's why. It was a real surprise to all of us when we realized it. When she first came into the department, Ann-Marie'd really hustled Betty, and it worked, Betty fell for it—hook, line, and sinker. Butter wouldn't melt in her mouth, as far as Betty was concerned.

She sometimes even compared the rest of us to Ann-Marie.
'If you all worked as hard as Ann-Marie,' crap like that,
you should excuse my French. The rest of us knew what
Ann-Marie was doing. Mostly, she wasn't doing her share,
that's what she was doing, she was just curled up at Betty's
feet, purring like a kitten. It was sickening. Some of us
figured if Ann-Marie hung around long enough, she'd be
running the office. Betty even used to invite Ann-Marie
over for dinner. She never did anything like that with the
rest of us; none of us ever saw the inside of Betty's house,
not that we'd want to. Looking at Iron Betty, you'd never
think she'd fall for somebody like Ann-Marie. Some of us
thought maybe, you know . . .''

"Do you think that's what it was?" I asked. "You
know?''

She giggled. "Well, Iron Betty's never been married."
She paused to let the deep significance of that sink in, but
all I could hear was Shaun's crying—to judge from the
volume, somewhere down around his mother's ankles.

I asked her when Betty's attitude changed towards Ann-
Marie.

"I don't know, so it must have been after Ann-Marie
left Biology. They were still real close right up to the time
she left, I know that. Betty was real sorry about her leaving. Some of us figured it must've been a lover's quarrel.
More than a quarrel, though, it must have been a real
knock-down-drag-out.''

"Well," I asked, "how did you *know* Betty started hat-
ing Ann-Marie?''

"Oh, because somebody—it wasn't me, honest!—asked
Betty how Ann-Marie was doing at her new job. Not that
any of us cared, of course, we just wanted to see if Ann-
Marie was still keeping in with Betty, now that she no
longer had any reason to. And pow! Betty got real upset,
like Joan had slapped her sunburn or something—Joan being the girl who'd asked her. She said she had no idea how
Ann-Marie was doing, wanted to know why Joan wanted
to know, acted like she thought Joan knew something and
was laughing at her to her face—which she was, sort of,
we all were, but we didn't know anything, it was just a

shot in the dark.'' She paused, perhaps to adjust the shackle around her ankles, or the volume.

"Can you recall about when that happened?"

"A long time ago—seven, eight months."

"Last summer sometime?"

"Yeah, right. But here comes the good part," Barbara went on, her voice gaining enthusiasm. "Ann-Marie comes back! Just strolls into my office as if she never left."

"When?"

"Like maybe the middle of November—it was right before Thanksgiving break, I'm pretty sure. Anyway, Betty happens to be standing by my desk when it happens. I'm sitting there looking from one to the other, very interested in what's going to happen now, because of course now I know how Betty hates her guts. Betty stiffens like she's seen a ghost and asks Ann-Marie what she wants. 'I'm looking for somebody,' Ann-Marie says, and kind of ducks her head and tries to act humble, but there's a little smile playing all over her mouth. 'This is a working office, Miss Ekdahl,' Betty says, in a voice so cold you could freeze meat with it. 'Unless you are here on business, you will have to leave.' "

"And she was there to see Mike Parrish," I said, hoping to hurry Barbara along a little. "How do you know?"

"How'd you guess? I heard you tell Iron Betty that Ann-Marie was going with Mike at the time he took his own life or whatever. That was news to me, but I wasn't surprised either." Shaun was really crying now, the steady existential crying of the three-year-old. "She wasn't involved with Mike when she was working in the Department. Like I told you, him and me used to talk sometimes. He would've said something, or I would've seen it."

I could believe that. "But . . . ?" I prodded her.

"But she called Mike up, maybe three, four days before she came in. I recognized her voice, even though she didn't say who was calling. She asked for Mike in that Swedish accent of hers you can cut with a cheese scraper. I pretended I didn't know who it was, said 'May I say who's calling?' That pissed her off because she knew I wouldn't talk to Mike before connecting her, I'd just put her on hold and buzz his phone. 'Just put me through, please,' she said. So I waited a certain amount of time and then did. They talked for a long time. His light was on, so I could see that. Before that, I didn't know they knew each other except to say 'hi' to. She left the department a couple months after he was hired.''

''You didn't listen in on the conversation, did you?''

''Me?'' She giggled. ''No, honest. I'm not like that. I just snoop a little when it's Iron Betty and I think it might be interesting. Besides, there was a call on another line. Anyway, that's how I knew she came in to see Mike, the day Betty caught her in my office. I didn't see her together with Mike, because Betty made her leave. In fact, I never saw her again at all.''

''Betty said that it was Professor Lock who filled out the evaluation forms for Ann-Marie,'' I said, changing the subject.

''Yeah, I heard that.'' She giggled. Shaun sobbed. ''Not really. Professors usually never fill out the evaluations, they're too busy. Maybe Betty asked old Lock how Ann-Marie was doing, but my guess is he wouldn't even understand the question. Betty did those evaluations herself, I'd bet on it. She gave them to me to type up. You should've seen them, were they ever sickening! God, how could Ann-Marie pull the wool over the eyes of somebody like Iron Betty? Betty must be starting to lose it.''

''Do you know why Ann-Marie quit?''

''Sure, she told us it was because she got this really good job offer from this guy she knew when she lived in Germany.''

''What?''

''That's what she said, anyway. She came in one day and told us she'd met this guy she used to work for in Germany and now he's here and he's a big shot in some company in town and he's going to offer her a job— although he doesn't know it yet, she said.''

''He doesn't know it yet,'' I repeated.

''That's what she said. Like, he didn't know yet that he was going to give her a job, but she was sure she could hustle one out of him. She must've, too, because thirty days later she was gone.''

"Did she say the name of the company?"

''Nope, just that it did a lot of business overseas and her Swedish and German would come in handy.''

I glanced down at the notes I'd made from Ann-Marie's personnel file, and darkened the circle I'd already drawn around the name of the German company she'd worked for.

"What was Betty's relationship to Mike?" I asked her.

''You mean, like maybe Betty and Ann-Marie were both after him?'' Barbara McKay gave a snort, then said, skeptically, ''Well, I guess it's possible—if Betty could fall for Ann-Marie, she could fall for anybody. But if she liked Mike at all, she sure knew how to hide it.''

That sounded pretty convincing. I couldn't think of anything else Barbara could help me with, so I thanked her and hung up. My ear was sore and I had a headache from all the background noise.

Barbara McKay and Betty Hall had told me a lot. Mike Parrish was unhappy with Biology because it was gradually learning how to do without his services. That could be a motive for suicide, except that Mike didn't seem to let it depress him; it had made him bitter instead. Ann-Marie had known him briefly during her stay in the Biology Department, but there hadn't been anything between them, according to both Betty Hall and Barbara McKay. But then Ann-Marie had called Mike up in the middle of November. Why?

There could be all kinds of innocent explanations for it, of course. She and Mike might have met by chance on the street and decided to get together, or they might have become friends at any time after Ann-Marie left Biology, and this was just the first time Ann-Marie'd had any reason to call him at his office. Mike might not have told Barbara McKay about his relationship with Ann-Marie because he knew what a gossip she was.

I didn't know what to make of the relationship between Ann-Marie and Betty Hall. According to Barbara, they'd been unusually close all the time Ann-Marie was in the Biology Department, but then, sometime last summer, Betty got upset when Ann-Marie's name came up and later when she saw Ann-Marie herself. It was always possible that Barbara's guess was correct and that it had been a love affair that went sour—there wasn't any reason why Ann-Marie couldn't be bisexual or Betty Hall gay.

Betty Hall had been keeping something back when she'd talked to me, I knew that. I recalled her words about how Mike Parrish hadn't done anything to incur the wrath of central administration, as if somebody she knew had. I wondered if she was thinking of herself.

I didn't know where to begin picking at any of that, so I decided to start with something simpler—trying to find out who it was Ann-Marie had met that she'd worked for in Germany. I had no idea where that would take me, but every time I tried to find a connection between Mike Parrish and Ann-Marie that might give her a reason for wanting him dead, the trail ended without leaving any indication of where to go next.

Ten

I put Carol to work. She'd called several times since talking me into investigating her brother's death, wanting to know if I'd made any progress. I'd put her off because I hadn't found out anything that added up to much, and I didn't want to share what little I had with her anyway. I could easily imagine her trying to get something from Terry Rhodes herself, and Carol in a porn shop looking for her brother's killer would be at least as disastrous as a bull in a china shop.

I called her when she got home from work and told her it sounded as if Mike had had a large chip on his shoulder over the way the Biology Department was treating him and that I'd also learned he was in danger of having his job reclassified into something with less responsibility and prestige.

Carol got very defensive. "So? I knew that. He thought they were using him—the professors, some of the graduate researchers. Getting him to put a lot of time and effort into their projects and then not giving him any credit for the results when they were published. You remember at Christmas, how he had to drive all the way down here from the farm because they needed him? Does that sound like he was just a flunky? But he wouldn't have killed himself on account of *them* any more than on account of Ann-Marie. He'd more likely take a punch at somebody over there."

I wondered suddenly what kind of emergency it could have been that made it necessary for him to drive all that way on the day before Christmas. It was something I'd have to ask Betty Hall about.

I didn't argue with Carol. I told her, "You're going to find out for me where Ann-Marie works."

"How can I do that?"

"You can follow her when she leaves for work Monday morning, just like in the movies."

There was a long pause as she thought about that.

"It doesn't really work like that, do you think?"

"Like what?"

"I mean, don't they catch on that you're following them—or else you lose them?"

"How would I know? I'm only a cop. I've only followed one person in my life and that was easy because he was too upset to notice."

My past heroics didn't interest her. "What if she catches me?"

"Don't let her. But if she does, just give her a weak smile and say you merely wanted to see if you could follow somebody and you chose as your first victim the woman you think murdered your brother." She didn't think that was funny, but I didn't care, since I did. I told her to put the name and address of Ann-Marie's workplace on my answering machine as soon as she learned what it was, or to call me around three, when I'd be awake. I didn't want her waking me up an hour or so after I'd gone to sleep. I hung up rather than listen to some more what-ifs and buts.

I called Ginny Raines next, my detective friend on the campus cops. It was Friday night and after seven, but she was home anyway, which was unusual since she leads an active social life. She told me I'd been busy lately, something I already knew, and asked me what I was doing to keep out of trouble. I gave her a brief description of what I was doing for Carol.

"What was that you called it," Ginny asked, "that thing you said you were?"

I knew what she meant. "Co-dependent," I replied.

"Didn't you tell me it's a disease—like alcoholism?"

"Sort of, yeah. But I'm working on it," I added.

There was a long, pregnant pause. I doodled a square on the notepad by my phone while waiting for her to decide where she wanted the conversation to go next. Finally she asked, "You really think her brother was murdered?"

"Pretty sure."

"Proof?"

"Nothing that would interest the police up north yet, and Buck Hansen isn't interested in a would-be murder that happened a long ways away." I told her the few facts I had and she listened and thought for a few moments and said that they wouldn't interest her either, if she were a homicide detective, especially if it hadn't even happened in her bailiwick. "It's still none of your business," she added.

"What is," I asked, maybe a little shortly, "besides eating, sleeping, and sex sometimes?"

"I saw Al last night," she said. "Speaking of sex sometimes."

"Al was speaking of sex sometimes?"

"You know what I mean. He was with a woman he introduced as Deirdre, at that new southwestern restaurant, Yupxican, or whatever it's called. He didn't look all that happy."

"Of course he didn't," I snapped at her. "He hates Mexican food. It gives him gas."

"Southwestern Mexican food isn't supposed to do that," she replied.

"Then maybe Deirdre gives him gas." I'd met Deirdre just once, at her house the night I took Al away from her at a party neither of us liked very much. It wasn't anything to brag about, anybody could have taken him away from that party, that woman. I changed the subject. "Terry Rhodes," I said, "Ann-Marie's husband, was holding something back, I'm sure of that."

"A guy like that is always holding something back, Peggy," Ginny said. "It's not sinister, it's a lifestyle. Okay," she went on, "so you're going to look for murderers as a way to—what's the word I want?—your sex urges until Al tires of Deirdre and comes back for more of your bleak, crabby company.''

"Sublimate," I said. Ginny knows how to hurt, she just doesn't know when to stop sometimes. "He proposed marriage, or a reasonable facsimile thereof, and I said I didn't want to talk about it. He took that as a definitive answer, and went away mad. Maybe I was a little more abrupt than usual.''

"Why this time? He's made those kind of noises before, hasn't he?''

"It's the first time he's made them this long after being with his kids. He usually wants to get married—or for us to move in together—for a week or two after he's seen them, and then he forgets all about it until the next time. So I took it as a bad sign. Do you want to know why I'm calling you?''

"Sure."

"I've got the name of a company in Germany, in Hamburg. I want to know more about it. What they do, what Ann-Marie did for them, and, especially, the name of a man who worked there who may be here now.''

"Why?"

I told her that my prime suspect in Mike's death used to work there. Terry Rhodes couldn't, or wouldn't, give me its name and Ann-Marie had apparently told Mike nothing about it, she'd said that she'd come to this country as a child. She'd named the company on her University job application, however, several years ago.

"Have you tried the University library? They'll have a phone book for Hamburg, I think. You can look it up. If it exists, call 'em and hope somebody there speaks English—unless you speak German.''

I told Ginny I didn't want to talk to anybody at Ann-Marie's old company directly, because I wasn't sure I wanted them to know I was interested in them, and I wondered if she knew of any other way.

"Why don't you hire a private detective?" she asked.

"It would be pretty expensive, wouldn't it, paying to send a private eye over to Germany? I doubt Carol has that kind of money, and—''

"You're really in over your head, aren't you, Peggy?" Ginny interrupted me. "Listen up. You don't *send* a private detective over there, you look up private detectives in the Hamburg phone book which, as I've told you, you'll probably find in the University Library, in whatever passes for the yellow pages in Hamburg. You hire one *there* to find out what you want to know about the company." She was speaking so slowly and clearly that I could almost see her lips moving.

She was right, I was in over my head. I thanked her for her advice, however sarcastically given, and hung up. I figured I could get Carol to go along with hiring a German private eye. After all, she was getting me for nothing and she made more money than I did—certainly enough to pay a private detective in Germany to do a routine check on a company there.

My watch said it was almost eight. That gave me time to get to the University Library, which closes at ten on Friday nights, look up the Manfred Stiller company, and, if it turned out to be real and still there, look up the names of private detective agencies. I didn't bother calling Carol to get her permission. If she refused to pay for the detective, I'd have an excuse to stop helping her.

I couldn't find anything that looked like yellow pages, but I found a fairly recent copy of a Hamburg phone book and found Manfred Stiller listed. I copied down the address. Then I looked under *Privat,* but found only one listing for a private detective. That didn't seem right for a town as big and bustling as Hamburg, but I thought that maybe the Germans are so disciplined and law-abiding that there isn't any market for private eyes.

I was writing down the number when a man standing next to me at the counter asked, "You know somebody in Hamburg, do you, Miss O'Neill?"

I looked up, recognized him: Professor Hamilton. I'd taken Intermediate German from him when I was a student, to satisfy the language requirement for graduation. He hadn't changed a bit. He was well over six feet tall, thin, stooped, fiftyish, a crane-like man with a cherry-red nose, protruding teeth, and only a few strands of long hair clinging to his head for dear life. He'd been a rotten teacher, spoke German with an English accent laced with Scotch, but oddly enough I'd liked him and he must have remembered me for that. He couldn't have remembered me for the excellence of my German.

"I wish I did," I said.

"What for, may I ask?" It wasn't so much that Hamilton showed his teeth as he spoke; they seemed to pop in and out of his mouth in a friendly, curious way. They'd fascinated me in class.

I told him I was trying to find a private detective in Hamburg. "I'm a campus policewoman," I said, "and it's part of a case I'm working on." He asked me why I'd decided upon this particular detective agency. I explained that, as he could see, it was the only one in town.

"Oh, no, no, no," he said, "you've just looked in the wrong place! It will be under *Detektiv*, not *Privatdetektiv*. Had you told me of your, ah, career goals when you were in my class, I'd have steered you to German detective fiction. Made German relevant for you, as it were."

Under *Detektivburo* there were plenty of detective agencies to choose from and I let Professor Hamilton choose one for me. He said it was in an area of the city he knew.

"Now what?" I said. I was thinking aloud, but I didn't mind if he heard me. "I don't suppose you'd be willing to call them and make arrangements for me, would you?"

He looked at his watch, said, "It's seven hours later in Hamburg—almost four A.M. Unlike your American private eyes—in books, at least—German ones must need sleep sometimes, or so I should imagine."

He suggested that I come to his office at eight on Monday morning, when I got off work, and he'd call Hamburg then—it would be afternoon there—and act as my translator. I accepted gladly and then he went loping off to the library stacks on his long legs, holding up a little pile of reference cards before his eyes, like a divining rod.

Eleven

I had the weekend to kill, while I waited for the seeds I'd planted to sprout, so I called Martin Reid. Marty. After all, I'd driven Al into the arms of a woman named Deirdre in part because I knew Marty was out there, so wasn't it time I collected my reward?

"I know it's kind of short notice," I said, "but I wondered if you'd like to go skiing tomorrow."

"Sure." He didn't sound at all surprised to hear from me. "I'm free all afternoon, but I have work to do at my office tomorrow night. I don't have to be there until a little before ten, though, so that's okay."

I was glad he had work to do. I had Saturday nights off, and I wasn't sure how long I wanted the first evening with Marty to last. We agreed we'd ski the trails at Nichols Park, a few miles out of town, and then go someplace for dinner.

I was waiting for him outside my apartment when he pulled up. He drove a white BMW. He put my skis next to his on the rack, and then held open the passenger door. It had been a long time since a man had done that—it's not an easy thing to do with a van, even if it would occur to Al in the first place. Of all the prestige cars, the BMW's the one I dislike least. It's not flashy, and it's not the car's fault that so many men who can't drive own them. Marty Reid's smelled new.

"I didn't realize associate professors made so much money they could afford BMWs," I said. "Especially professors who have to use the supercomputers during off-peak hours.''

He took his eyes off the road to look at me. Why not, since the car seemed to drive itself? ''Not all my priorities are in order,'' he said, smiling. He added, ''It's a five-three-five-eye,'' which made no sense to me.

''What is?'' I asked, looking at him. As he had the first time, he looked a little like a younger Al—if Al felt comfortable in the fast lane.

''This car.'' He explained that it was a 535i. ''I'll keep it a couple years,'' he added, ''then trade up for something in the 7-series, or whatever the equivalent is then.''

''Ah.''

''I don't have any other vices, Peggy,'' he said, reading my mind.

''That wasn't what I was thinking,'' I lied. ''I was just thinking how I'm starting to be overtaken by technology: supercomputers, modems, radio telescopes, scanners, five-three-five-eyes, stuff like that.''

He skied well. I had trouble keeping up with him and finally stopped trying. He let me catch up at the top of the highest hill, which isn't all that high, but then, with a full-body shrug, or twitch, he set off down the other side, apparently expecting me to follow. After I'd caught my breath, I skied down after him. He was wearing the latest in cross-country ski outfits, bright and expensive and extruded from a European machine. His body looked good in it. I was wearing jeans, and a heavy sweater I'd bought at a yard sale.

It was about six when we got back to his car. We dropped off my skis at my place and then drove to the Science Tower, where Marty parked in the underground garage. Then we walked to a restaurant he liked not far from campus, a Cambodian place.

When we'd ordered, I asked him how he'd gotten into Astronomy. He told me his dad had been an astronomer, so it must have been in the blood. He said his dad's name as if I should know who he was, but I didn't.

''He was here at the U for about twenty years,'' Marty explained. ''He died about five years ago, still pretty young. He did a lot of good work, but he wasn't the show-man Lucas Calder is—Lucas' opposite in just about every way, in fact, although they were friends. They name build-ings after the Calders of the world, not the Reids,'' he added.

"Speaking of whom," I said, "Calder's sitting at a table in a corner behind you. You can look, if you want—he's got his back to us."

I'd spotted him almost as soon as we sat down, on ac-count of his size and his mane of black hair streaked with white. The man he was sitting with, facing me, was at least as tall as Calder, but physically his opposite in every other way: thin, long blond hair. About thirty-five. He would have been strikingly handsome had there been any life in his pale face. He'd been staring at me, I thought, and that made me uncomfortable, but when Marty turned to look, he shifted his eyes to Calder.

I asked Marty if he knew who the blond man was. He shrugged. "Lucas knows everybody," he said.

"Is it true he went bankrupt a few years back?"

"Those of us who want to get promoted to full professor have forgotten all about that, Peggy," Marty replied, low-ering his voice.

"It doesn't seem to have slowed him down any. Those parties of his must set him back a lot of money. The last one made the society pages: nobody but Nobel Prize win-ners allowed."

"Oh, they aren't that exclusive. I usually get invited, of course, and other people in the department he likes. Be-sides, it's possible a lot of the expense comes out of the Astronomy Department's entertainment budget. Lucas makes contacts at those parties that are useful to the Uni-versity. And they're his way of keeping his influence alive, now that he isn't doing as much research as he used to. He's become quite a wheeler-dealer."

It didn't sound as though Marty cared much for Calder. He must have seen that in the look I gave him because he added, "As you can tell, he's not my kind of guy, even though—I admit it—I owe my position at the U to him. To his friendship with my father, I should say."

"Don't you and the other research scientists at the University also owe him the Supercomputer Institute?" I asked.

He looked at me in surprise, as if he didn't expect me to know that. "Yeah," he answered, "I guess that's true. If he hadn't come up with the idea for the Supercomputer Corporation, and sold the University administration on it—and the state legislature, too—we wouldn't have much in the way of supercomputers. We wouldn't be able to afford them without outside money."

"It was a pretty cynical idea, wasn't it?" I said. "Everybody knows the Corporation's just a way to skirt the rules prohibiting secret research on campus."

"Cynical? Why shouldn't the University do secret research? Just about every other major university does. And what does 'secret' mean anyway? How long do you suppose they could have kept the invention of the wheel secret? Do you think there's anything going on in scientific research now that's easier to conceal? Lucas Calder's 'pretty cynical idea,' as you put it, was necessary, given the shortsightedness of the administration." He jabbed at a mushroom on his plate with a chopstick, angry about something.

"And there's no going back, is there?" I said. "Back to the days when you sat in front of a telescope and studied the stars and jotted down your observations—"

"With a quill pen, on a piece of parchment? No, there's no going back. There never is—and why should there be? What was so great about the past anyway? We don't even know what it was. Like everything else, it's just what the last person you talked to said it was. You think Galileo wouldn't trade places with me?"

I wondered about that, but I only said, "You have a nice way with words." I was a little taken aback by the flow.

"I assume you were a humanities major in college," he said.

"Yep."

"I remember reading something that might interest you, then, about the new Symore, the supercomputer we just got: if you fed *War and Peace* into it, it could tell you in ten seconds how many times Tolstoy used the word *and*. With the older supercomputers, it takes a minute.''

"Why would I want to know how many 'ands' there are in *War and Peace?*" I asked, opening my eyes as wide as I could.

He laughed, trying, not very successfully, to hide his annoyance. "A humanist cop, just what the world needs more of! No wonder you were so easy on Jason Horn. Nuisance, troublemaker—caught red-handed breaking and entering, and bashing a professor to boot—and you didn't even want to arrest him.''

"He wasn't going anywhere," I said, on the defensive suddenly, wondering how Horn had gotten into the conversation, "and I don't like taking people downtown and booking them. It's depressing down there, a dungeon. Besides, you could have made a citizen's arrest, forcing me to take him to jail.''

"I guess I could have, at that," he answered, smiling at me. "Maybe I'm too soft, too.''

He asked me if there'd been any word from Horn since the last time we'd talked. There hadn't been. Horn had made no effort to contact relatives in other parts of the country. I'd heard that the relatives didn't seem particularly concerned, one way or the other.

"Nobody's grieving, is that it?" Marty asked.

"You make it sound as if he's dead.''

"I think he is. Don't you?" Before I could answer, he said, "I don't suppose you have any new theories about what he was doing in Calder's office, either?''

"Just the same old one, that Horn hoped to find something in there that would embarrass Calder or the University.''

Lucas Calder's voice suddenly boomed: "I knew somebody was talking about me, my ears were ringing.'' We both looked up to see Calder smiling down at us.

Marty started to get up—Calder seemed to command that kind of respect from him—but caught himself and stayed where he was. "We were just speculating on why that fellow Jason Horn was in your office," he said. "You remember Peggy O'Neill, the campus policewoman who—''

"Of course I remember you," Calder said, turning his attention to me. "In fact, I hope you won't be offended, Marty, if I tell you that it was Ms. O'Neill, not you, who first drew my attention to this table." He was looking at my hair. Maybe someday I'll change the color, become invisible like Jason Horn. Back to Marty he said: "Not campus policewoman. Campus cop. Get with the times, Marty." He laughed smugly. "And is this a business dinner, or strictly for pleasure?"

"I'm always on duty," I replied. "Justice never sleeps." I looked around for his companion. He was standing at their table, putting money on it.

Calder stayed a few minutes longer and then asked Marty, "Will you be in your office later tonight, as usual, or do you have other plans?" Calder's eyes were small and bright and merry and they bounced between Marty and me.

"I'll be at the office, Lucas," Marty said.

Calder nodded to both of us and turned and headed for the door. I watched him make his way among the tables, trying not to knock them over with his bulky coat. People looked up as he passed, leaned to whisper.

He reminded me of something. At first I couldn't remember what it was, and then I remembered the print that Ann-Marie had given Mike Parrish at Christmas, in which a troll was demolishing a town not because it was evil, but only because it was so huge and ungainly. Calder seemed to be like that, I thought, in his passage through life.

He paused at the cashier's desk for a mint or a toothpick and, as he was standing there, his companion joined him. They walked out together, talking.

Marty and I lingered over our tea and then compared fortune cookies and walked back to the Science Tower together. It was cold, but the stars were out and there wasn't any wind.

I was missing something, an arm around me. Marty's

arms were as long as Al's. Long arms are important in the winter here, when you're both wearing bulky coats.

As we came up the walk to the Tower's entrance, Marty said, "I've got two tickets to a hockey game next Friday night. Would you like to go?"

"You like hockey?" I asked. The question started out as a cry of dismay but at the last possible moment I turned it into a question.

"Why? Don't you?"

"I can take it or leave it," I said, hedging, lying. "I've got tickets to the Marx Brothers film festival for Friday." They were tickets I'd ordered back when Al was still around. Al's as much a Marx Brothers fan as I am.

"I could never understand what was so funny about them," Marty said.

Thud. He didn't seem to hear it, just waited expectantly.

"Hockey, then," I said. "What time?"

"I'll pick you up at your place at seven, okay?"

"Fine."

We stood at the door for another couple of seconds, and then I touched his coat and said, "Friday," and walked away, conscious of yet another small self-betrayal.

It was a little after ten, but I wasn't in any hurry, the night was mine. Yes, I thought, I was glad Marty had to get "on" his supercomputer that night. If I'd agree to go to a hockey game with him, I'd probably agree to anything.

When I got on the bridge that goes across the river to the Old Campus, I stopped and leaned on the railing and looked down at the ice. It was frozen hard and there was trash on it that people had thrown off the bridge—the same creeps who let their gum fall from their mouths into drinking fountains—but no bodies, no Jason Horn. If he'd jumped, Lawrence had said, he'd bounce and then just lie there.

I glanced back at the Science Tower, a couple of hundred yards behind me. A man was walking up the path I'd just come down, heading for the entrance. He wasn't wearing a hat, in spite of how cold it was, and the moon hanging over downtown glittered off his long, bright hair.

He was too far away for me to be sure, but he looked like the man who'd been with Lucas Calder in the restaurant. He paused at the door, then opened it and disappeared inside.

I wondered how anybody could like professional hockey, could enjoy watching toothless men fight with sticks, their feet so deformed and calloused they could file them into blades and play without skates.

Marty hadn't looked at the stars through a telescope since he was a child. Now the stars were just a complex mass of numbers, he'd told me at dinner, that he fed into a supercomputer he'd never seen either. Strange world we live in.

Bleak and crabby, as Ginny'd said I was, I straightened up from the railing and continued on my way, wishing I knew what the hell to do with the rest of the night.

Twelve

Monday morning, I hung around the squad room until almost eight and then walked over to Professor Hamilton's office. It was in Frye Hall, an ancient, ivy-covered building on the Old Campus that I liked a lot, in spite of the fact that I'd once found a corpse in an office in there. Some buildings are strong enough to survive their histories.

Hamilton and I arrived at his office simultaneously, a few minutes after eight. He let me in, plugged in his hot water pot, and then sank into his chair and propped his long crane's legs up on his desk. He seemed tired, his nose was even pinker than it had been on Friday, and his cheeks were crisscrossed with a delicate network of angry veins. I notice things like that, though I wish I didn't.

We made polite conversation until the coffee was ready. He asked me if I'd ever had any use for my Intermediate German and I said I'd spent a couple of days in Germany a few years back. I didn't mention that I'd discovered that nobody there spoke Intermediate German. He told me he was working on a book on Thomas Mann. The large photograph on the wall behind him was Mann himself, he added. Mann looked a lot like a successful accountant. Professor Hamilton had been working on a book on Thomas Mann back when I took his German course, too, and I wondered if it was the same book he was working on now.

He dialed the long distance operator, gave the number of the private detective agency in Hamburg he'd selected for me, and charged the call to my phone number. There was a brief pause and then he was spouting German. Even with his English accent, I didn't understand much but the words "Manfred Stiller" and "dollars." As he rattled on, he jotted down figures, then turned to me and said, "Their minimum comes out to be about a hundred and fifty dollars. He says he doesn't think it will be such a difficult assignment and shouldn't take long."

I said that was fine and told him I wanted to know what the Stiller company did, whether or not Ann-Marie Ekdahl had ever worked there, and when, and in what capacity. I also wanted to know the names of everybody in Stiller's management in the years Ann-Marie was supposed to have been with the company. "And all the dirt they can find, tell them," I added.

When he'd hung up, he told me the agency would call him when they had something to report, probably in three or four days.

When I got home my answering machine was winking. I pressed "Messages" and listened to Carol's report. She sounded quite pleased with herself.

"I followed her all the way to work," she said. "The freeway was pretty crowded—she takes the freeway—so I had to stick pretty close and even then I almost lost her. She works in one of those big new office buildings out by the airport. The parking lot was almost full when she got there and I had trouble finding a place to park, and by the time I did, she was disappearing into the building. She was going pretty fast but that was because she was late, not because she saw me. I went in and looked around, but I didn't see her anywhere. A lot of businesses have offices in there. How about tomorrow I'll get there before her and wait inside and see where she goes? I could wear a disguise, you know. I don't mean a false nose, or moustache," she added hastily, "just something so she won't recognize me. She's never seen how I look dressed for work, so I'll probably blend right in. I want to do it, Peggy."

She sounded happier than she had in a while. I went to bed before I'd decided whether I wanted her to get involved any deeper, even if it did help her get over her brother's death.

There was another message from Carol waiting for me when I came out to the living room that afternoon. It was short and to the point. "I'm going to do it, Peggy. I'll be careful. Talk to you tomorrow." I was glad she'd taken the decision out of my hands.

The next morning the message waiting for me told me to call her at work. I called the number and a secretary put me through.

"The good news is," she said, "I found out who Ann-Marie works for. The bad news is, she recognized me and I think she guessed that you're looking into Mike's death, too."

"What'd she do?"

"She looked surprised for a second. Then she laughed, but she was mad, too, Peggy, I could see that. She gave me that nasty little smirk of hers and said, 'Playing detective?' "

"What else?" I asked.

"Nothing right then. We were in the elevator and it was crowded. I didn't want to ride up with her, but I didn't have any choice, there were too many other people getting on, so I wouldn't be able to tell where she got off if I didn't get on too. I'd dyed my hair, Peggy. I thought that would be enough."

I couldn't help laughing. "What color?" Carol's a blonde.

"A henna rinse, maybe a little overdone. But it doesn't look too bad, actually, and I've been getting compliments on it all morning. I was wearing sunglasses too, but it didn't fool her."

"You were wearing sunglasses a lot at Christmas," I reminded her. "I think the sunglasses disguise only works if you *haven't* worn them before around the suspect."

"She didn't act surprised to see me or anything, but as I said, I could tell she was pissed. The elevator ride seemed to take forever, with her staring at me the entire way, but there were too many people for her to say anything else. When we got to her floor, she just got off and went down the hall to her office. I think she was surprised that I followed her because when she got to the door she turned and looked back and there I was, practically breathing down her neck. I looked at the name on the door and then looked at her and gave her a little wave and mouthed a 'hi.' She said, 'You are wasting your time, Carol. *Both* of you are wasting your time.' She said 'Both of you,' so that means she guessed you're mixed up in it, too.''

That didn't come as a surprise since her husband, Terry Rhodes, would have told her about the visit I'd paid to him. "What's the name of the company, Carol?" I asked.

"Ed. Tech." She spelled it. "It stands for Educational Technology."

The name didn't tell me much. "Do you have any idea what they do?"

"No. I didn't go in, and that's all there was on the door."

"I'll try to find out. I can't think of anything else for you to do right now, Carol. I'll call again when I have anything new to tell you. If I do," I added.

"Oh, you will, Peggy! Let me know if there's anything else I can do to help."

"You can check your doors and windows, to make sure they're locked properly before you go to bed."

"You, too, Peggy. Ann-Marie knows you're involved, too."

"I checked mine a long time ago," I told her.

Professor Hamilton called on Thursday to tell me that the detective agency had phoned him. They had the report I wanted and he'd arranged for them to call his office at eight A.M. the next morning—three o'clock in the afternoon in Hamburg.

He was already in his office when I got there, at his desk, reading. He gestured at the coffeepot, and we sat and talked as we waited for the phone to ring.

He listened for a while to the metallic German noises coming over the phone and then started writing. He wrote for two or three minutes, asked some questions and waited for some answers and said a few more things and then hung up.

He turned to me. "Here's what they've found out. If you want more, we can call them back." He put half-glasses on his ravaged nose in order to read what he'd just written down. "Manfred Stiller is a small import-export company. Exports primarily to Holland, Belgium, and Scandinavia, imports for the most part from the Far East—Japan and China—*now.*" Hamilton put extra emphasis upon "now" and gave me a sly grin. "You knew something about them that you didn't tell me, didn't you?"

I shook my head, baffled.

"A shot in the dark then, eh, when you asked for all the dirt they could find?" He didn't really believe it was just a shot in the dark on my part, so I tried to look knowing and inscrutable and waited for him to tell me what he thought I already knew. "Well, in any case," he went on, "Stiller used to import technology from the States—but they don't anymore."

"Why not?"

"Their license was revoked! Apparently Stiller had purchased some sort of American gadgetry—I have here 'a big VAX computer,' whatever that is, complete with spare parts and something called 'software.' Your Pentagon didn't want those things to go behind the Iron Curtain or to any other country that might use them against the U.S. in some way. Stiller signed an agreement promising not to sell them to any country on the Pentagon's naughty-boy list. However, a couple of months after Stiller got this computer and its accoutrements"—Hamilton smacked his long thin lips over that word—"it turned up lock, stock, and barrel, in, of all places, Bulgaria. Tsk, tsk! It was the CIA that ferreted that out, according to our detective friends. Stiller's license to import from the U.S. was revoked in 1987 by your Commerce Department. For a time, the Stiller company was in serious financial difficulties on account of it, but they seem to be recovering nicely. It was not company policy to do that sort of thing—at least, that is what they are now trying to make the Americans believe. The man responsible may have been working on his own. Or, of course, Stiller may have made him the scapegoat in order to avoid ruin. In any case, he was discharged, and seems to have vanished. The company is appealing to get its license to import from the U.S. back again. According to the report, there's a good chance they will.''

Hamilton paused, emptied his coffee cup with one swallow, and sat back.

"Did they find out anything about Ann-Marie Ekdahl?"

"Nothing very interesting, I'm afraid," he replied. "She's listed among the company's employees—she worked there from 1984 until the end of 1986, when she left to get married and come to this country with her husband, a U.S. soldier. She was a secretary. She knew a number of foreign languages useful to the company, was paid a handsome salary, and her supervisors thought highly of her. The detectives were unable to unearth anything of a criminal nature concerning her. She seems to have been exactly what she was—a highly competent secretary.''

He slid his notes across his desk to me. "I hope you can read my handwriting. Those are the names of the people working for Stiller at the time Ann-Marie worked there. That fellow"—his index finger hit a name—"was the one they fired for getting Stiller in trouble with the U.S.''

The name was Eric Fridell. Hamilton pronounced it "Free-*dell.* ''

"It doesn't sound German," I said.

"Oh, it's Swedish, I'm sure. Which makes sense, doesn't it, since the company does a lot of business with Scandinavia? Besides, the Germans and the Swedes have always been thick.''

And Ann-Marie was Swedish, too, of course. I've never liked coincidences since, by definition, they defy reason.

"And he's vanished, you say?"

"Nobody who knew him at Stiller seems to know where he's gone to, at least," he replied.

I was curious to know more about Eric Fridell, but not so curious that I wanted to spend more of Carol's money asking the Hamburg detectives to look for him. Not yet, anyway. I folded the piece of paper Hamilton had given me, stuck it in my pocket. He explained how I was to pay the detective bureau when I got the bill. I got up to go and thanked him, using Intermediate German. He didn't seem to notice.

"Does this help?" he asked, showing concerned teeth. "Is this news about the company having its export license revoked the 'smoking gun,' as you Americans say, you're looking for?"

"I don't know. I don't know what's a smoking gun and what's not."

"I don't suppose I'll ever find out the end of this," he said.

"Maybe I won't either," I replied.

Thirteen

Friday night I went to the hockey game with Marty Reid. It was a disaster, as I'd known it would be and, no doubt, the fault was mine. I cast a pall over the evening because I wasn't able to participate fully in the mindless violence. In fact, I wasn't able to participate in it at all. As I sat there drowning in the crowd's, and Marty's, excitement, I was reminded of the one time I'd watched a cockfight. It was in Puerto Rico when I was in the Navy and determined to experience everything before I died, because I couldn't think of anything better to do with my life.

We stopped off someplace for drinks afterwards and I had a Coke for which Marty insisted on paying, and then he grumbled over having to pay so much for something that didn't have alcohol in it, and finally he drove me home. He parked and kissed me and, feeling a little guilty about the evening and curious about him and about myself, too, I let him do that.

When he was back on his side of the car and restarting his fine, quiet engine, he said, "I'd have done better, wouldn't I, if we'd sat in a theater without air conditioning and watched four guys in baggy suits being silly, instead of dragging you to a hockey game?" The muscles were showing around his mouth, somewhat marring his Tom Sawyer looks.

"I guess." I didn't know if that was true or not, I just said it to cover my retreat. I thanked him for the evening and he thanked me, and our smiles were like flowers at a mob funeral.

* * *

I killed the rest of the weekend paying bills, balancing my checkbook, and ice skating with a friend on Lake Eleanor. I'm not a good skater and I fell hard and bruised my butt, but at least Al wasn't there to see it. Al's a great skater because he grew up near here.

Monday afternoon, I called Educational Technology, where Ann-Marie worked.

I listened carefully to the voice that answered before I said anything, just in case it was Ann-Marie, and when I was sure it wasn't, I told the receptionist that my name was Deirdre and I was calling from the Filbaugh Management Corporation. "We're an apartment management firm," I explained, "and a woman applying for one of our apartments has listed Educational Technology as her employer. I'm calling to verify that."

She asked me the employee's name and I told her. It might have been my imagination, but I thought there was a drop in voice temperature at the other end of the line as she said, "Yes, she's an employee here."

"Can you tell me how long she has worked for you?" I asked.

"I'll have to check her file. Is that necessary?"

"It is indeed," I replied. "We are only interested in renting to a stable clientele, and we like to know a little something about people before we admit them to one of our neighborhoods—for we think of our apartment buildings as neighborhoods, you see. And we've found that a person's work record—when viewed in conjunction with his or her credit rating—is a virtually certain indicator of character. We are an equal opportunity renter," I added, just for the hell of it.

She told me to wait and went away, hopefully to get Ann-Marie's file.

"She started here in April of 1988," she said when she returned. "Her record doesn't say what she did prior to that. She married an American somewhere abroad and came here as his wife."

"She has been with you, then, for almost two years," I said. "She's foreign, of course. Swedish?"

"Yes."

"A stable people, the Swedes. By the way, just to satisfy my curiosity, what is it exactly your company does? The name, Educational Technology—much less Ed. Tech—doesn't speak volumes, does it?"

"We design, manufacture, and sell technology for use in education," she replied, as if reading from a stock prospectus. "Videos, tapes, slides, educational software. We do a big mail-order business all over the country, as well as abroad. One of our salesmen told me once that we sell the modern equivalents of McGuffey Readers, chalk, erasers, and blackboards."

I'd never heard of McGuffey Readers, but I had heard of software. "Computers," I said.

"Oh, yes, certainly. These days, computers and computer programs are big items in education. We adapt computers for use in education."

I'd been encountering computers a lot lately on my daily rounds. Lucas Calder and Marty Reid and their supercomputers. Mike Parrish, the computer technologist. And now Ann-Marie Ekdahl, Mike's lover, worked for a company that dealt in computers and stuff necessary to their care and feeding.

"Abroad, too, did you say? You export?"

"Yes, in the past several years—just since I started here—we've doubled our export business."

"Germany, for example. And Sweden?"

"Yes, all of Europe, parts of Asia, the Middle East, Africa."

"I suppose Ms. Ekdahl is useful for her knowledge of German and Swedish."

"I guess she is," the receptionist replied, almost making it a sniff. "She certainly has no trouble typing her boss' correspondence."

My heart skipped a beat. "He writes in—?"

"Both languages. German and Swedish."

"Her boss," I repeated, trying to stay in character. "That would be . . . ?"

In the background, I heard a man's voice ask a question and she broke off suddenly, then said to me, "Wait a moment," and put me on hold. I counted ten, wondering what was going on at her end. I thought about hanging up, but you don't learn much doing that.

There was a click and a man's voice said brusquely, "Who is speaking, please?" He had an accent like Ann-Marie's.

I started to get smart, say "Mr. Fridell, isn't it?" because I would have bet money on it, but instead I told him my name was Deirdre. I was about to go on with the rest of my story when he interrupted with, "Deirdre what?"

What's good enough for the receptionist isn't good enough for the boss, apparently. I snapped off Al's last name without a pause. "May I ask to whom I'm speaking?"

"Fridell," he said. "May I ask why you are making inquiries about one of our employees?"

In Professor Hamilton's office, I'd wondered how I was going to find out where Eric Fridell had disappeared to, after he'd left or been fired by the Manfred Stiller Company. Now I knew. I had him on the phone and, for once in my life, was at a loss for words.

"Well," he demanded angrily, "are you there?"

"No, not yet," I managed to say as I hung up.

Fourteen

The next afternoon, I was drinking coffee and looking out at the piece of Lake Eleanor I can see from my living room window. Boys and girls, just home from school, were skating on the rink where I'd been skating, too, on Saturday. They reminded me of a jigsaw puzzle I'd had as a child, of children skating on a pond in some place simpler and more innocent than where I lived, their brightly colored scarves floating on the air behind them. There'd been a piece missing from that puzzle. There was more than one piece missing from the puzzle I was working on now.

According to Barbara McKay, Ann-Marie had boasted that she'd met a man she used to work for in Germany, and she planned to hustle a job from him, one in which her Swedish and German would come in handy. A short while later she'd quit her job in the Biology Department and gone to work for Ed. Tech. The man she'd met must have been Eric Fridell, who'd been fired by Manfred Stiller in Hamburg for illegally exporting technology behind the Iron Curtain, and now both of them, Ann-Marie and Fridell, were working for a company that exported educational equipment, computers included. Six months after going to work for Ed. Tech, Ann-Marie had left her husband, and a year later she'd gone after Mike Parrish, a computer specialist.

What was Eric Fridell doing in this country—and under his own name, too—if he'd done something that violated our national security? How was all of this connected with

Mike's death? And what had Ann-Marie been doing in the year between leaving Terry Rhodes and taking up with Mike?

My doorbell rang. I got up and glanced through the front window, but whoever was on the porch was turned away and too bundled up to recognize from where I was standing. It was just a woman in an expensive camel's-hair coat.

It was Ann-Marie. She was wearing a soft fur hat that matched the coat's soft, tawny collar. It made her look caressable except, perhaps, to birds and small, scurrying things. The smile on her mouth was tentative, telling me she hoped I wouldn't turn her away. I opened the door, told her to come in, and stood back to let her open the storm door herself. She slipped her suede boots off on the porch, holding on to the storm door with one gloved hand for balance. The boots were long and took a while to slide off her legs. I took her coat and hung it in my closet.

She said "yes" to coffee and then seemed to forget me as she looked around my apartment. She took her time. "You have a beautiful place," she said finally. Her eyes fastened on a large picture I have on one wall, of a blue door in an alley in Morocco, taken by a photographer whose work I like. Just about the only original art I can afford on my salary is photography, and even photography's starting to get too expensive for me. "I wonder what's behind it," she said, meaning the blue door. I did, too, so we did have something in common, Ann-Marie and I.

She continued to wander about my living room, pausing to look at some of the things I've collected. I don't like clutter, so there's not a lot. The knit suit she was wearing was the kind you buy when you're a secretary and have to spend a lot of money on clothes.

I asked her if she used cream or sugar. She was standing at the window that looks out onto Lake Eleanor, and the low western sun bathed her in a soft, yellow glow. Her back was to me, her body still and slightly slumped, and I thought to myself that she looked like an actress who'd come too early to the theater, or stayed on after the curtain had fallen.

"Neither," she said, which jolted me until I realized she was answering my question, not my thoughts.

When I brought the coffee, she sat down on the couch and I took the chair by the window.

"What you're doing for your friend Carol is, I'm sure, very admirable," she said, "but it isn't very nice for me. You can see that."

"Maybe it was a little annoying," I replied, "discovering that Carol was following you. But—"

"That was just one little thing," she said, barely shrugging, speaking so softly that it didn't even feel like an interruption. "I am thinking of more serious things, things that you are doing. Talking to my ex-husband. Asking about me at my place of work."

"Terry Rhodes isn't your *ex*-husband, according to him," I said.

"Don't split hairs, Peggy. Terry is my ex-husband in everything but name, and that will change soon, too."

"But he has his uses. He provided you with a nice alibi for the time of Mike's death."

"I did not need an alibi for poor Michael's suicide. And Terry and I are still friends."

I said, "Mike was also your friend."

"It is too bad about Michael. No man has ever killed himself on account of me before, and I did not really believe anybody would ever do it. Men should not kill themselves over a woman, or the other way around, either. I want my lovers to remember me as a happy interlude."

" 'Sex is just an extension of my friendship.' "

"Terry told you that." She smiled in recollection of something, perhaps the moment when she'd told him that. "Yes, it can be that. Has it never been that for you?" She saw me wince and said, with a smile, "You just don't like hearing the words."

"Terry doesn't seem to remember you as . . . what shall I say? . . . a happy interlude," I said, mimicking her accent, because she'd made me mad. "He seems to think you tricked him. You pretended to love him, just to get into this country.''

''Is that what he thinks?'' She shrugged. ''I wanted to come to this country, to live here, and he provided the means. I thought it was clear to him, the deal we made, but apparently it was not.''

''You told us, up at Mike's parents' place, that you came to the U.S. as a child, with your parents. Why'd you lie about it?''

''I tell different stories to different people,'' she said. ''I create myself, sometimes as I go along. Life is a lot more amusing that way, I think. Who wants to play the same role all the time, day in and day out?'' She looked at me, said, quite earnestly, ''You should try it, Peggy. Or do you like who you are?''

I mostly do, I think. I said, ''You cheat people who think you're one thing and find that you're something else—or maybe nothing at all.''

''It's obvious that you do not have the faintest idea of what I'm talking about. People cheat themselves, in that they so often think what they want to think, rather than recognize what *is*. But I did not come here to defend my life, only to try to convince you to stay out of it. Your talking to Terry was annoying, Peggy. Calling Educational Technology was upsetting. I want you to stop what you're doing.''

''How do you know it was me who called Ed. Tech? It could have been Carol.''

''Don't play games with me, please. It makes no difference. You are behind it, in any case, and if you stop, Carol will. I'd like more coffee, please.''

She held out her cup. As I poured, she leaned over the coffee table and said to me, softly, ''I don't like to be suspected of murder, Peggy, but I cannot do anything about that. I also don't like to be hounded—by you or by Carol—and to have my private life invaded.''

Her voice never quavered and when I glanced up at her, her large blue eyes were gazing at me steadily.

''I can sympathize with you,'' I said, trying to match the steadiness of her voice. ''But in my invasion of your private life I've stumbled across a few things that interest me. Since you have nothing to hide, I wonder if you'd mind satisfying my curiosity."

She sipped coffee, watching me for a moment, and then nodded.

"In Germany," I said, "you worked for a company called Manfred Stiller, an import-export company."

To my surprise, her face seemed to stiffen slightly, but she managed a shrug and kept the little smile on her face. "I should have guessed that you would use—or did you misuse, I wonder?—your authority as University policeman to get to my confidential records. Well, no matter. . . . Yes, I did work as a secretary for a company in Germany that did import-export business. What of it?"

"The company," I went on, "lost its license to do business with the United States."

She sat up, said, "Yes. However, I left before that happened. I was not involved."

"If you left before it happened, how do you know about it?"

"I have friends who work there still. They have written and told me all about it."

"You have a friend here who knows about it, too: Eric Fridell, the man who was fired for getting the Stiller company in trouble. It's because I spoke with him yesterday that you're here today—not because I talked to your husband or harassed you at work."

"Mr. Fridell is in this country legally," she said, her voice rising slightly. "If you know so much, you must know that, too. He was not charged with anything criminal in Hamburg. He has a right to be here, to start over."

"Start over doing what?"

"He is a businessman. That is all he is. He is no ideologue, no communist. He is good at what he does, which is selling electronic technology. He learned about Educational Technology from friends in Hamburg, after he was unjustly discharged, made a scapegoat by Stiller. He decided to leave Europe, to start over here. Ed. Tech was happy to have him because of his many contacts in Europe, and also his experience." When she stopped she was slightly out of breath, as if not used to talking so much, so fast.

"Unlike you, he didn't have to marry an American to get here."

She shrugged. "No. It was easier for him."

"If he's here legally, so that I can't blow the whistle on him and get him deported, then why are you afraid?"

"I am not afraid," she replied. "I am upset that you are trying to cause trouble for me—and now for Eric—Mr. Fridell—too."

"What'd you do," I asked, "you and Eric—Mr. Fridell, I mean? Agree to meet again in this country? 'I'll find an American sucker and marry him and you get your green card, and we'll meet again on the other side of the ocean?' "

"No. Stop mocking me, please. It was purely an accident, our meeting here," she said. "But when we met, he offered me a job, a better job than I had at the University."

"That was in, let's see, April, almost two years ago, wasn't it?"

"Perhaps. What difference does it make? But if you say so, it is probably correct."

"And you left Terry in November of that year."

"What does it matter?"

"You'd become Eric Fridell's lover by then, of course?"

"Of course." She tried to say it in my voice.

"According to your husband, you'd had a number of lovers in the two years you were together. What made Fridell so special that you'd leave Terry for him?"

"I didn't leave him for Eric," she replied. "I just . . . left him."

"To go on to better things. That's what Terry said you left him for. I've driven by your apartment, Ann-Marie, I've seen it. The builder must have been told about mansard roofs by a blind man. You've been in the Land of Opportunity for over three years, but it doesn't look like it's paying off for you. Was Eric Fridell supposed to be the prize? What happened?"

She got up. "No, you are just making wild guesses,

stupid assumptions.'' She looked around the room. ''My coat. Where is it?''

''And then,'' I went on, staying where I was, ''out of the blue you call up Mike Parrish at the Biology Department—last Thanksgiving, or a little before—and the next thing we know, you're dating him and he thinks it's serious. When I met you at Christmas, you were acting as if you *were* serious about Mike: that he was more than just a—what shall I say—a happy interlude.''

She was still looking around the room, but not for her coat now. She was looking for something other than the truth to tell me.

She fastened on the least important thing. ''It may have seemed that way to you,'' she answered finally, ''and to poor Mike. But I was never serious about it.''

''You don't have to tell me that,'' I said. ''What made you think of Mike just when you did, Ann-Marie, over a year and a half after you'd left the Biology Department?''

''There was nothing sinister in that,'' she said, on track again. ''We met by chance, on the street. He recognized me and said hello, reminded me of where we'd met before. He seemed interesting, or perhaps I was bored, I don't know. So a few days later, I called him up at the Biology Department. That's all there was to it. You're trying to make something out of nothing.''

''I didn't realize just how small a town this is,'' I said. ''You seem to bump into lots of old acquaintances on the street who then become your lovers,'' I said. ''First Eric Fridell and then Mike Parrish. Both involved with computers.''

She remembered then where her coat was and went to the closet to get it. ''I think,'' she said, ''that if you snooped into anybody's life the way you have snooped into mine, you would find coincidences that would seem significant to your very creative imagination, Peggy.''

''Tell me about it, Ann-Marie! Not everybody's life leads from Terry Rhodes to Eric Fridell to Mike Parrish and finally to Mike's death. It wasn't *my* 'very creative imagination' that made all those colorful connections.''

Her face suddenly went old and gaunt, like a haunted

house. "I'm going to the police," she said, "if you don't stop hounding me. I mean it. For I do not believe you are carrying on this investigation in any official way." She looked at me, half-defiant and half-pleading, and walked quickly to the door.

I followed her out onto my porch. "There's something else I'm curious about," I said, looking down at her blonde head as she bent to pick up her boots. "You seem to have made quite a hit with Betty Hall, the Biology Department's executive secretary, during the time you worked there." I didn't mean to stop there, but Ann-Marie's reaction startled me. She straightened up quickly and stared at me, suddenly more interested in what I had to say than in tugging at a boot.

"Yes?" she said, her eyes burning into mine.

"You even became her friend—which, I understand, is a remarkable feat. But whatever your relationship was with Betty Hall, it came to a screeching halt. I was talking to her about Mike's death—his murder, Ann-Marie—and when your name came up, she got a look in her eyes that reminds me a little of the look in yours right now. You wouldn't care to give me some idea of what happened between you?"

It was cold on the porch and a cold wind was blowing into my apartment. There was no color at all in Ann-Marie's face. She continued to stare at me for a long moment, her lips parted, her perfect white teeth bared.

"Nothing happened," she said finally, and she composed her face and returned to pulling on her boots. She cleared her throat and said it again, to make sure I heard it clearly. "Nothing happened! Say I got bored with her—with her *grayness*, with her *need* for me! Say whatever you want." She stomped down hard on my porch floor with her boot and stared at me. "But find something else to amuse you, Peggy O'Neill," she said. "You will be sorry if you don't."

She didn't wait to hear if I would answer her. She turned and walked into the late winter afternoon, walked into it fast. She didn't look nearly as elegant as she had when she'd first arrived, and under the Swedish accent that sounded phony, and the beauty that was meant to be seen from a distance, I'd seen something real: fear, the kind that comes when you realize you've burned all your bridges, and you want very much to find a way back to the shore.

It had startled her that I'd learned about Manfred Stiller. It had frightened her a little when I'd told her I knew of Eric Fridell's past. But she'd been more than startled or frightened when I'd mentioned Betty Hall. For a moment, at least, she'd been terrified.

Fifteen

The phone woke me up. I squinted at the clock on my bedside table. I'd managed to get five hours sleep, a couple less than I wanted. The light filtering through my bedroom curtains told me it was a sunny afternoon. The voice on the phone told me it was Ginny Raines.

"Sorry to wake you up, but Bixler wants to see you in his office at three. He also said to tell you he didn't mean 3:10 or 3:20."

"How about 3:05?"

"He didn't say."

"Good. I'll be there then."

"He's serious, Peggy." There was laughter in her voice, but caution, too. We sometimes play games when it comes to dealing with Lt. Bixler; it's the only alternative to finding new jobs. Bixler wouldn't mind that at all, at least as far as the women cops go. He's the cop who caused the uproar on campus last year when he stated that personally, and in his own opinion, women who drink are just asking to be raped. When the uproar showed signs of leading to meaningful changes—getting him fired, for one—he said he hadn't really meant what he'd said and besides, he'd been misquoted. And everything returned to normal, the way it usually does.

I got to headquarters at three and was at Bixler's door a few minutes later. It was open, so I walked in. I was expecting to find out that Ann-Marie had made good her threat to complain to my supervisors, but I was wrong.

Bixler wasn't alone: two men were with him. They

looked like missionaries, the kind who go door to door with loving smiles and cold eyes. One of them was black and one of them was what's technically termed white.

The white one said they were U.S. Customs agents and they wanted to talk to me. They both, as if on some prearranged signal, brought out wallets and dangled them in front of me so I could see that they were telling the truth. I nodded, then looked around for some place to sit down, but there wasn't a vacant chair.

The black one turned and gave his loving smile to Lt. Bixler and asked him if they could talk to me in private. Bixler's eyes bulged just slightly more than they normally do. "Since you already know the gist of what we have to discuss with Officer O'Neill," the black one added.

Bixler was faced with a problem. If he left the room, I might take his swivel chair, sit down behind his desk. That would be the reasonable thing, since there wasn't another chair in the room. But it was clear that there was no way he was going to let me sit at his desk. His dilemma was written all over his big red face under the toupee that didn't match his real hair.

I started to say, "You can take your chair out with you," but before I could, the black agent said smoothly: "Perhaps Officer O'Neill would take my chair if you'll permit me to take yours, Lieutenant."

Since he dislikes blacks almost as much as he dislikes women cops, Bixler had a tough pill to swallow there, and it took him a while to get it down. He looked from the agent to me and back, then nodded and heaved himself out of his chair. At the door he turned to me. "I'll be wanting to talk to you afterwards, O'Neill, so don't go away."

When I was a rookie, I used to watch him warily at all times when we were in a room together, and nod too eagerly at whatever he said to me. But that was then. Now I just sat down in the chair the Customs agent vacated and shoved myself around so I could keep both of them in sight. I couldn't imagine why I was there, but I hid my curiosity behind an expression that implied that this kind of thing happened all the time in my line of work.

"My name's G. B.," the black one said.

"I'm George," the other one said. His glasses also helped distinguish him from G. B.

"I think G. B. used to stand for something," G. B. said with a smile, "but if so, I've forgotten what it was."

"There aren't any nicknames for George," George said.

My neck was starting to ache, from moving left to right and back again. What a pair—Tweedledum and Tweedledee. "What can I do for you?" I asked.

"We have some business to discuss with you, Officer O'Neill," G. B. said. "Peggy's a pretty name, by the way. It would be nice if we could call you Peggy."

"Sure."

"Call me G. B.," he said, "and I'm sure you can call George George."

George nodded and said, "I didn't think I was going to like you."

"Why's that?" I asked, thinking that this was getting stranger with every passing moment.

"My sister," he explained. "Lenore. When she was little, she had to tap dance to a record of you."

"A what? Oh," I said, catching on, and laughed. "I'm sorry about that."

"What's the joke?" G. B. asked.

"It's no joke," George told him. " 'Peggy O'Neill' is a song. We had it on a 78 RPM record." To me he said, "Lenore was very small and round and she wore a pink tutu when she danced to it."

It was a dreadful image. I managed to pull my eyes away from George and asked G. B., "What kind of business?"

"Confidential business," he replied. "Very confidential. About a company called Educational Technology."

"Does that ring a bell?" George asked.

"Eric Fridell," G. B. added, thinking maybe that would jar my memory.

I managed to keep my face blank. "What makes you think I know anything about them?"

"We've got their phones bugged," G. B. explained.

"Why?"

"We can't tell you that," George said.

"Because Educational Technology is involved in illegally selling stuff overseas that we don't want going there. Smuggling. They're what's called 'techno-bandits,' " G. B. said.

That's what the Manfred Stiller Company, in Hamburg, had been caught doing, according to Professor Hamilton. Recalling Hamilton's words, I said, "Stuff like a big VAX computer and its accoutrements?"

G. B. smiled, nodded. "We didn't realize you knew about the Manfred Stiller Company. In fact, it wouldn't matter if somebody sent the Russians a VAX computer today: it's old and slow compared to the newer models. But it was one of the fastest at the time and we didn't want the Soviets to have it. They got it anyway, thanks to Eric Fridell and the Stiller Company."

"But that's the sort of thing Ed. Tech's involved in, is that it?" I asked. "Techno-banditry?" Saying the term felt like braces springing loose in my mouth.

"Right. But they don't deal in the big stuff, like mainframe computers. Ed. Tech uses its legitimate business—exporting educational technology—small computers used in the classroom, educational software programs, things like that—to smuggle out new technology that we don't want the Russians to have: microchips, operating manuals for new computers, and spare parts, among other things."

"Toasters that actually work?"

George took the question seriously. "If it contained some new technological advance that might aid the Soviets militarily, yes. Once, years ago, we banned the sale of personal computers to the Russians on account of all the new microcircuitry that went into them."

"That's silly!" I said. "It wouldn't be hard to smuggle a small computer out of the country—or a toaster."

George shrugged. "In large quantities, it would."

"They'd only need one," I argued. "Then they could copy it."

"At that time, they didn't want to. They had other uses for their computer engineers. So they wanted to purchase PCs from us."

"There's a list—a blacklist—of things the government decides it doesn't want going behind the Iron Curtain," G. B. explained. "For every American out there who's trying to steal military secrets and sell them to the Russians, there are twenty or thirty Americans willing to smuggle blacklisted items to them."

"They steal them?"

"Sometimes, but not always," George said. "Usually they buy what they want, just like everybody else does. They might set up a dummy company that places an order with the manufacturer for something on the Soviet Union's shopping list. They claim they're going to use it here, in some legitimate business. When the dummy company gets what they've ordered, they repackage it, give it a phony label, and the next thing you know, we find out that it's hard at work in Minsk."

"Or a real company somewhere abroad—South Africa, for instance, or Sweden, Holland, or Germany, just about anywhere—can order it," George went on. "That's what happened in the case of the Stiller Company. They imported the VAX from us, claiming it was for use in Germany. Then they exported it behind the Curtain."

"So we *can* sell this kind of technology abroad—just not to the Iron Curtain countries?"

"Right. And a few other countries that make us nervous."

"But once it's sold abroad, you have no way to prevent its resale to the wrong people?"

"It's virtually impossible," G. B. said.

"So why try?"

"It's the law," George answered glumly.

"You guys happy about your careers?"

"Sometimes," George replied, staring out Bixler's window at the sunlight on the snow. Then, his face brightening at some memory, he went on, "A few years ago, for example, we heard about a shipment of microchips that was about to leave the country illegally for Iraq. We made a switch at the airport—replaced the good microchips with defective ones—and then, when they were safely on their way, we arrested the people who were involved here, confiscated the money they'd been paid, and closed down their company! So once in a while we get lucky."

"I'll bet those are fun times," I said. "And then what happens—to the people you catch, I mean?"

"They go to jail for a couple years," G. B. replied with a shrug. "At best."

"It's not as if they were stealing military *secrets*," George explained. "That can get you life in prison, maybe even electrocuted, gassed, shot or hanged." He paused, reflected. "Or lethally injected."

"It's just *business*, after all," G. B. went on. "Most American manufacturers are in favor of selling what they make to whoever has the bucks to pay for it, regardless of politics. They say that if we don't do it, somebody else— the Japanese, probably—will. And it stimulates the economy and creates jobs."

I made a show of looking at my watch. "Okay," I said. "I've got a meeting scheduled with Lt. Bixler and I'm beginning to look forward to it. Where do I come in?"

"You don't," George said. "That's the point."

"The real point," G. B. said, "is that you've upset some of the people at Ed. Tech."

"The ultimate point—the nub—is that we don't want you to upset them any more."

"Why not?"

"Because we aren't ready to close down Ed. Tech just yet," G. B. said. "On Monday, you called them and, under an assumed name, asked questions about the company, even talked to Eric Fridell. Yesterday, one Ann-Marie Ekdahl, Fridell's secretary, came calling on you, and she stayed nearly an hour. This made us nervous. So we made inquiries about you. One of your supervisors thinks you're a man-hating feminist with a chip on your shoulder, a smart-ass, and a troublemaker."

"I don't hate men," I said.

"The other thinks you're smart, rebellious, insecure, but a good cop."

"If handled the right way," George reminded his partner.

"We liked the man who gave you the good recommendation," G. B. said. "He was very convincing."

"We've told you what we're up to. Now we'd like you to tell us what you're up to," G. B. said.

"But why don't you want Ed. Tech upset?" I asked. "Why aren't you out there closing them down, or sneaking around in their warehouse, replacing cartons of blacklisted items with sand, or something?"

"George and I—Customs—would, if we had our way," G. B. said. "That's what we're paid to do. But we can't have our way—not this time. Another agency of the Government wants to keep Ed. Tech alive and well. Apparently, they're using—"

"G. B.?" George interrupted his partner. To me he explained, "We operate on a need-to-know basis."

G. B. ignored him. "Another agency of the Government—we're not at liberty to tell you its name—is using Ed. Tech for its own purposes."

"Like what?"

"Smuggling things behind the Iron Curtain that the Russians *wouldn't* want, if they knew exactly what they were getting. That's all we can tell you about it. Now it's your turn, Peggy."

"What kinds of things?" I persisted.

"G. B. . . ." George cautioned.

G. B. was oblivious. "You've heard about computer viruses, Peggy, haven't you?" he asked. "Who hasn't, these days? Well, suppose we knew the Russians were in desperate need of a certain microchip for a computer they'd acquired from us illegally. What good's a computer, if you can't get spare parts for it? And suppose we were able to engineer a virus onto some of the chips destined for the Soviet Union? A virus, say, that was designed to make one mistake, at random, every 50,000 operations or so. The Russian engineers would go crazy, trying to pinpoint what was wrong!"

"You're using Ed. Tech to play dirty tricks on the Russians," I said.

"In a word, yes," George replied. "We want to discourage them in their smuggling, tip them off balance and make them nervous."

"Now it's your turn, Peggy," G. B. said.

I didn't mind telling them what I was up to. After all, the only reason I was involved was because I couldn't get Homicide interested in Mike Parrish's death. Customs wasn't Homicide, but it was a law enforcement agency. So I told them everything I'd found out.

When I'd finished, G. B. nodded, said, "We know about Mr. Fridell, of course. He's not a nice man. He told several lies about his past on his visa application. However, we aren't going to report him to Immigration yet, however much George and I, personally, would like to. Our friends—"

"Your friends don't want Ed. Tech. upset," I finished it for him. "The CIA."

Both men pretended they hadn't heard me. "Miss Ekdahl and Fridell knew each other in Germany," George went on, putting unnecessarily heavy emphasis on the verb, "when they were both working at Stiller. But their private lives, singly and together, weren't any business of ours, and they still aren't. We checked out Ekdahl and her husband, Terry Rhodes, when she popped up two years ago at Ed. Tech. as Fridell's secretary, but as far as we could tell, she was just a lover who'd followed him to this country, nothing more. Apparently, they're no longer lovers. Now she's just his secretary."

"I think," I said, "Mike Parrish was murdered. And Ann-Marie's the most likely suspect. I can't think of any reason why she'd waste time on a guy like him, unless she saw some profit in it, and the only thing Mike had going for him, at least as far as she was concerned, was that he knew computers. Aren't you wondering about that, even a little—considering how world peace hangs in the balance, and all? Ann-Marie seems to be a loose wire in the nice machinery of Ed. Tech., at least as you two soldiers and your 'friends' see it. Doesn't that bother you?"

G. B. shrugged off my sarcasm, which always annoys me, and shrugged off my questions, too. "Sounds to me," he said, "as if Ann-Marie's had quite a varied erotic life.

You can't be sure it wasn't some other facet of the guy's personality that turned her on. Or maybe stringing this Parrish guy along for a while was the turn-on for her. I don't think it's any of our business, in any case. We're not the morals police.''

"Morals police! I'm not talking morality, I'm talking murder! Don't you want to catch whoever killed him?''

"What we're doing is more important than the individual,'' George said.

"You're sounding like a communist,'' I said, "or an ant.''

"Sometimes,'' George said, "you have to take on the colors of the enemy in order to beat them. Camouflage.''

"It seems reasonable to me,'' G. B. said, "that one of her lovers is going to blow his brains out, sooner or later.''

"Law of averages,'' George explained.

They were watching me, waiting for me to say something. I was at a loss for words, for the second time in three days. I hoped it wasn't going to become a habit.

I heard a sound from the wall separating Bixler's office from the office next to his, like somebody overweight testing a wooden chair to its limits. The office next to Bixler's belongs to the chief, who was out of town. All the walls are thin in the old building.

"I'm at a dead end,'' I said finally, speaking loudly and clearly, so Bixler could hear every word. "After all the running around I've done, I've got more questions than I had before. The only question you've answered is why Ann-Marie came to see me yesterday, and why she was so nervous when the conversation turned to Eric Fridell. I thought it was because she was a murderer. Maybe I was wrong.''

I didn't know if I was telling the truth or not and I didn't spend any time thinking about it before I spoke.

"You *were* wrong,'' G. B. said, his voice enthusiastic. "So you're going to drop it. That's good.''

I didn't say anything.

"There's just one more thing,'' George said. "What we've told you is confidential, of course. So you won't be telling this woman, the dead guy's sister, about us. She sounds like the hysterical type to me—not like you at all. She sounds like she could fly off the handle at any moment and do something *we'd* regret, like go to Ed. Tech and confront them, maybe tip them off to what's going on. We don't want some crazy woman upsetting the applecart.'' George's eyes avoided mine when he said that.

"Whatever the applecart is,'' I said.

"It sounds,'' G. B. said, "as if Ann-Marie Ekdahl's satisfied that all you're interested in is the death of her ex-boyfriend. That's good. Maybe you should call her up and tell her you're sorry and you won't be bothering her anymore.''

"And you *won't* be bothering her anymore, of course,'' George said, taking his glasses off and polishing the lenses carefully, watching me with sad, nearsighted eyes. "You'll *mean* it when you tell her that.'' It wasn't a question.

"Of course she'll mean it, George,'' G. B. said. "She's a good cop. She gave it the old college try, so to speak, but she knows when to quit.''

My hackles were up. I licked my lips in order to keep from biting them or thinning them into a sneer. Tweedledum and Tweedledee watched me for a moment and then, apparently satisfied with what they saw, they went away.

Sixteen

Bixler was back in his office almost before the two Customs men had turned the corner down the hall. I didn't wait for an invitation, I sat back down and faced him as he settled into his big swivel chair. I was curious to see what he'd do: try to pretend he hadn't heard every word, or come right out and admit it.

"You've been meddling in something that's none of your business," he said, starting out calmly. "Again."

"I was doing it on my own time, too," I pointed out, just going through the motions, knowing that nothing I said would make any difference to him.

"Maybe so, but maybe not on your own authority. You wouldn't by any chance have passed your snooping off as police business, would you, anywhere down the line?"

I said I hadn't. I didn't tell him I'd come close on a couple of occasions. Like George, I operate on a need-to-know basis.

"Murder is Homicide business," Bixler plowed on. "Especially when it's got no tie to the University."

"Murder?" I asked, blinking innocence. "What murder?"

The blood flooded his face, making its resemblance to a half-filled hot water bottle all the more striking. "Don't fool with me, O'Neill! You know what I'm talking about. Some guy who killed himself over some bi—woman. That's what brought Customs over here. Your butting your nose in where it doesn't belong almost ruined something important, something that maybe involves national security.''

''Uh-huh. The *bi*—the woman involved used to work here. The guy who got killed was working here when he died. So it does have a connection to the University.''

''Remote, O'Neill, remote. It's a big place, the U. People who work here get in trouble just like people who work other places. You're going to leave it alone. That's a direct order.''

I thought, God, this man has a way with words! I nodded, got up wearily. I hadn't got my required amount of sleep, I'd been batted around like a badminton birdie by two refugees from *Alice in Wonderland,* and now Bixler was trying to sit on me. ''All right, Lieutenant,'' I told him. ''I got the message from them. And I'm sure you heard my answer.''

''Yeah.'' Points of light flickered in his sly little eyes. ''Right! I heard how you made them *think* you were going to stop your meddling. I noticed they even left here thinking you'd *promised* to stop your meddling. But it's a strange thing, O'Neill: I didn't actually hear you *say* it.''

I suppose even dinosaurs acquired a measure of cunning, as the millenia passed and their food supply dwindled.

''What do you want me to do?'' I asked him. ''I told them I didn't know where to go with it next. What more do you want?''

He rose from his chair, slammed his palms down on his desk, and half-roared, half-whispered: ''Even if you thought you *knew* where to go with it next, even if you find a clue so big you have to carry it around in a wheelbarrow, you're *still* going to stay out of it, O'Neill. Understand? You're not going to stay out of it because you don't know where to turn next, you're going to stay out of it because I'm *telling* you to stay out of it. Get it?''

I nodded. And to prevent him from shouting something like ''I didn't hear your answer!'' I added: ''Got it.''

He was having trouble breathing as I left his office. I've had that effect on him before.

I managed to get away without promising him anything, either.

The trail had led me to Ed. Tech and straight into the arms of the two Customs men, and I couldn't see any way around them. I was more certain than ever that Mike Parrish's death was murder and that Ann-Marie had something to do with it. I was also sure Mike's death was related to what was going on at Ed. Tech—even though the Customs men didn't seem to think so—and to his knowledge of computers. Ann-Marie must have wanted that knowledge for something.

The Customs men had given me something new to think about, too, possibly another piece of the puzzle: whatever Ann-Marie had used Mike Parrish for, it had to have been without Eric Fridell's knowledge since, if Ann-Marie and Mike had been part of what was going on at Ed. Tech, Customs—or their "friends"—would have known about it. They seemed content to believe that Ann-Marie had been no more than Fridell's lover, and wasn't even that now. And they obviously hadn't heard of Mike until I told them about him. Lover's quarrels and crimes of passion aren't important in the international game of spy versus spy—and nobody but Carol and I thought Mike's death was murder anyway.

I had to call Carol and give her the bad news, and I had to do it without making her suspicious of Ed. Tech. G.B. had been right in thinking she might try to solve the mystery of her brother's death on her own, by going out to Ed. Tech and doing God-knows-what that would only get her hurt or in trouble.

I called her up and told her I didn't know what to do next. She said, "You'll think of something, Peggy," but I could tell from her voice that she knew what was coming.

"Maybe," I hedged, finding I didn't have the guts to come right out and say I wouldn't and wasn't planning to. "But nothing comes to mind at the moment. I'm going to give it a rest."

"What about Educational Technology? Did you find anything out about that?"

"They sell educational equipment. They seem perfectly legitimate." That was one of the harder half-truths I've ever told anybody.

"But you still think Mike was murdered?"

I told her yes, but that I hadn't been able to come up with anything to prove it. We'd never get the case reopened with what I had, I said. That was true, we couldn't get it reopened even with what I had that Carol didn't know about. "Carol," I said, "you know hardly anything about your brother's past, after he left home and before he came back here. There might be a lot of people you've never even heard of who had a reason to kill him, not just Ann-Marie."

"You're giving up, aren't you?" she asked.

"I guess so," I replied. And then: "Yes, I am."

"You've only been working on it two weeks. You've found out a lot."

"Goddamn it," I flared, releasing anger I didn't know had been building, "that's long enough, isn't it? I'm no private eye. I told you, I'm at a dead end. I'm sorry, but *I* didn't kill your damned brother." I tried to get myself back under control. I said, lamely, "I have other things to do, Carol. I have problems of my own."

"I'm sorry, Peggy."

I said I was sorry, too, and I lied and said that I'd give it some more thought and maybe come up with something. I hate it when I say cowardly things like that. We'd keep in touch, I added miserably.

She said that yeah, sure, we'd keep in touch.

I thought it was over then.

Seventeen

I didn't find Jason Horn's body, Lawrence Fitzpatrick did. That seemed appropriate since, at the time Horn had disappeared, Lawrence had prophesied that he'd turn up—in the spring, he'd said, under the snow. It wasn't spring yet, but it was on the way.

A few days after my little chat with G.B. and his pal George, there was a thaw. It lasted almost a week, left the whole city noisy with its dripping, and turned streets into shallow lakes where the drains were still clogged with ice.

It was the first week of March and I was in a squad car, splashing down the poorly lit Old Campus streets, when I heard Lawrence, who was driving the other squad car that night, call the dispatcher. Lawrence is a nice guy, the nicest on the force, next to Jesse Porter. It took me a while to realize that. I hadn't been predisposed to like any man who insisted on being called "Lawrence."

"I'm in Corridor Four," he said. His voice sounded strained. "There's a body in a snowbank here and it's a murder. Call Homicide." There was a pause, and then he added, as if trying to talk something out of his mind, "But they don't have to hurry, if they've got anything better to do. It's been here a while."

The dispatcher called my number and asked me if I'd heard the message and I said yes and that I was already on my way over there. I switched on my flashers, but at 4 A.M. there wasn't enough traffic to warrant using the siren.

We've divided the campus into corridors whose numbers change periodically. It's a way for us to keep the dispatcher informed about where we are, without sharing the knowledge with people who might be listening in for reasons of their own. Corridor Four was the Farm Campus, two miles north of where I was. It was a quick drive.

Lawrence was standing by his squad car when I walked up to him. I said "Hey!" and gave him a shove, and he said, "There's no reason why you should have to see it, so don't go over there."

"Chivalry isn't dead," I retorted, trying to keep it light. "That's nice."

"That's not what I meant," he said, but I was already walking over to see what he'd found.

It was a man's body, on its back, but I didn't recognize him. Snow covered part of his face, filled his eyes, resembled so closely his lamb's-wool hair and beard that it looked as if his head were made of snow. His torso was naked, his arms hidden behind his back; the lower part of his body was still buried, one bare foot sticking out of the snow. His chest and belly were crisscrossed with dark lines that, when I bent to look more closely, looked like slashes made with a knife.

I was so engrossed in studying the corpse, half emerged from winter, that I didn't notice the sirens until they stopped. I straightened up and turned, and saw Buck Hansen coming toward me.

He nodded and I stepped aside so he could see what it was I'd been looking at. "You found this, Peggy?" he asked. I said no and nodded to Lawrence, who was coming over to join us.

"I was on patrol," he said to Buck. "I almost missed it. But something made me shine my light over here and I saw the foot. I dug through to the face and torso and then stopped and called it in."

Two other cops were setting up lights around the scene and others began cordoning it off. A car door slammed behind us and a man carrying a black bag came up, nodded to Buck. Buck told him to go ahead and they went over to the corpse together. I trailed along behind, maybe because my memory was trying to jog my consciousness.

The man from the Medical Examiner's office used his glove to brush snow off the corpse's face.

"It's Jason Horn," I said.

Buck looked at me, started to ask who Jason Horn was, and then remembered. "Do you recall when he disappeared?" he asked me.

"Early January." I said. "I'm not sure of the exact date."

The Medical Examiner had brushed enough of the snow off Horn so that we could see that he was wearing pajama bottoms and that both feet were bare.

"It wouldn't bother me a bit," Lawrence said, "if we moved away from here." He looked at me as if I'd somehow offended him by not being as affected as he was. He was right: I was feeling fairly detached. I'd been shocked by corpses before, but they had been still warm, newly dead, when I happened on them.

I pictured Horn in my mind as I'd last seen him, at the beginning of winter, humiliated, walking out of Lucas Calder's office. I'd felt a pang of guilt then, even if he had brought it on himself. It wasn't easy to relate that man to this frozen thing in the snow. It was somehow unreal, like a curious piece of sculpture. I don't think there's any inherent connection between a body when it's living and when it's dead; the only connections are those the survivors want or need to make.

Buck looked down at the body, as if to see what could be upsetting to Lawrence about it, then shrugged and moved away, and we followed him. The Medical Examiner called after us, "His hands are tied behind his back." With the help of a Homicide cop, he'd lifted Horn far enough out of the snow to see that.

I asked Buck if he needed us anymore and he said no. Then he remembered that I'd been involved with Horn before, and added that he wanted to talk to me the next day. I said he could call me anytime and he replied that he'd wait until I got a good day's sleep and then I could call him. It didn't look as if there was any urgency about trying to find out who'd murdered Horn, he added, since the trail was probably just as cold as Horn.

I didn't sleep very well. A little after noon the next day, I called Buck to make sure he'd be in, and then drove downtown to police headquarters. I nodded to the duty officer, who'd seen me before, and walked down the hall to Buck's office. It's a brightly lit hall and there's an institutional ring to your footsteps that's probably meant to be hell on the nerves of the guilty. The sign on Buck's door tells you he's Mansell Hansen, but he hasn't been called that by anybody since the day he was baptized, and even then, it was only the minister.

He'd already read my report on the break-in at Calder's office and the report Ginny Raines had filed when she'd interviewed Lucas Calder and Marty Reid, right after Horn had disappeared.

"The only person," I told him, "to come up with a theory about why Horn was in Calder's office is Lawrence Fitzpatrick—the cop who found his body. At the time of Horn's disappearance, he said it was because Horn was working for the Russians, or somebody like that, and was rummaging around in Calder's office looking for Star Wars secrets. When he got caught, his masters killed him."

"Lawrence have any grounds for thinking that?"

"Yeah, he reads lots of suspense novels. The big weakness in his theory is that Lucas Calder probably doesn't do secret research. Nobody at the University does, much less astronomers. How about those fringy organizations Horn belonged to? Have you started checking them out? Some of them must have some pretty unstable members."

"My men have been out questioning people who belong to those groups," Buck said, "but I'm praying we can solve this one before we have to open that can of worms! It'd take a year to investigate all the kooky organizations that man belonged to. Hell, he was even a charter member of a group that 'investigates' things like haunted houses and reports of close encounters, did you know that?" He shook his head. "I'm glad I'm not a campus cop, having to deal with the kind of weird folk you have over there."

I said it was stuff like that that kept professors off the streets and out of our hair, so we encouraged it.

"Apparently, not every group Horn belonged to was eager to have him," Buck went on. "But they couldn't throw him out. They just tried to minimize the embarrassment he sometimes caused them."

"Or so they say."

"True. How weird do you have to be, do you think, to embarrass people who think they can improve the quality of wine with a piece of crystal?" Buck sounded as if he really wanted to know.

"If it's true," I said, "it'll put the French wine industry out of business. Maybe one of their agents killed Horn. It sounds like you've been reading up on the New Age."

"Have to, in my line of work. We're trying to get help from the FBI, but they're being their usual cagy selves about admitting they've got plants in any of Horn's groups. Time will tell."

"The FBI must have a pretty hefty dossier on Horn, too," I said, "even though everybody, at least on campus, has always assumed he was just an eccentric and harmless gadfly."

"Not anymore," Buck replied. "A death like Horn's really changes your perception of a person's life."

Now, at least, Horn was being taken seriously. "How long had he been dead, can they tell?" I asked.

"He was a block of ice. The ME says he thinks it's a good bet the body was already frozen, or nearly so, when it was buried in the snow, since it didn't melt the snow around it. There weren't a lot of signs of decay, either, so that means he was kept in cold storage somewhere for a while after he was killed. We determined that he was buried when there was about four feet of snow on the ground. There wasn't that much snow until almost two weeks after he was reported missing."

"That gave them plenty of time to torture him all they wanted to," I said.

"You noticed that, did you?"

"Was it as bad as it looked?"

"Easily. Horn had something somebody wanted. He'd have to have been quite a guy not to have spilled his guts, if that's what it was all about. Of course there's always the chance that we're up against a psychopath, but they mostly go after women."

I asked Buck what he knew about Horn's private life. I knew he'd never been married.

"He didn't have much of a private life. He was a loner. We can't even find anybody he was especially close to in any of those groups he belonged to. Maybe they're hiding something, or maybe they're just trying to put distance between themselves and a murder, we don't know yet. He did have a long-time relationship with a woman who works on campus, a secretary, but they broke up last summer sometime. I've got a man out talking to her now. I suppose it's always possible he threw her over for another woman and she killed him."

"And tortured him first?" I asked skeptically. "She'd have to have quite a monumental ego problem to take rejection that hard."

"I'm sure you wouldn't take it like that, Peggy," Buck said, smiling.

"You're right," I agreed. "I hope you're collecting alibis for certain *important* people on campus at the time Horn vanished, and not just secretaries—say from January eighth, when he was last seen, to January tenth, when he was reported missing?"

He laughed. "What're you thinking, that Lucas Calder needs to account for himself during that period?"

"Horn was caught breaking into Calder's office," I reminded him. "Maybe Calder had some pressing reason for wanting to know why."

"We'll ask him, Peggy. Very politely. Any more advice?"

"Marty—Martin—Reid."

"Did I hear you say Marty? How's Al?"

"Al's got indigestion."

Buck gave me a thoughtful look while he considered that, then decided to stick to business. "He was the guy who blew the whistle on Horn in the first place, wasn't he? You have any reason for thinking he's a suspicious character?"

"He prefers hockey to the Marx Brothers."

Buck laughed. He's got wrinkles at the corners of his eyes, like a lizard, a lizard with a good sense of humor. "I'll have him brought in and held for questioning," he said.

We talked a few minutes longer, made a tentative date to have dinner at my place soon—I can do a pretty good lasagna, salad, and garlic bread, if I have to—and then I got up.

"You making any progress in the death of your friend's brother?" he asked, following me to the door. He's about three inches taller than I, but somehow never seems to be looking down at me when we talk.

"Not anymore. I crashed into two guys from U.S. Customs who don't want me badgering my chief suspect. She works for a company that does business on the side—with Russia. The CIA's involved too, I think."

"It sounds like more than just a simple homicide," Buck said.

"It's still homicide," I retorted, "no matter how complicated it sounds: somebody I know, who's dead, a friend's brother, a human being."

"You promised these guys you'd stay away?" he asked, unaffected by my moral heat.

"They think I did."

"Keep the promise they think you made, Peggy." He put his arm around me, and we walked down the hall together. He's one of the few men who can put an arm around me and keep it attached to his body. When I didn't say anything to his last remark, he added, "Failing that, be careful."

Eighteen

I had time on my hands. I spent some of it wondering about Al. Ginny'd seen him last week with Deirdre, eating Mexican food and looking miserable. I missed him, but not so much that I'd marry him or let him move in with me. I like being alone when I want to be alone, damn it! Has anybody ever heard of a married person having that privilege? In my experience, a married couple doesn't have good friends, just a set of people they can both get along with. I tried imagining waking up and going to bed with Al, every night, every morning, all the rest of my life. I tried the same exercise with a movie star I thought was good looking and possibly intelligent and witty. Life with either of them quickly became beige. Maybe I just have a beige imagination, maybe that's the problem.

On an impulse, I called him. He should have been home, waiting by the phone, but I got his answering machine instead. Al's one of those jerks who makes a number out of it, so you have to wait a long time to leave a message. I hung up in the middle of it, during his juggling demonstration.

Except for Al, my life started to return to normal. I played a little racquetball for the first time since Mike Parrish's death, and lost a rung on the ladder at the gym. I skated with a friend twice on Lake Eleanor and went skiing once alone. I watched old movies on my VCR—including a Marx Brothers' I almost have memorized—and caught up a little on my reading. And then one afternoon, a week after Lawrence had found Jason Horn's body, I met Betty Hall, the Biology Department's executive secretary. We crossed each other's path on the mall across from the library.

She looked smaller than I'd remembered, and at first I thought that must be because her overcoat was too large, but then I saw the dark rings under her eyes and how pale she was. I thought she must be sick.

I said hello. She didn't recognize me, or pretended she didn't, until I told her who I was, and then she gave me a smile without pleasure, told me she was in a hurry, and she proved it by walking away quickly. I watched her until she disappeared.

She was one of the pieces of the puzzle I'd been working on, but wasn't permitted to work on anymore. I thought about her, as I continued on my errand, and about the inexplicable change in her feelings toward Ann-Marie. I recalled Ann-Marie's reaction, at my place, when I'd brought up her relationship to Betty Hall. I'd asked her what had happened between them, and Ann-Marie answered that nothing had happened, but she'd looked frightened when she said it. She didn't want me looking in that direction.

The thought of Betty Hall and Ann-Marie made me think of other pieces of the puzzle: her lover, Mike Parrish, and computers; Ed. Tech and computers. Jason Horn's tortured body came into my mind then, a piece from some other puzzle that didn't concern me—and then I saw him standing in Lucas Calder's office, the office of the man who, more than anybody else on campus, had been responsible for the Supercomputer Corporation and the good health of the Supercomputer Institute.

Somebody tapped me on the shoulder, said in a joking way, "Hey, wake up! It's your turn."

I was standing in a line to pay the fine for an overdue book I'd borrowed from the University library. I put down some money and walked away. Somebody ran after me with the change I'd forgotten. I was looking for a telephone, before I even knew why.

When I'd talked to her, Betty Hall had told me that

Mike Parrish wasn't going to be fired: *he* hadn't done anything to incur the wrath of central administration, she'd said. She'd stressed "he," as if somebody she knew *had* aroused the administration's ire. The odd way she said it puzzled me at the time, but she'd said she didn't mean anything in particular. I didn't believe her.

Something else had struck me as odd, too. When I'd told her that Mike Parrish and Ann-Marie Ekdahl were going together at the time of Mike's death, she'd said, quite flatly, "That's impossible." Why was it impossible?

And finally, as I dropped a quarter into the pay phone just inside the library doors, I thought of something Buck Hansen had told me, that Jason Horn had had a long-lasting relationship with a woman who worked on campus, and that they'd broken up last summer.

That was the order in which these things emerged into consciousness in my head, even as I dialed Homicide and asked to speak to Buck. I asked him the name of the woman Horn had been involved with. I had to wait a few seconds for him to find it among the papers on his desk. I hung up as he was asking me why I'd wanted that information.

I looked up Betty Hall's address in the Student-Staff Directory, and drove over there. If she'd been on her way home from work when I'd bumped into her on the mall, she'd be there by now.

For most of the winter, I'd been involved with the life and death of Mike Parrish. In the background, meanwhile, the mystery of Jason Horn had been developing on its own. And now I'd just come to the irrational conclusion—the certainty—that the two stories converged at one point: Ann-Marie.

I glanced at myself in the rearview mirror to see if what I felt going on in my mind could be read on my face, and it could, I'm not at all sorry to say: if I were a driver in another car on the road, and saw that face, I wouldn't have cut in front of me. The words of the two Customs men echoed in my head: *She's a good cop if she's handled the right way. She gave it the old college try, but she knows when to quit.*

Sure I do, I thought, grinning back at my image in the mirror and almost rear-ending a station wagon stopped at a light in front of me. I'm not investigating Mike Parrish's death now, I'm investigating Jason Horn's. G.B. and George didn't tell me I couldn't do that, did they?

I gave Buck Hansen a long, sober thought: this might be something important, something I should turn over to him. One of his men had talked to Betty Hall about Horn's murder, but apparently she hadn't told him anything. But he hadn't known about Ann-Marie's connection to Horn—how could he, since it only existed in my head?

If I found out that it existed in reality, too, would I tell Buck and let him handle it? I'll decide that after I've talked to Betty Hall, I told myself. Buck might feel obligated to tell his superiors about the Customs connection, and then he'd find himself shut out of investigating a murder, just as I had been. That would make him miserable, maybe even give him an ulcer. I wanted to spare him that.

Nineteen

Betty Hall lived on a street of small homes that looked as if they'd been built in an age when builders cared about people. They were old homes, one-and-a-half- and two-storied, and they looked carefully maintained. Lamps glowed in the front windows of many of them, in Betty Hall's, too.

I rang the bell and after a few moments, a curtain at the side of the door stirred, and then she opened the door and said, "This is a surprise, twice in one day. What can I do for you?" She didn't look any better than she had when I'd seen her on the mall an hour or so before, or any happier to see me.

I told her I wanted to come in and talk to her about Jason Horn.

Annoyance replaced the surprise on her face. "Why? The police have already been here. I told them all I know."

I shrugged and smiled. "I'd like to hear it, too."

"Ask them," she said, and started to close the door.

"If I do that," I said, "I'll also tell them what I know about Ann-Marie Ekdahl. And what I suspect."

Her head went back as if I'd slapped her and she let go of the door. Before she could recover from the shock, I stepped inside. She backed away and I closed the door behind me. The hallway was dark; she hadn't turned on the light.

"I can't imagine what you're talking about," she said.

"She broke up your relationship with Jason Horn. I'm talking about that."

"Jason and I ended our relationship last summer. It was a mutual decision. I haven't seen him since. That woman played no part in it."

She was a pretty good liar, except for the "that woman." I said, "The last time I talked to you, we discussed Mike Parrish. You were quite relaxed, as long as he stayed the topic of our conversation, but you turned to ice when the subject of Ann-Marie came up. Then you murdered a ballpoint pen, and got ink all over your hands. I think I know why, now."

"I don't believe you know anything," she replied.

"I know that you and Ann-Marie were good friends for a long time while she was working for you. But then, at some time after she left the Biology Department, your friendship went sour. The last time she showed up in your office, you acted as if you hated her guts."

"I should have known that nothing goes unnoticed by Barbara McKay. But I'm afraid she misunderstood, as gossips always do. There was nothing between us, Ann-Marie Ekdahl was just a common, garden-variety secretary, the kind that is always coming and going at the University."

"No, she wasn't. I've seen the evaluations you put in for her. You didn't think there was anything common or garden-variety about her when you wrote those."

"How did you—?"

"Illegally," I replied, "very much so. And I can get into a lot of trouble on account of it. But I'm investigating a murder, the murder of Mike Parrish, my friend's brother. He's supposed to have killed himself over Ann-Marie Ekdahl. Or don't you remember my telling you that? You seemed quite startled at the time, and for some reason, you refused to believe they'd ever been together as a couple."

"I remember that the police have called Parrish's death a suicide. I have no reason to doubt that verdict."

"I think I can interest Homicide in the likelihood that Ann-Marie Ekdahl broke up your relationship with Jason Horn. If I do, they'll turn your life inside out. They'll talk to the secretaries in your department—and not just Barbara McKay—and if it's true that you used to invite Ann-Marie here, they'll find plenty of witnesses to confirm it. They'll talk to Ann-Marie, too. And my guess is that she'll be glad to have you as a fellow suspect in Horn's murder. Maybe she'll tell them about how she broke up the relationship between you and Horn. And then Homicide will come looking for you for his death, since you'll have one of the oldest motives there is for murder.''

Her reaction surprised me. She laughed. ''You think there's a chance I murdered Jason in a fit of rage over being tossed over for another, a younger woman? And tortured him first and then threw his body out in the snow?'' She was still laughing when she said that, but there were tears in her eyes, too, I could see that in the dim hall light.

''No,'' I replied, ''I don't.''

She gave me a startled look, hearing that. ''Nor will the police.'' Instead of asking me to leave again, she turned and walked into her living room and I followed her. She offered me coffee, but didn't sound interested in making it; it was more a form of clearing her throat.

''I admire your tenacity,'' she said. ''I've always thought tenacity should be rewarded.'' She looked better than she had when I'd first arrived at her door.

''It's true that Ann-Marie broke up your relationship with Horn?'' I asked.

''Yes. Yes, I suppose she did. But he never said so. At first, he merely stopped coming over here so regularly.''

He stayed at her place three nights a week, she explained. They'd evolved that routine over the years. Not many people on campus knew of their relationship: Horn hadn't cared, but he thought that she would be embarrassed by that kind of association with him, and that it might make her job more difficult.

''And then he called me one night,'' she said, ''last summer. He told me he wasn't coming over and that he wanted to 'put our relationship on hold.' Those were his words. I asked him why, but it was clear that he didn't want to tell me. I guessed, of course, that there was another woman, although it never occurred to me that it was Ann-Marie. It's still hard for me to believe. But later, one of my friends told me she thought she'd seen them together, going into a theater, Jason and Ann-Marie.''

''You introduced Ann-Marie to Horn back when Ann-Marie was still working for Biology?''

''Yes. Here, in this house.''

''Do you remember when he stopped coming over here regularly?''

''Of course I do. It was early August.''

''That's almost a year and a half after she stopped working for you.''

''I'd have known,'' she said flatly, ''if they'd become involved any sooner than that. Jason's no good at lying. He couldn't keep something like that from me. Oh, Ann-Marie flirted with him when we were together, and Jason flirted back—but neither of us took it seriously. That was just her way, I thought, and didn't mean anything. And it made Jason feel good. He knew it wasn't real, too—at least, that's what I thought at the time. He sometimes called her 'the anima woman.' He said that meant the same as *femme fatale*—the sort of woman who projects an image of being whatever a man wants her to be—a kind of mirror. She often doesn't know it herself, he said, doesn't realize her power. Jason recognized her power, he could even tell me about it, but he underestimated it.''

Ann-Marie's husband, Terry Rhodes, had said something like that about his wife, too. A needy lady, he'd called her, the kind that attracts men who can't save themselves, so they decide to try to save her. Maybe that's all a *femme fatale* is.

''You must have underestimated her power, too,'' I said. ''I don't think you make a habit of inviting the people who work for you home.''

''No, I don't.'' She got up and moved around her living room as she spoke. ''She was a capable worker, almost compulsive about it. And creative, too. But the other women in the office didn't like her, and at first I didn't either. But she didn't act as if she cared, she seemed to take that reaction as given—as if she'd earned it somehow, and it made her special. But one day I saw her standing in the hallway. She was with someone taller than she, a man, smiling up at him, one of the professors who was talking down at her. There was light falling on her face from a hall window and I could see something about her I'd never noticed before, in her or in anybody. She looked so *awkward*, as if she didn't really know how to stand or walk or talk in this world, on this planet, she was only faking it, wearing a disguise.'' Betty Hall's voice trailed off. She turned quickly to me, as if to see if I'd left, or was looking at her oddly, which I hoped I wasn't. "After that," she said, "I liked her. Or maybe I just wanted to get to know her better."

"Did you ever meet her husband?"

"Terry—Rhodes, I think it was?" she replied, the spell broken. "Yes, she brought him here once. We obviously bored him, and neither Jason nor I liked him. They'd only just gotten married, you know—they'd met in Germany, I think she said, where he was in the Army. I couldn't imagine what she saw in him and it seemed obvious that Ann-Marie regretted having married him. He had a custodial job at the U., too, as I recall. He worked nights, and on a few occasions he dropped into Ann-Marie's office just at her quitting time. She discouraged that, and he stopped coming."

That was news. When I'd talked to him, Terry Rhodes didn't mention anything about working at the U. He was in school, he'd told me.

"Can you tell me what you think Ann-Marie saw in Horn?"

Betty Hall looked at me. She was a gray woman— Ann-Marie had described her that way, too—she seemed to cultivate gray as a way of life, the protective coloring of gifted women from an age that had no use for their gifts. But suddenly she gave me a little impish smile that was as unexpected as it was beautiful. "At the time, I thought maybe she saw in him what I did," she said, and then she heard what she'd said and looked quickly down at her hands. "But we both know better than that." When she looked back up at me, her face was composed.

"A couple of months after you think she went after him," I said, "he broke into Lucas Calder's office. He got caught. A month or so later, she started going with Mike Parrish. My guess is that she dumped Horn after he was caught in Calder's office."

"Yes. She must have."

"Why do you think so?" I expected her to say that he'd come crawling back to her.

She looked down at her hands twisting in her lap. "I called him," she said reluctantly, "when I read in the student newspaper about what had happened."

"*You* asked him to come back?"

"Not in so many words. But he knew that's what I wanted. He said he was ashamed, that he needed time to deal with what had happened to him. The University was trying to get him fired—they'd been trying for a long time and now it seemed certain they had what they needed to do it. He said he didn't want to involve me in all that. He was still thinking he might try to fight the University, but he was also considering resigning and moving away. He'd always wanted to live someplace warmer than here." She looked at me, added, "When he disappeared, I just thought he'd walked away—from everything."

"When you phoned him, did you ask him why he'd broken into Professor Calder's office?"

"Yes, but he didn't tell me very much. He said he'd been absolutely sure he'd find something in there that would embarrass Lucas Calder—and the University, too."

"Like what?"

"I have no idea. Jason had lots of odd ideas over the years, Peggy. He was jealous of Calder, of course. Calder's everything that Jason wasn't—that Jason didn't think he was. And it infuriated him that Calder made fun of the things Jason believed in, or at least that he kept an open mind about. Jason had also heard the rumors that Calder took money from some of the big defense contractors, to lobby for the creation of the Supercomputer Corporation."

"I've never heard those rumors," I said.

"That's all they were," she said, shrugging. "There wasn't any proof. Jason had heard some of the other faculty gossiping about it, the way they do."

"He broke into Calder's office," I said, "looking for something that would embarrass Calder *and* the University. Where did he expect to find it? In a file labelled 'Secret'? Lying out on his desk?"

She paused for a moment before responding, and then, as if she'd made her mind up about something, said, "He may have thought he'd find it somewhere in the files in Calder's computer."

The hair started to rise on the back of my neck as I saw what was coming next. Betty Hall waited for me to ask the next question, a smile playing around her mouth.

I asked the next question. "How was he going to find it there?"

"I don't think it would have been hard for him, Peggy, if there was anything to find. Jason knew more about computers than almost anyone on campus. He had more knowledge in his little finger than Michael Parrish had in his entire body."

Twenty

She liked my reaction to that.

She savored her pleasure for a moment, and then went on, as if she hadn't exploded a bomb at my feet. "Computers were Jason's hobby. He always liked tinkering with things. When he was a kid, he told me, he built model airplanes and crystal sets, and when he was grown up he built a computer—he knew them inside out. He called himself a hacker, making a joke about it—but that's exactly what he was. Not too many professors—at least outside the hard sciences—know the first thing about computers, even today. They have computerphobia, Jason called it. He even belonged to a computer club for a while. And do you know what else he did?" She was smiling now as she spoke, as if talking about a son, to forget he was dead. "He sometimes broke into computer systems, he told me—all over the country, not just here. Just for the fun of it. He never did any harm, he just wanted to see what they were up to. Banks. Big corporations. He told me that once he even broke into the phone company's system and read the correspondence of the company's big shots."

"What do you mean," I asked, "he 'broke into computer systems all over the country'?"

"Jason said he could go from his computer—you know, a desktop computer just like the ones we use in our offices—to other people's computers, by way of some kind of telephone hookup. Using a modem. He had one of those. They aren't very expensive."

Marty Reid had mentioned modems, too. He'd called a box-like thing next to his computer a modem. I said, "I don't suppose the phone company big shots would have slept well, knowing a New Age Marxist revolutionary was rummaging through their files from the privacy of his apartment."

"That's what he said, too. And when the kids started doing that kind of thing—the hackers—and started damaging the computer systems of corporations that had extensive computer networks, Jason stopped. He knew that if he got caught, he'd be punished worse than other hackers, because of his politics and his reputation. And he knew what the University would try to do with it, too, if he was ever caught. So he gave it up. I don't think he even owns a computer now—owned one at the time of his death, I mean."

I asked her if Horn had talked about his knowledge of computers in front of Ann-Marie.

"Oh, I'm sure he did. Jason was proud of his knowledge. He was very childlike, in many ways."

That was the understatement of the evening. Horn must have bragged to Ann-Marie about his computer skills. When, later, she'd wanted somebody with those skills, she'd known where to turn. And still later, she'd turned to Mike Parrish, a computer specialist.

"It doesn't make sense," I said, thinking aloud.

"What doesn't?"

"That Jason Horn broke into Calder's office because Ann-Marie wanted something in there."

"There's no reason to think he did it for Ann-Marie," Betty said. "He may have done it entirely on his own, just to try to prove something to himself."

"Two men are dead," I reminded her. "Both with computer knowledge, both involved with Ann-Marie, and neither of them her type. Those are reasons enough for me. There are also the keys Horn had to the Science Tower and to Calder's office. Would he have gone to that much trouble, just to try to prove something?"

"You didn't know Jason. He was capable of anything, once he got a bee in his bonnet."

More than a bee in his bonnet had gotten him tortured and murdered. "He got caught in Lucas Calder's office on November first. A few weeks later—sometime in late November—Ann-Marie started hustling Mike Parrish."

"How do you know that's when it was?"

Because Barbara McKay'd told me. But I didn't want to get her into any more hot water than she was probably already in with Betty, so I replied that I'd learned if from Mike's sister Carol.

"When you talked to Horn on the phone, did he say if he'd found what he was looking for?"

"It sounded to me as if he hadn't," she said.

"Because he got interrupted by Professor Reid."

"No, I don't think so. He sounded disappointed, as if he hadn't found what he thought he'd find in there."

We sat in silence for a while. I remembered something else I'd wanted to ask Betty about. "Christmas Eve day, Mike Parrish came back to town from his parents' farm, about a hundred miles north of here. He said some kind of emergency had come up and he was needed in the Department. He was gone all day. Do you remember what it was?"

"Are you sure that's what he said?"

"I'm sure, yes."

"I can't believe anybody was here, much less doing research that would have required immediate help from Parrish. But if he did come back to work that day, he'd certainly have put in for overtime for the hours. I'll look into it and call you if I find a record of it, but I don't think I will."

I didn't think she would either. I was sure he'd come back, that one day of the year when the campus would be virtually deserted, to do something else, something for Ann-Marie that had later gotten him killed, just as Jason Horn had done before him.

Betty asked me if I was going to tell the city police what I'd learned from her.

I was wondering the same thing. I'd confirmed the connection between two dead men: Ann-Marie and computers. That would be enough to start Buck Hansen looking into Ann-Marie's life with a vengeance, and looking into Ed. Tech, too, and Eric Fridell, her once and future boss. Then bells would start ringing in the heads of the two Customs men, G. B. and George, Tweedledum and Tweedledee. A discreet word from them—or from their "friends," almost certainly the CIA—to Buck's superiors, and the next thing you know, Buck and I would be reminiscing in a coffee shop somewhere about the feeling you get when a rug is yanked out from under you. National security, you know. There are people willing to turn the country into a banana republic in the name of national security.

As long as I confined myself to Jason Horn's murder, and kept Buck out of it, I wouldn't have to look over my shoulder all the time to see if G. B. and George were stalking me, since they didn't know about Horn—or about the University connection at all. And maybe I'd get lucky and—just by accident, of course—be able to pin Horn's murder on Ann-Marie before the Customs men caught on to what I was doing. Once she'd been arraigned for one murder, not even the CIA would be able to protect her. After all, it would look pretty fishy to the Russians if a murder indictment against somebody working for Ed. Tech were suddenly quashed.

There was also Lucas Calder, the University's most colorful scientist, a media personality and author. The University wouldn't like having him badgered by the cops. I was starting to believe that there was something in Calder's office that Ann-Marie wanted—it was certainly worth looking into, at any rate—and that when Jason Horn had been unable to find it, she'd turned to Mike Parrish. It might be easier for me than for Buck to check that out without attracting Calder's—and the University's—attention.

I'd made up my mind not to tell Buck what I'd learned from Betty Hall, but that didn't stop me from overrationalizing the decision. After all, I reasoned, I didn't have any *proof* that Ann-Marie was interested in Mike just for his computer skills or that she'd been interested in Jason Horn for his, or that she'd been behind either of them breaking into Lucas Calder's office. I didn't even know for sure that Mike Parrish *had* broken into Calder's office, it just seemed likely.

Betty Hally stirred and I looked up. She said she'd never seen anybody so deep in thought before in her life—even after a quarter of a century at the university.

I headed for the door and she followed me. On the front steps, I said, "No, I'm not going to tell the cops what you've told me. Not yet, anyway. I want to do some more looking into it on my own first, undisturbed. If I turn it over to Homicide, I don't think we'll ever find out what Ann-Marie was up to."

We were standing on her front steps. She said: "Is this really very important to you, Peggy?"

"Yes." I blinked. "Isn't it to you?"

She smiled. "I'll call you, if I find that Michael Parrish put in for overtime Christmas Eve."

I waited for her to say something more, but she just turned and went back into her house. As I expected, I never heard from her again.

Twenty-one

I knew so little about computers in general and supercomputers in particular that, to me, it wasn't outside the realm of possibility that Ann-Marie was involved in trying to steal a supercomputer, with or without the support of Eric Fridell and Ed. Tech. I didn't even know what a supercomputer looked like—which wasn't surprising, considering Marty Reid had told me he didn't either.

The day after I talked to Betty Hall, I got up early and called Marty. I hadn't talked to him since the disaster of our hockey date, but he was the only person I knew who seemed to know a lot about computers.

He didn't sound too frosty when I told him who was calling, so maybe he'd taken our date as a learning experience, too, the kind some people need occasionally. I explained what I wanted and he asked me what my sudden interest in computers was all about. I told him I was looking into Jason Horn's murder and I thought there might be a connection.

"Officially?" he asked.

I was starting to hate that question. "No."

"Then why are you doing it?"

"Because I'd like to know why somebody murdered him, and what he knew that was so important that he was tortured for it before he was killed."

"And because you feel responsible for his death, too, because you almost arrested him once. What do you think you can do that the cops aren't doing? They've been here, of course. They were here the day after you found Horn's body, questioning both Lucas and me about it. I told them I couldn't imagine how Horn's death could be connected in any way with the break-in at Lucas' office. Lucas told them that, too, in somewhat stronger language and in a louder voice. After all, Horn must have been involved in just about every fringe movement on or near campus. Did you read his obituary, Peggy?''

I said I didn't mind sharing a planet with harmless nuts; it's sort of comforting to know there are people in the world who think the dead would while away eternity throwing china out of the cupboards of strangers.

"You're missing my point," Marty said. "Horn was a nut who palled around with a lot of other nuts. Not all nuts are harmless, even if Jason Horn was. His death might easily be connected with one of the weirder organizations he belonged to—hell, it might even be a ritual killing of some kind.''

That was a new theory. "I don't think he belonged to anything that weird," I replied. "But if he did, the city police will find it out. They're good at that sort of thing. I'm working on the possibility that the reasons he was murdered had something to do with computers. Specifically, the University's supercomputers.''

There was a long pause. I waited it out. Then Marty said, "You must think you know something the city police don't. Or else you're making wild guesses. Which is it?''

"I know that Jason Horn was probably as good with computers as you are. Computers were his hobby. He was a hacker, apparently a very good one.''

There was another pause. Finally, Marty asked me how I knew that.

"It doesn't matter. But it changes things a little, doesn't it? It means that, when he broke into Calder's office last fall, he didn't have to just stand there staring at Calder's computer with his jaw hanging open, like a caveman gaping at a cigarette lighter.''

"If you're right, Peggy, it means I was lucky to catch him before he could get into Lucas' computer files, maybe damage or erase some of his stuff. Not that that would be such a loss to science, but it would be a loss to Lucas," he added dryly.

"Why wouldn't it be a loss to science?"

"Because Lucas doesn't do research, basic research, anymore," Marty answered.

I recalled that, at the Cambodian restaurant, he'd said much the same thing, but at the time I didn't pick up on it. "He's one of the University's most prominent scientists," I said. "What do you mean he's not doing real research?"

"Prominent, yeah. Productive, no. Not anymore. Now he's just a name, living off his past successes. He's a scientific *personality*, speaking and writing for the masses, making the universe 'conversational.' "

His voice was tinged with contempt. Maybe he was thinking of his father, who'd toiled in the groves of academe, in Calder's shadow, until his death.

"But he does have access to the supercomputers from his office, doesn't he?" I asked him. "Just as you do?"

"Sure, but he doesn't really need it."

"Then why does he have it?"

"For show. Prestige. Because he worked so hard to get the Supercomputer Corporation here."

"Indulge me, Marty," I said, trying to hide the excitement in my voice. "Give me the names of a few journals that'll give me some background on computers and problems with computer security, things like that, in a language I might be able to understand. I've read a little in the papers about computer viruses and what they do, but I don't know anything other than that there are such things."

"You aren't planning to annoy Calder with this investigation of yours, are you?" he asked, hesitant, almost putting quotation marks around "investigation." "He's tired of hearing about Jason Horn. I wouldn't like him thinking I've encouraged you in any way."

"I wouldn't dream of annoying Calder," I said, not knowing if that were true or not, since I rarely remember my dreams.

Reluctantly, Marty gave me the information I wanted, but added that he thought I was just wasting my time.

I spent two hours in the library and, armed with notes and questions, went over to the Supercomputer Institute, a smaller version of the Science Tower—granite and glass that, like smog, made no concessions to the eye of the beholder. A receptionist sat at a desk in front of a glass wall and, on the other side of it, a uniformed guard stared out blankly.

I asked the receptionist if I could see Dr. Swanson, the Institute's director. I had to tell her that it was police business and show her my shield. She apprised her boss of my presence over her intercom and then buzzed me through the wall. I was surprised the guard let me pass without frisking me. I followed the receptionist's directions past the guard and down a hall even more luxuriously carpeted than my apartment, knocked on Dr. Swanson's door, and went in.

He rose from some kind of ultra-modern chair and came to meet me, ready to shake hands, a small, lean man of about forty. He looked like a jockey in beautifully tailored tweed and he wore his thick gray hair brushed up from his high forehead in a pompadour. The curiosity in his eyes gave way to pleasure as he saw me staring through the glass wall behind him. The whole place seemed made of glass.

"Those are the supercomputers," he explained, leading me over to the wall and pointing down at things that resembled large gray filing cabinets. "And over there is the newest one, the Symore." He pointed to another large object that looked marginally more interesting, hexagonal in shape. I contemplated it briefly, wondered if it was speed reading *War and Peace* in search of adverbs.

"What are those bubbly things?" I asked, amazed at the swiftness with which we'd taken on the roles of tour guide and tourist.

"Coolant pods. Heat exchangers that cool the liquid that keeps the supercomputers from burning up. They generate a tremendous amount of heat—enough to heat this entire building all winter.''

''What about in the summer?'' I asked.

''We vent it outside, of course.''

''Adding to the greenhouse effect that's going to change the planet in ways that nobody can predict,'' I said.

''It's being studied,'' he replied. ''Even now, a super-computer somewhere—if not one of those down there—is wrestling with just that problem.''

I'll sleep better at night knowing that, I thought. I came away from the glass, and in that way drew him away from it, too. When we were seated, I explained that there'd been a break-in in the office of someone who had access to the supercomputers, and I was working on the theory that it might have had something to do with the supercomputers.

''Whose office?'' He was suddenly all business.

''Lucas Calder's.''

''Lucas'? Ah yes, he mentioned to me that somebody had broken into his office, but he didn't attach much importance to it. It was that odd fellow who got himself killed, wasn't it? I don't recall the name.''

''Jason Horn.''

''That's right. Rather one of the fringe element, wasn't he? You think he might have had it in for Lucas because of Lucas' advocacy of the Supercomputer Corporation, is that right?''

I said yes, and was about to go on when he cut in with: ''But that doesn't explain his getting murdered, does it?'' Dr. Swanson was shrewder than I'd given him credit for being. ''I mean,'' he went on, aiming a finger at me, ''it's one thing for a silly man like Horn to want to hurt or annoy a man like Lucas Calder. It's quite something else if the silly man gets murdered. You see my point, don't you? You aren't suggesting that Lucas Calder murdered Horn?''

''Of course not,'' I said, backpedaling fast. ''The most likely theory is that there's no connection at all between Horn's breaking into Calder's office and his getting murdered. But there's always the possibility, however remote, that Horn was acting on somebody *else's* orders when he broke into Calder's—''

"Ah," Swanson said, and relaxed back into his chair, which accepted him without comment. "Spies, perhaps, or one of those radical groups this Horn seemed addicted to. And they—what's the expression I want?—eliminated him, once his usefulness to them was over."

"Yes." I was pleased to discover that Dr. Swanson must read the same thrillers that Lawrence Fitzpatrick read.

"But why?" Dr. Swanson asked, becoming shrewd again. "Why would they want to break into Lucas' computer? He didn't do classified research."

"Maybe they didn't know that," I said.

He thought about that. "Well, perhaps," he said doubtfully. "Ask your questions, then. However, I do have an appointment at three-thirty." He pulled a large, old-fashioned watch out of a pocket and looked at it and put it away again.

I told him I knew that, since the creation of the Supercomputer Corporation, scientists all over the city now had access to the supercomputers.

"All over the *state*, you mean," he corrected me. "But most of the businesses and industries interested in using our supercomputers lie within a radius of a few miles of here, of course. The big electronics companies, several of the larger banks, research hospitals."

"Anybody who's got the necessary cash can buy time on the supercomputers?"

"Well, not anybody, of course. You have to have a bona fide *project* to work on, and you must be either a member of a department authorized to use the supercomputers or affiliated with one of the outside companies that has bought time from the Supercomputer Corporation."

I asked him to tell me a little about the Corporation.

Its offices, he explained, rented space from the University. They were just down the hall from his. The Corporation had its own director and acted as a kind of middleman between the University and the outside community. It could sell time on the University's supercomputers to anybody it wanted to. A part of its profits were paid to the University, which in turn used them to maintain the Supercomputer Center.

"The Corporation launders money for the University, so to speak," I said, to make it easier for me to comprehend.

"Launders—?" He understood what I meant then, and barked it away with a wooden laugh. "That's a good one," he said.

"And you have no idea what kind of research is going on down there," I said, nodding at the glass wall behind him, "to heat this building and pay for the care and feeding of the supercomputers?"

"None of all," he said, his good mood restored.

"Your job, then, as director, is just to make sure the trains run on time."

"Yes." He drew the old-fashioned watch out of the little pocket on his trousers again and looked at it. "Odd you should call it that," he said. "My father worked for the railroad all his life. He left me this, his railroad watch."

"That's nice. All right, let's say I have permission to do research using your supercomputers. What do I need to get access to them from my office?" I didn't care if "access" had become a verb to the likes of Marty Reid, it wasn't a verb to me.

"Well, we provide you with a modem and a key box and that's it, you're in business."

In one of the journals Marty had recommended I'd read that a modem is a box-like thing connected to your computer that allows your computer to communicate, via telephone, with another computer someplace else. With a computer and a modem, you can, say, dial into a library's card catalogue, if it's been computerized, and search for a book without leaving home. You can also dial somebody else's computer, if you know the number, and give that computer a message that will cause it to print out "Merry Christmas" on Christmas Day—or cause it to self-destruct.

"You can buy a modem in any computer store in town," I said.

"For ordinary computers, yes, of course. But not for

use with supercomputers. Our subscribers are issued special modems.''

"What's a key box?"

"Along with the special modem, the access code, and the password, the key box is our main line of defense against unauthorized use of the supercomputers. When somebody buys time on the supercomputers, a key box is installed between his modem and his telephone. It's the key to the supercomputers. Without it, you can't access them.'' Anticipating my next question, he went on: "The access code is just a budget number for your project that you type in. There's nothing secret about it, it appears on your monthly bill. The secret part is your password.''

"It's sort of like a money card, then,'' I said. "Somebody might steal the card—the access code—but it's no good without the owner's secret number, the password.''

"Exactly. People usually choose such things as their wife's or husband's name, or their place of birth—something easy to remember. Researchers have notoriously bad memories, most of them, and it makes things difficult if they forget their passwords.''

"You don't keep a list?''

"No. The password is just between the user and the supercomputer. The first time you access the supercomputer, it asks you to give it a password. After that, you have to use that password or the computer will act as if it doesn't know you—and it's not just an act, either.''

"Then it comes down to this,'' I said. "If I had one of your special modems, a key box, somebody's access code, and his password, I could break into *his* supercomputer file from the computer in *my* office. I wouldn't need to do it from his office. Right?''

Dr. Swanson frowned suddenly, thinking he'd caught on to what I was getting at. "Is that what you believe? That Jason Horn might have broken into Calder's office to try to use Lucas' access to somebody *else's* supercomputer files?''

"Is it possible?'' I asked, not answering his question.

"Do you really think Horn knew computers that well?'' he asked, not answering mine.

"What if?"

"Why from Calder's office? Why not from somebody else's?"

"If that's what he was doing," I said, "he had to choose somebody's office, since he had no access to the supercomputers himself. So why not Calder's, especially since he didn't like him?"

"You're thinking that Jason Horn might have been something of a—a *hacker*," Dr. Swanson said, uttering the word as if it tasted horrible. "And that he wanted to break into the program of one of the scientists outside the University who's doing classified military research—wanted to steal it perhaps, or harm it. Is that it?"

I didn't say anything, just looked expectant.

"How'd he get the key to Lucas' key box?" he asked, not very hopefully.

"Would that be so difficult?" I asked in return.

Dr. Swanson gave me a sad look. "No," he said. "No, you're right. You're very quick to pick up on things, aren't you? Lucas, of course, was totally unimpressed by the need for security. I'm a friend of his, you know, I've been in his office many times. He leaves his key in the box—which renders it useless as a security measure, of course. In his favor," he added, "I have to say that he's not the only one. Until the coming of the Supercomputer Corporation, there was little real need for security here. Now that we have the Corporation, it's virtually impossible to teach the old dogs new tricks."

He got up and moved around the room, glanced nervously out his window and down at his supercomputers, brooded on them.

"Scientists," he blurted out suddenly, at his reflection in the glass, or mine, "don't give a *shit* about security!" He turned back to me. "It's not just us, either, you know, it's the same everywhere—even in government research institutes. I've seen them, I've talked to other directors. Scientists are a pain!" The overhead light glittered on his high forehead, shinier now than when I'd arrived.

"Yours must be a very frustrating job."

Returning suddenly to the subject, he asked: "But how

would a man like Jason Horn get the passwords of scientists working for off-campus defense contractors?'' His face shone with triumph, or at least with hope. "Tell me that!"

I couldn't. I also didn't think that's what Horn had done. "I don't know," I said.

Dr. Swanson liked hearing that a lot. "And how often could a trespasser—any trespasser, not just a Jason Horn— break into Calder's office and use his computer for any length of time, without being caught?" he demanded, pressing his advantage. "As, indeed, Horn *was* caught."

"You're right, of course," I said, agreeing with him entirely. "It would be a very chancy business. You certainly couldn't make a career of it."

"Exactly. Exactly!" Dr. Swanson scrutinized me closely, as if suspecting I had more up my sleeve, so I went over to the glass wall and looked down at the supercomputers.

One of the journals I'd looked at described what hackers do, once they've managed to break into somebody's files. They stroll through them, pausing to investigate promising byways, sniffing the occasional flower here, the odd herb there. The gentle hackers mean no harm, they're just looking for a technological high. Jason Horn had been a gentle hacker, according to Betty Hall, before he'd given it up as too dangerous.

But somebody could also stroll through supercomputer files looking for classified research to sell. Somebody who didn't need access to the supercomputers in his own work, but had it anyway.

"You said passwords are usually something pretty obvious—a wife's name, or a lover's, or a child's?"

Dr. Swanson nodded reluctantly. "Alas, yes. And I see what you're driving at, that it might not be hard to get passwords from researchers—strike up a conversation with one in a bar, at a party, whatever. However, we do what we can to minimize the danger from that quarter. Supercomputer users are required to change their passwords every two months. The computer automatically notifies them of this and, if they don't, they're barred from entering their own files until they do. So whoever was breaking into their files would have to steal their passwords over and over again.''

''Unless the trespasser, the first time he got into somebody's supercomputer files, opened a secret door of his own that he could use later? At will?''

Swanson's eyes looked haunted. ''You came prepared, didn't you, young lady?''

''Yes.''

''That's why the key box is so important,'' he said, ''and why it's so important to keep your password secret!''

He was right that it would be virtually impossible for a man like Jason Horn to get the passwords he needed. But it wouldn't be hard for supposedly bankrupt Lucas Calder.

Calder was a friend—or a friend of a friend—of most of the scientists in the area. His parties were famous, his guest lists an international *Who's Who* of distinguished researchers. And he had the other necessities: the special modem and the key box.

I said: ''Right now, somebody somewhere on campus could be browsing through supercomputer files down there that aren't his own, couldn't they?''

''If he could get through the obstacles we've discussed, yes.'' Swanson looked at his railroad watch, pointedly. He didn't like me anymore. Then his face lit up. ''But we'd still catch him, sooner or later—and sooner, rather than later, too, I imagine. Because every time you log onto a supercomputer, the date and time are automatically recorded. For billing purposes, as well as for security reasons. If somebody called up a file through—to use your example—Lucas Calder's computer, the next time Lucas called it up, he'd see that last date and time and he'd wonder about it, since he'd know he hadn't been using it then. And he'd also be charged for that time, of course—and time on the supercomputers is expensive. So, sooner or later even the most absent-minded scientist would figure out that somebody'd been accessing his files.''

Goldilocks and the three bears for the 1990s. *Who's been accessing my files?*

I got up. Swanson followed me out the door, down the hall, clearly happy to see me on my way out.

"It's too bad," I said, "that Professor Calder's not doing research anymore, just when—thanks to Calder himself—the University has all the new supercomputers."

Dr. Swanson frowned. "He'll come back to it one of these days. He's just taken a little time off. Most researchers have fallow periods, you know, but they usually come out of it. Right now, he's playing the role of grand old man of science to the hilt, enjoying the limelight. You can't blame him for that." Dr. Swanson's view of Calder's "fallow period" was considerably kinder than Marty's had been, I thought. "And, of course," Swanson went on, "he's got that big book project, *The Birth of the Universe*, which takes an enormous amount of his time."

"Another popularization. Somebody I know calls it 'making the universe conversational.' "

"That's not a very generous assessment, I'm afraid," Dr. Swanson replied. "It's a very ambitious project, very worthwhile, in my opinion. There's nothing wrong with explaining to the general public, in language it can understand, the latest results of science. Calder's new book is even going to include a software program, I understand, that people with a little computer knowledge can use to create and destroy their own galaxies, pixel by pixel."

"He can do that?" I pricked up my ears at the word "software." "He can design software of that complexity?"

"Perhaps, but it's time-consuming. He's working with a local software company on that aspect of it. Someone there is doing the design work."

We'd come up to the guard, who was standing at the glass wall exactly where I'd left him, when the full impact of what Swanson had just said hit me. "You wouldn't happen to know its name, would you," I asked Dr. Swanson, "the software company Calder's working with?"

"No. Why?"

I poked the guard absently, just to see if he was real. He was. "Just curious," I said, and thanked Swanson and left.

All by itself, that piece of information meant nothing, since there were lots of companies in town involved with computers and computer software. Ed. Tech wasn't the only one, it might not even be the only one that created educational software.

But it wasn't a piece of information all by itself. I'd learned from Lawrence, from Marty Reid, that Calder liked money, spent it lavishly, and had even declared bankruptcy once. I'd learned from Marty and Dr. Swanson that Lucas Calder wasn't doing any kind of research now that required the use of supercomputers. I'd just learned that he could go from the computer in his office to the supercomputers and—assuming he was able to overcome a few technical problems—go undetected into the files of other scientists, scientists who were doing secret research.

Even that didn't have to mean anything, until you added in the fact that Ann-Marie Ekdahl had hustled two men who were good with computers, and at least one of those men—armed with illegal keys—had broken into Lucas Calder's office. And Ann-Marie, of course, worked for Ed. Tech, an educational software company that was engaged in illegally smuggling sensitive technology—computer parts, software, among other things—out of the country. Ed. Tech could also be smuggling out classified research provided by Lucas Calder.

Twenty-two

It was after three when I got out of the Supercomputer Institute. I didn't have time to try to find out if my hunch that Calder was involved with Ed. Tech was right—and I wasn't even sure I'd be able to, not without upsetting the two Customs men, G. B. and George. But, if I hurried, I could check out my guess about where Jason Horn had gotten the keys he'd used to break into Calder's office. Betty Hall had mentioned that Terry Rhodes, Ann-Marie's sometime husband, had worked as a custodian at the University at the time Ann-Marie was working in the Biology Department.

I called Rick, my friend in Personnel, and asked him if he had a file on Rhodes. After a few seconds of keyboard tapping, he said: "I have a Terence Michael Rhodes who worked as a maintenance engineer part-time from February 1987 to January of '89. Then he went full-time, and that lasted until September '89 when he quit. That's it. End of record."

"Do you know where on campus he worked?"

"Nope, but his supervisor would. His name's Irving Prior, and you can find him in Building Maintenance, as could your father and grandfather before you. Prior's been around since the University was built. He's in charge of all the maintenance engineers."

"Maintenance engineers?"

"We don't have custodians anymore, Peggy. We've got maintenance engineers. We've also got color engineers now. Guess what they do."

"Empty garbage cans?"

"No, silly, sanitation engineers do that! Gotta run. The Gorgon's drifting my way."

Terry Rhodes had worked part-time at the U. from when he and Ann-Marie arrived from Germany until about the time they broke up. Presumably he was in the Business School at the time, if he was telling the truth about that, and working part-time to supplement his educational benefits from the military. He'd switched to full-time shortly after Ann-Marie'd left him, which probably meant the end of his academic career. And finally he'd quit in September of '89. Something else had happened about that time: Ann-Marie had gone hustling Jason Horn—if my hunch was correct, to get Horn to break into Lucas Calder's office.

I took the inter-campus bus over to the Old Campus and then walked to Building Maintenance, hoping to catch Irving Prior before he left for the day.

I found him tilted back in a swivel chair, his feet up on a battered desk, a long, thin man of indeterminate age with a graying flattop, who was studying a sheet of paper through reading glasses. He looked as if he'd been put together by a pipe fitter. I told him who I was and that I was making inquiries about a former employee, a maintenance engineer named Terry Rhodes.

"Rhodes wasn't a maintenance engineer," he said. "He wasn't even a custodian. He was a janitor."

"It's so hard to keep up," I said.

"I know what you mean. I've been here a long time, seen a lot of changes, all cosmetic. What's he done?"

"Nothing, I'm just—"

"That's what he did for us, too," Prior said.

"It's just a routine inquiry," I said. I was trying not to grin. He wasn't having that problem at all.

"In this light, you look like a candle in a dusty attic," he said. He said it as a fact, one that needed no comment.

"I'm trying to find out what building Rhodes worked in, if he worked in any one particular building."

"He did, they all do. They're assigned a building, they stay there forever unless they want a transfer for some reason or other. They get to know it real well, they work faster and better—'cept Rhodes, of course. Nothing we could think of made him work faster or better.''

"You don't seem to have any problem recalling the man.''

"That's right. I bet Mr. Rhodes don't have any problem recalling Irv Prior either.''

"Why not?'' I looked at the big clock on the wall over Prior's desk. I'd hoped it was time for him to go home and that he'd be in a hurry to get rid of me, but it wasn't working out that way. Then again, it was possible that the warehouse *was* his home.

"Most of the time he worked for us, we were on his ass. He was a goof-off. We canned him, finally.'' The recollection brought his feet down off his desk. "You see, it's kind of hard, canning people around here, about as hard to fire a civil service employee as it is to get rid of a professor. Rhodes'd done okay when he just worked part-time—he was going to school then, I guess. But when he quit school and went to work for me full-time, he changed. Couldn't get hardly a jot of work out of him. We found him sleeping on the job, sometimes.''

"So you fired him.''

"We didn't, actually. That was just me boasting. I gave him a choice: quit or I'd call you people, the cops.''

"For sleeping on the job?''

"No, for being caught red-handed smoking marijuana. I gave him the choice, and he quit. A lot simpler than having to can him. A lot less paperwork involved, believe me.''

"Which building did he work in?''

"The Science Tower, over on the New Campus.''

"And he had keys that would open any door in the building?''

"How else would he get in and out of all the rooms? Knock?'' Prior shot me a look of sudden interest. "Why?''

"It's just part of the investigation,'' I answered, grinning, knowing he wouldn't grin back.

He didn't. "Yeah?''

"Yeah.''

"You want to know my feelings about him?" Prior asked me suddenly, as I got up to go.

"Sure, go ahead."

"He ain't the criminal type. If there's stuff missing from the Science Tower that I ain't heard about, Rhodes didn't take it. Leastwise, not anything bigger'n you could put in your pocket. He was just too lazy. Being a thief requires initiative. That man had less initiative than anybody I've ever known and I've known some doozies, believe me."

That fit with my estimation of Rhodes, too.

" 'Course," Prior went on, "he could've known people involved in burglary, loaned 'em the keys to the Tower—which is what you come here to find out, ain't it?" He didn't wait for me to reply to that, just went on. "It don't take long to make copies of keys, and it don't take a criminal mastermind to find someone who'll copy a key stamped 'duplication prohibited' for a price." He lifted his long body up out of his chair and followed me to the door. "I ain't heard of any burglaries in the Tower recently," he said to my back. "Nearest thing to a burglary was that fruitcake professor breaking into Lucas Calder's office back in November. The fruitcake that got murdered," he added, to be sure I understood which fruitcake he meant.

I repeated that it was just part of an investigation we were making, thanked him, and left him looking after me with a grin on his skeptical, knowing face.

It started to snow while I was walking my beat that night, one of the late winter/early spring storms we often get here, and by the time it stopped, new snow was clotted in the bare tree branches like homemade ice cream in the dashers. The temperature hovered right at freezing, which was almost balmy compared to the winter that had gone before. The wet snow made walking hard, and I was dead tired when I finally got home.

The red light was blinking on my answering machine, something it hadn't been doing for a while. I considered not answering it, just taking a hot shower and drinking a cup of tea and crawling into bed, but after I took the shower and made the tea I did listen to it, and it was Carol.

Her voice was slurred. "Somebody broke into my house and I got mugged. My head hurts, my face hurts." She continued, "I'd appreciate it if you'd call me."

Those were the same words she'd left on my answering machine nearly two months ago, when she'd called to tell me her brother was dead.

She answered on the first ring. Her enunciation wasn't any better live than canned. She told me she'd gone to a movie the night before and when she'd entered her apartment she surprised somebody in there who'd hit her in the face and run out.

I asked her if she was okay, and she said the police had taken her to the hospital for observation but she'd refused to stay the night. "I'd like you to come over," she said.

"Why?"

"I want to show you something."

I looked outside at the morning grayness, thought of the streets, not all of which would be plowed yet, and asked, "Can't you just tell me?"

"No. Please."

So I drove over. The roads were lousy, but I'm a better driver in bad weather than the natives of this state—at least the ones trying to drive to work that morning.

Carol's mouth was swollen and she spoke with difficulty, but that didn't stop her. "I always leave a light on inside when I go out, but it was off when I came home. I noticed that from the street, but I just thought the bulb had burned out, the way people always do in the movies and you think they ought to know better. That was the last thing I thought, when I knew somebody was in the darkness with me, that it was just like in the movies."

"Interesting," I said wearily. I looked around her apartment, couldn't see anything missing. "What'd he take? Or she," I added, mindlessly ideological.

"It wasn't a simple burglary, Peggy. He didn't even touch my color TV or VCR or CD player or stereo. My jewelry box was in plain sight on my bureau; it's still there. I think the cops wondered if maybe I was a crack dealer or something, and that whoever broke in here was a customer, trying to rip me off."

"You probably just interrupted him before he could get started," I suggested.

"No! I know what he was after. I found out after I got back from the hospital. Come on, I'll show you."

She led the way down her hall to a room in the back. It was full of boxes that I recognized from the last time I was at Carol's—her brother Mike's belongings.

"I never felt like going through his stuff," she explained. "I just jammed it all in here."

"You think he took something of Mike's." All of a sudden I wasn't feeling so tired.

"You remember the picture he had, Peggy, of the troll? The one Ann-Marie gave him for Christmas? It's gone! It was over there, on the wall. I took down another picture and put the troll up in its place, so it wouldn't get broken or something. And because I wanted to see if I could stand to keep it, because I like the damned thing in spite of who it comes from. It's not there now. See for yourself."

I ignored the absurdity of that last remark, glanced over where she was pointing. "You're sure? You've looked for it?"

"Of course I'm sure, Peggy. That's where it was, now it's gone. And it's the only thing missing."

It had been a nice print, and nicely framed, too, but it wasn't valuable enough to steal. Whereas Carol did have, as she'd mentioned, her share of the expensive technological toys we all seem to need these days.

I asked her if she'd gone through everything and she said she had, and as far as she could tell the print was all that was missing. It was as if the thief had known exactly what he was looking for and when he'd found it, he'd taken it and left.

"You call the burglar 'he,' " I said. "How do you know?" I was thinking that maybe Ann-Marie had wanted her gift to Mike back, and broken in to get it.

"I could see enough of him for that. He was tall, way taller than me. He had longish hair, blond, I think—light from outside glittered in it. And women don't hit the way he did either. I'd probably recognize him again, if I saw him.''

We went back to the living room. That's where my involvement with her brother's murder had started. It seemed like a long time ago. It was a long time ago, almost a winter.

''You told the police about the print, of course.''

''Naturally! As soon as I discovered it missing, I called them. They listened politely. And that's what you're doing, too, Peggy, isn't it? Listening politely, as if it doesn't really concern you. Thank you very much.'' She added, defiantly, ''I just wanted you to know, that's all.''

I looked at her and thought of telling her what I'd been up to—partly on her behalf, but mostly on my own now—and decided against it.

''How'd he get in?''

''He kicked in the back door. It's got a good lock on it, but the door itself must be made of balsa.''

''I hope you've had it fixed.''

''Why? He won't be coming back. He got what he wanted.''

''Get it fixed anyway. Maybe there's something else in Mike's stuff he wants and you interrupted him before he could get it.''

She looked scared and said she hadn't thought of that. I left her there, apparently thinking about it, and drove home and went to bed.

Twenty-three

I was still in bed when the phone rang that afternoon. I thought it was my alarm and tried to make it stop, but it wouldn't. The clock said it was a few minutes after three. I picked up the phone and said hello and recognized the voice of G.B., one of the men from Customs, and he got right down to business. "Something's scared them," he said, "and I'm wondering what you've been up to lately. You're not still sniffing around the death of your friend's brother, are you?"

I didn't say no, because I don't believe in lying if the truth will serve the same function. "I've been looking into the murder of a professor on campus," I told him.

"Who?"

"Jason Horn."

There was a brief pause while he mulled that over. "Rings no bell," he said finally. "Maybe you're not lying to me, but how do you explain this? Eric Fridell at Ed. Tech gets a call, it's from a guy who's sounding upset, very upset. He wants to know where his wife is. You know who we're talking about here?"

"Terry Rhodes. Ann-Marie."

"Yeah. Fridell tells this Rhodes to calm down, that Ann-Marie's in Europe for a few days, on business for the company."

"Is she?"

"We don't think so. She's run errands like that for Fridell before but we usually hear about it. But Rhodes doesn't sound like he believes it, he tells Fridell she would've told him. Fridell asks, 'Why would she bother, Terry?' Rhodes doesn't like to hear that, he gets mad. Fridell tells him to shut up, he doesn't want to discuss it over the phone, he'll call Rhodes when he's got time to talk about it.''

"I didn't know Rhodes was involved in this,'' I said.

"Before he found his niche in life at a porn shop, he was a part-time driver for Ed. Tech, an errand boy. But he got himself fired.''

"Drugs.''

"He doesn't seem to be able to function long without them on any given day.''

"You seem to know quite a lot about the inner workings of Ed. Tech.''

"It's our business to know *everything* about Ed. Tech, Officer O'Neill. It's one of our most important customers,'' he added, the irony heavy enough to cut with a dull ax.

"It doesn't sound to me like anybody's spooked at Ed. Tech. Just Terry Rhodes.''

"Yeah, is that how it sounds to you? Well, you're wrong. The owner of Ed. Tech, a happy merchant by the name of Judd, seems to have decided to take a vacation. On the spur of the moment, so to speak. He's in South Africa, where he has a villa by the sea. I've seen pictures of it, taken from the air, you know, or maybe from higher up than that. He's got a dumpy-lumpy wife and two dumpy-lumpy kids in a nice house here, but you ought to see what he's got there! There's a lot of money in educational software, did you know that? We don't know why he's there now, he's never been prone to sudden vacations before. So we think maybe he smells something, and doesn't want to be around when it comes out of the snow in the spring.''

"Do you mean anything special by that?''

"By what?''

"That image: something coming out of the snow.''

He sounded puzzled. "No, why? You into imagery now, too?'' It was too good to be an act. "Another thing that points to something being wrong is that Ann-Marie didn't go anywhere on company business. We think her husband-in-name-only has very good reason to be concerned."

"How do you know?"

"The receptionist, Judy—the one you talked to. She's on our payroll. She says Fridell didn't send Ann-Marie anywhere on business that she knows about. Ann-Marie's just not there, and she's missed almost a week of work."

"I haven't done anything recently," I told him, "that could have anything to do with that."

"Maybe so, O'Neill, maybe so. We haven't been getting any blips from you on our radar, so you might be telling the truth. I'm just checking. But I'll tell you this, George and I don't think our operation is in the best of health right now."

"What would you say," I asked him, "if I told you that Ed. Tech was funneling secret research, stolen from the defense contractors in this area, behind the Iron Curtain—aided and abetted by you guys and your CIA friends who think Ed. Tech's only sin is indulging in a little techno-banditry?"

"Can you prove it?"

"I'd need some help."

"What kind of help?"

"I'd need somebody who could do what I think two other men have done, or have tried to do: go into Lucas Calder's supercomputer files and see if—"

"Who? The guy you see on television sometimes, the scientist? You think he's involved in this harebrained scheme of yours?"

"Yes."

"And you want somebody to break into his supercomputer files—to look for what?"

"I'm not sure, exactly. Something that'll prove he's stealing the research of scientists outside the University who are doing classified research for the military."

"Holy shit, O'Neill! 'You're not sure, exactly.' And what if you're wrong? How do we explain it, if we get caught breaking into the computer files of a scientist that I'll bet even George has heard of? You need a search warrant to do things like that," he went on piously. "You've heard of those things? You have enough evidence so I can go get a search warrant to search Calder's files?''

''No.''

''Then back off, O'Neill, back off. Same simple rule pertains as before: you stay out of it.''

That *was* simple. I hadn't really thought it would do any good to tell him my theory without anything solid to back it up, but I'd pretended to think it would be worth a try. Now, whatever happened would be his fault, at least in my mind.

''Here's something else for you,'' I said, giving him one final chance to be a good guy. ''Mike Parrish's sister, Carol—her apartment was broken into last night. She was beaten up and something belonging to Mike was stolen.''

''So?'' He said it the way people who are picking their noses say ''So?''

''Doesn't really move you, does it? I think it's related to Parrish's murder and to Ann-Marie. And that means it's related to Ed. Tech.''

''If it's really connected with Ed. Tech,'' he replied, ''it tells me something's bothering them, which I already know. Maybe it has to do with why Judd decided to take a vacation in sunny South Africa all of a sudden, and why Ann-Marie's dropped out of sight, too.''

''What it tells me,'' I said, ''is that there are some nasty people at Ed. Tech. Two people have been murdered already, and my friend's been beaten up.''

''I don't know about that, Officer O'Neill. What's Ann-Marie want to commit murder for, tell me that? And Eric Fridell's just a dishonest businessman out making a buck selling electronics equipment to the Russians.''

''What does he look like? Fridell?''

''Why?''

''I'd like to avoid him if I ever come across him,'' I replied. ''Electronics salesmen scare me.''

''That's good. Well, I shouldn't, but here goes: He's tall. Got a youngish-old face that's taken too much sun over the years, eyes so blue you'd think they were good quality glass. Thin mouth. Expensively cut blond hair that he probably keeps in place with mousse. Judy tells me the ladies around the place really go for him, but he gives her the creeps.''

''The man who broke into Carol's apartment fits that description.''

''Yeah?'' G.B. sounded hopeful. ''Well, I just hope he got what he went after, and that solves their problems.''

''So you can get back to business as usual.''

''You got it.''

''You're a cold-blooded bastard, aren't you?''

''So were the dinosaurs.''

''And they're extinct,'' I retorted.

I walked right into it. ''Yeah, but it took millions and millions of years, Peggy. You think warm-blooded animals'll do as well?''

He hung up. At least he was back to calling me Peggy.

I turned on the coffee maker, showered, and dressed in jeans and a sweatshirt, and by the time I'd drunk a couple of cups of coffee and spooned down some microwaved leftovers, it was after four.

I put on my boots and down jacket and drove over to the porn shop where Terry Rhodes lived and worked. The sky was overcast, but it was still light out. The days were getting longer now.

I wanted to talk to Rhodes about a lot of things: Educational Technology, since he'd worked there for a while; his career in ''maintenance engineering'' at the University, which he'd been too modest to tell me about at our earlier interview; and his wife's unlikely trio of lovers: Eric Fridell, Jason Horn, Mike Parrish. I didn't think there was much risk that Rhodes would blow the whistle on me to the University police or to anybody else. He was apparently too worried about Ann-Marie for that. My only worry was the two Customs men: I didn't want to show up as blips on their screen. That could be fatal to my social life for a long time to come. Not that it was much to speak of anyway.

Twenty-four

I parked a few doors down from the porn shop. Two old men, unshaven, in overcoats too thin for the cold that had returned in the wake of the snowstorm the night before, were buying tickets outside the adult movie theater. On the other side of the street, a car slowed and stopped and a slender man detached himself from a doorway and crossed to the passenger's side. Hands touched briefly, and then the car drove off and the man sauntered back into his doorway. The entire transaction took maybe twenty seconds, from darkness to darkness. That's a journey too, a life.

None of the people on the street appeared to be paying any attention to me, and the drug salesman didn't seem to think I was anybody he had to worry about either, but it wasn't a good place for a woman to be alone for long, not even in daylight. I got out of the car and walked to the porn shop. I was about to open the door when, glancing through the window, I saw a man standing at the display counter talking to Terry Rhodes.

He was blond, tall and thin, and fit the description Carol had given me of the man who'd invaded her apartment. He also fit G. B.'s description of Eric Fridell. And I'd seen him before. He'd been sitting with Lucas Calder in the Cambodian restaurant the night I'd eaten there with Marty Reid.

I turned away and walked back to my car. Safely inside, I locked the doors and sat and waited, not knowing what to do next.

After a few minutes, the porn shop door opened and Fridell came out, followed by Rhodes, who looked angry and worried. They talked briefly in the cheap yellow light from the sign above the porn shop. Fridell was smiling, and then he offered Rhodes his hand. Rhodes didn't take it. Fridell shrugged, said something else, and then turned and walked down the street away from me. Terry Rhodes looked after him, as if he didn't want to let him go, and then went back into the porn shop.

A car pulled away from the curb in front of me, something recent and nondescript—American or Japanese. Fridell was driving. I started my engine and followed, kept my distance until another car turned in between us. The snowplows hadn't been down these streets yet and nobody was driving very fast. Clumps of dirty snow made Fridell's license plate unreadable.

After about two miles, he turned off Central and drove in the direction of the railroad tracks and the freeway. A few blocks beyond the tracks, he turned onto a street that ended abruptly at the sound barrier that runs along the freeway beneath it. I didn't follow him down that street; I parked at the intersection and watched. He turned into the driveway of the last house on the block, an old, two-story building almost nestled against the high, wooden sound barrier.

Fridell parked in the driveway and went in, but the house stayed dark. As I sat there, trying to decide what to do next, the side door opened and Fridell came back out. He was carrying something that looked like a long tube. He climbed into his car and backed into the street, tires spinning in the new snow. He headed toward me, so I ducked down a bit, until he'd cleared the intersection and the car disappeared back the way it had come.

I got out, flipped up the hood on my jacket, and walked down the dead-end street to the old house at the end. Few of the houses gave any sign that people lived in them anymore, and the sidewalk hadn't been shoveled all winter. In places, I had to crawl over icy hills of snow thrown up by the plows after earlier storms. The only noise was the windy hum of the cars passing on the freeway beyond and below the sound barrier that had failed to save the neighborhood.

I walked up to the house, climbed the wooden steps to the porch that ran the length of the front, and peered through the curtainless window in the front door. In the gray evening light the room seemed almost bare: no rugs, a sagging overstuffed chair, a table and two wooden chairs that looked like a display in a Salvation Army window.

I tried the front door but it was locked. The side door was locked, too. I walked around the back of the house, wading through snow, sinking up to my knees in places. I tried to avoid walking under the enormous pointed icicles that hung from the eaves, some of them almost to the ground. Where the back of the house met the sound barrier, there was just enough space to squeeze through. The traffic on the freeway seemed much closer there.

I crouched at the first basement window, my back almost touching the sound barrier, and cleared away enough snow to peer in. The basement was empty. I kicked in the window, flinched as I heard glass hitting the floor, pushed out the remaining pieces of glass in the frame, then crawled through and dropped to the basement floor. When my eyes had become accustomed to the gloom, I found a wooden box and moved it over to the window, in case I had to leave in a hurry.

I made my way carefully up a flight of wooden stairs which led to the kitchen. The house was as cold inside as it had been outside. The kitchen was filthy, not with dirty dishes, but with the dust and grime that collects in houses that aren't used for a long time. The only sign of human habitation was a telephone on the wall by the side door.

The dining room and living room both looked the way I'd seen them from the front porch through the window. The only evidence that anybody had been in here recently was an ashtray with five or six cigarette butts in it, on the floor next to the overstuffed chair.

I went upstairs, moving quietly even though I was sure there was nobody in the house but me. The bathroom at the top of the stairs was filthy. The front bedroom contained a bed and mattress without bedclothes, and a dresser, empty. I went down the hall to the room at the back. The door was open, the room was empty of furniture, but in one side was a narrow door that led to the attic. I opened it and climbed the steep, narrow flight of stairs.

The rafters were high enough that I could stand up straight. Icicles hung from the roof like stalactites in a cave, in some places all the way to the floor, where they puddled in small, frozen lakes. In a corner was a bed that seemed to be held up by icicles that had formed around it. They glowed softly, picking up the night lights of the city, stray lights from the freeway below us.

Ann-Marie was lying on the bed, her arms and legs tied to the frame with rope. Her camel's hair coat and expensive boots had been tossed carelessly into a corner of the room along with her other clothes. Her shoulder bag was lying there, too, its contents scattered over the floor.

In the pink, translucent light, she looked alive. She was staring straight up at the ceiling, wide-eyed, and there was a smile on her face, the smile that others—Carol, her husband Terry—had said looked like a cat's. I'd never been able to read it, any more than I could read the smiles of cats I'd known.

There were cuts on her breasts and belly, crisscrossed the way they'd been on Jason Horn, and dark blood, and a deeper, darker cut above her heart that I knew had been the one that had killed her.

She looked so young and doll-like, but a doll with defective eyes: they're supposed to close when you lay them on their backs, but this one's eyes were still wide open. I wanted to close them, but I didn't try. She'd been dead awhile; she was as cold as ice to my touch.

Next to her, on the floor beneath the window, lay an aluminum picture frame in a pool of broken glass. It looked as if somebody had smashed it against the bed. The picture itself was missing but I knew what it had been—the picture Ann-Marie had given Mike for Christmas.

The night before, Eric Fridell had taken it from Carol's apartment. He'd brought it here, to Ann-Marie. And then he'd killed her. He could have killed her first, of course, but I didn't think he had. He must have brought the picture up to the attic for some reason: to show it to Ann-Marie, I thought, to destroy it before destroying her.

A piece of cloth caught my eye, on the floor in a corner. It was flannel, and I recognized the pattern. I'd seen it on the pajama bottoms Jason Horn's corpse had been wearing when he'd been dug out of the snow. I stuffed it into my jacket pocket.

I realized that somebody had come into the house and was already on the second floor. I'd been so engrossed in what I'd found in the attic that I hadn't heard anything until now.

I looked around the attic, but there was no place to hide, unless I wanted to crawl under the bed Ann-Marie was lying on, and I didn't want to do that. I tried the window next to her, but it was frozen shut. Finally I went over to the door, flattened myself to the wall next to it, and waited. I could take him by surprise, even if he came up armed, I thought.

I heard the soft footfall of somebody entering the room below, heard my own breathing, saw my breath in front of my face. He was on the attic stairs, coming up here. And then, partway up, he stopped.

Liquid gurgled from a can and, even before smelling it, I knew what it was and I knew what was going to happen next. I assumed it was Eric Fridell, who'd returned to burn the house down and to make sure that whatever was left of Ann-Marie after the fire would be hard to identify. But he should have come all the way up here, doused her body, and then trailed gasoline down the stairs and through the rest of the house. Why stop partway up the attic stairs?

The answer was the sound of the attic door closing below me, followed by a click as a key turned in the lock.

It wasn't Ann-Marie who was being locked in.

I looked around, puzzled, and then saw a small chunk of dirty ice that my boots had left behind me. Fridell may not have known who it was, just seen a trail of melting ice and snow and knew somebody living was up here. Perhaps he thought it was a transient.

I grabbed up Ann-Marie's coat for protection and ran down the attic stairs to the door. It was old and the lock was old too, and I thought I could smash the lock or break down the door, but the stairs were too steep, the space too narrow. And then I heard the noise of the fire burning in the bedroom beyond the door, realized I was standing on old wood drenched in gasoline, and fled back up the stairs. A moment later they were on fire and the fire was chasing me.

I smashed in the window next to Ann-Marie and leaned out over the narrow windowsill, which looked rotten, no good to stand on. The eaves were too far above my head to reach even if I dared trust my weight to the sill, and what could I do on the roof anyway?

About ten feet below me and four feet away from the house was the top of the sound barrier. On this side it was just a tall fence, maybe fifteen feet high, but on the other side the fence ended on a concrete restraining wall that fell another thirty feet to the freeway itself.

The fence was my only way out. Even through my down jacket, I could feel the heat on my back.

I cleared jagged glass out of the bottom of the window frame and crawled onto it, crouched there a moment. I took a last look back. Ann-Marie, grinning as if enjoying something immensely, surrounded by flame, seemed to be rising from the bed, her hair on fire. I looked quickly away and, hugging her coat, launched myself, almost sideways, out the window.

I smashed into the snow on the fence and grabbed into it with both arms and legs for something solid to cling to, fighting the momentum that wanted to keep my body going over the fence and down onto the freeway. I came to rest on top of the fence, not breathing at all until I realized my body wasn't sliding anymore, and my face was buried in the snow beneath the thin icy crust. I raised my head up and spit the snow out of my mouth. I'd done this once before, as a child—jumped off a garage onto a fence, using an air mattress as a shield, just for the hell of it. I still have a scar on my left knee as a reminder of what can happen when you do things just for the hell of it. I'd done better tonight, protected by the snow, my down jacket, and Ann-Marie's coat.

I stared down at the freeway and the cars and trucks streaming by on it. I didn't like that view at all. In the other direction, the fire was blowing out from the broken windows and licking at me. The icicles hanging from the eaves that guarded the old house were melting fast. I looked down at the space between the house and the fence but all I could see was the snow that had collected there all winter and the footprints I'd made coming around the house, and I thanked whatever controls the weather for one of the snowiest winters on record, and for last night's storm as well. I swiveled around and hung by my hands from the top of the fence, prayed that there wasn't something sharp hidden in the snow, and then I let go and dropped.

Twenty-five

People had come from nowhere to watch the old house burn, and they watched me, too, as I stumbled out from behind it and down the driveway. I could hear sirens getting louder and shriller in the distance.

"Was there anybody else in there?" somebody hollered at me, a man, his face red and deeply etched in the glow from the fire. It wasn't necessary to holler, I thought, but people learn to do that in situations like this, from movies and television. He looked as though, if I said yes, he'd run in and try to rescue them.

"Not really," I replied, and then changed it to "no."

"You okay?" somebody else, a woman, asked me. "How did it start?"

Another woman said somebody'd moved into the house earlier that winter, a young man, but they almost never saw him, he came and went at odd hours of the night. Her husband thought he was a drug dealer, except there wasn't a whole lot of traffic, so he probably just made the stuff there—crack—and sold it someplace else. She'd never seen me before, she added suspiciously.

I didn't think I wanted to be there when the firemen came, have to answer their questions, explain what I'd been doing in the house. I needed time to consider what I was going to do next. The crowd gave me space to stand alone so they could watch me out of the corners of their eyes and point to me when the fire trucks arrived. The man with the intrepid red face stayed close enough so he could grab me—apprehend me, he'd say to the reporters—if I tried to run—that is, flee. Crowds at disasters always make me nervous.

The fire trucks pulled up then, a big ladder truck and a smaller one, and a fire marshall's car. The fire marshall jumped out and started giving orders, and the firemen began to do things with their hoses and ladders.

John Wayne bustled over to the fire marshall and put his hand on his arm and tried to say something over the dying roar of the sirens, and as he did I stepped back into the crowd, pointed to the house and said, "The roof's catching!" which it was, and everybody turned to look.

The fire marshall gave the neighborhood hero a glare, shook off his hand, and used his body to push him out of the way, and I turned and ran up the street, following the deep tracks of the fire trucks. I glanced back once, to see who was coming after me. Nobody was.

I turned the corner, jumped into my car, and started the engine. I had to wait for a cop car to scream past me and disappear down the way I'd come, and then I drove out of there and lost myself in the side streets until I got back to Central. I stayed within the speed limit on the way home. I passed the porn shop, saw that it was still open and saw the back of Terry Rhodes' head in the window, but I had no compelling desire to talk to the widower now.

I showered, made coffee, and sat in my window trying to figure out what had happened and what to do about it.

I looked at my watch. It was a few minutes after seven. I'd been awakened by G.B.'s phone call just four hours before—it seemed like a lot longer than that.

I picked up the phone and called Buck Hansen at his home. I asked him if he'd meet me somewhere near campus for coffee. He caught the need in my voice and said okay. Half an hour later I was at a table in a coffee shop, contemplating a donut with little candies stuck all over it that were like the colored rocks you see in fishbowls. Buck came in, bought himself a cup of coffee, and came over to where I was sitting.

I told him everything that had happened to me that day. Because it didn't make a lot of sense in isolation, I had to tell him everything else too: the connection I'd made between the deaths of Mike Parrish and Jason Horn and the theory I'd come up with to explain it, the entrance of the Customs agents, and, finally, the discovery of Ann-Marie's body in the abandoned house, the house where Jason Horn must have been tortured and killed, too. Buck didn't say much, just listened, and twice took our cups back to the counter for refills.

When I'd finished my story, he sat there for a long time, rubbing his chin and staring at me. Then he said, "You stink of fire and smoke and damp ash."

"No I don't. I showered, washed my hair."

"Then maybe it's your natural fragrance, I just never noticed it before." He was trying to be funny, I guess. He went on: "I don't know how you do it, Peggy. I—" He stopped, shook his head, then looked at me in despair. "It wasn't any of your business," he tried again. "You were told to stay out of it, and you still nearly got yourself killed."

"I wasn't told to stay away from Jason Horn's murder," I flared. "That was out of it—at least at first. And when a friend of mine gets beat up, that's my business. Nobody else seemed interested."

"You can jerk me around a little if you want to, Peggy," he said mildly, "just don't jerk yourself around. Once you knew Horn's murder was connected to Parrish's, you should have come to me."

"I did plan to come to you," I said. "Eventually," I added lamely. "It's just that I didn't think you'd be able to help, if those Customs guys got to your boss—and they would have, once they found out you were getting interested! And it pissed me off that nobody would take Mike's murder seriously down here, not even after somebody—Eric Fridell—broke into his sister's house and punched her in the face. She's lucky to be alive, Buck. I started wondering if maybe you'd been warned to stay away from Parrish's murder, too."

"I haven't. You know I was never involved in that investigation. He died up north, and they listed his death as a suicide. I don't have any jurisdiction up there, and I've got all the murders I can handle down here.''

"Right. But you've got Jason Horn's murder down here, and now I've *given* you Ann-Marie's. What are you going to do about her?"

"I'm going to put people to work finding what's left of her body first," he replied, not letting me rile him, "since you didn't tell the firemen about her. I'm going to discuss Jason Horn, Ann-Marie, and Mike Parrish with Betty Hall, too—something I would have done sooner, if you'd told me about it."

"I've already done that," I pointed out impatiently, "and we both know what the next step is: Lucas Calder. And when you get to Lucas Calder, you're going to have to look into his connection with Eric Fridell. And when you do *that,* you're going to appear on the radar screen of two very sweet guys from Customs, Tweedledum and Tweedledee, aka G. B. and George—or their friends in the CIA. Then what are you going to do, Buck?"

"I don't know, Peggy," he replied quietly. "I'll take it one step at a time."

"Until you run into 'national security,' and that'll stop you in your tracks."

"Will it?" he answered, still softly, but there was an edge in his voice. "We'll have to wait and see. In the meantime, I'm wondering what we should do about you." He saw the expression on my face and held up a hand. "No, I don't mean holding you as a material witness, although that's kind of an attractive idea, as a way to keep you out of danger. You can't be sure Fridell didn't know it was you up there with Ann-Marie's corpse."

"I'll be careful, Buck."

That wasn't what he wanted to hear. "Something's upset these people, Peggy. Both Jason Horn and Michael Parrish were killed in January. Nothing happened after that for over two months. Then suddenly, according to your Customs friends, the owner of this company of yours, Ed. Tech, leaves the country and the Ekdahl woman is tortured and killed the same way Jason Horn was. Eric Fridell, you think, breaks into Carol Parrish's home and steals a picture that Ann-Marie gave to Parrish, and finally he commits arson to hide the evidence of murder. It sounds to me like something's out of control and these people are starting to panic.''

''That's how it sounds to me, too,'' I said.

''Unless Fridell found what he wanted in the picture he stole from your friend,'' Buck continued. ''In which case, maybe they're content now, and with Ann-Marie dead and gone, things will go back to being the way they were before for them.''

''I *don't* think Fridell found what he'd hoped to find in the picture,'' I replied. ''But if you're right, then it'll be business as usual for all of them, including G. B. and George. Three unsolved murders. A happy ending.''

''They'll be caught eventually,'' Buck said, not letting me get to him, or at least not letting me see if I had. ''I'd like you to still be alive when it happens.''

''Justice only happens if somebody's stubborn enough to make it happen. Or stupid enough.''

''Somebody as stubborn and stupid as you are, you think? Maybe I *should* take you in as a material witness. After all, you're the only person besides her killer who knows Ann-Marie's dead.''

''The fire department'll recover enough of her body to identify her.''

''Maybe, if her teeth survive the fire, and if she had dental work in this country. You'd be safer in jail.''

''I won't do anything to attract attention, I promise,'' I said. ''I'll keep away from it for a couple of days—maybe a week. Then I'll call you, to see if you've made any progress. And I'll know, Buck, if the Customs men have been to see you and you've been warned off the case. You won't lie to me.''

''Can't, you mean. You can tell when somebody's lying to you, Peggy—even when they're not.'' He smiled at me when he said that. He has a beautiful smile. I don't understand how a man who's spent so much time with murder can keep a smile like that.

''All right,'' I said, returning his smile with the best one I had available. ''Nothing happened this afternoon, nothing at all. A house burned down. There may have been somebody inside. Somebody unknown who might stay that way.''

"How do you know all this?''

"I read it in the papers.''

He nodded, finished his coffee in a gulp, and set his cup down firmly. He got up, gave my shoulder a long, hard squeeze, and started to walk out.

"Here," I said.

"What's this?''

It was the scrap of Jason Horn's pajamas I'd found in the old house. "A clue, Inspector Hansen, or a souvenir.''

I sat there for a while after he'd left, staring out the plate-glass window at the people hurrying by, students mostly in that part of town. A red neon sign across the street flashed "Pizza" and reminded me of a dream I'd had that afternoon, a very bad dream. Of fire and ice and blood.

And maybe that's all it had been, a dream. How can you know for sure?

Twenty-six

Before going to work that night, I called Carol to find out if she'd had a new door put on her apartment yet. She said the landlord had told her a carpenter would be coming in the morning.

"That's not good enough." I told her I wanted her to stay at my place until she got the new door. She said no, that whoever had broken into her apartment had gotten what he came for and wouldn't be back.

"He may have gotten what he came for, but I don't think that was what he wanted."

"How do you know?"

"You'll have to take my word for it. I want you to stay at my place tonight." I wasn't ready to tell her about Ann-Marie being dead yet.

She said she'd think about it. I told her where I hid my spare key and then went to work, stopping at a *faux* food place for dinner, a little box of salted batter with bits of chicken in it.

I was assigned to patrol the New Campus on foot. That was just as well since, because I hadn't been getting my usual six hours of sleep lately, I'd probably fall asleep behind the wheel of a car. But at least the sidewalks had been shoveled, so it wouldn't be as hard slogging as last night.

Paula Henderson had one of the squad cars and she gave me a ride over to the New Campus. She told me I looked like shit and I said "Thanks," and she replied that I shouldn't be burning the candle at both ends, partying all day and trying to be a cop at night. She was joking, but the image of the burning candle made me shudder.

At about a quarter to two I was outside the Science Tower and decided to take a break. I let myself in and went down to the basement lounge for a cup of coffee and a donut from the machines. I wondered if Marty Reid was in his office tonight, but decided not to go up to see. I was too tired to socialize, too full of fire and smoke and damp ash. I sat with my coffee in the darkness of the lounge and tried to think about the puzzle I'd been involved in throughout the winter that was almost over.

I'd managed to fit a lot of the pieces together so that they added up to a kind of story: Ann-Marie had quit her job at the U when she'd met her old lover from Germany, Eric Fridell. Or she may have agreed, while they were still in Germany, to meet him here; it didn't matter which. She'd gone to work for him at Ed. Tech. Later, they'd broken up. I suspected Fridell had dumped her, and she was taking revenge on him, using something she'd thought she could find in Lucas Calder's office. Even before I'd discovered that he'd killed her, I was convinced that whatever she was doing didn't involve Fridell. If it had, the Customs men would have known about it, but I didn't believe they had any interest in Ann-Marie and her doings at all.

She'd hustled Jason Horn for his computer skills and then, when Horn hadn't gotten what she'd wanted from Calder's office, I was sure she'd sent Mike Parrish in to try to get it at Christmas. She'd taken on more than she could handle: I'd seen that in her fear, when she came to see me in my apartment to try to get me to stop my investigation into Mike's death.

The answer, I felt sure, lay in Lucas Calder's office, fifteen floors above me. What had Ann-Marie wanted there? What did Jason Horn know that somebody wanted so badly they'd tortured him for it, and killed him, and later tortured and killed Ann-Marie? Why hadn't Mike been tortured before he was killed? And where did the troll picture fit in?

Across the river, on the Old Campus, the bells in the

campanile struck twice. I got up to go back outside and resume my patrol.

Marty Reid came through the door then. He started when he saw me, said, "Jesus, you scared me! Why didn't you turn on the lights?" I apologized, asked him what he was doing down there. I'd seen a coffee maker in his office.

"I'm out of coffee," he said, "so I had to come down for a cup of this watery shit. Care to join me?"

I said no, and started to leave.

"How's it going with your computer education?" he called after me.

I turned back. He didn't seem to want me to leave. I told him I'd take him up on his offer of coffee, and watched him as he dropped money into the machine.

I'd promised Buck I'd give him a few days, maybe a week, before doing anything more. But what if I could persuade Marty Reid to help me now? With his help, I might be able to find out what role, if any, Lucas Calder played in all of this. For somebody who knew computers the way Marty did, that wouldn't be hard to do.

"It's not true," I told him, when he'd handed me the cup and sat down at the table opposite me, "that Jason Horn broke into Calder's office for some foolish reason of his own."

"You're still on that kick, are you, Peggy? You don't seem to know when to quit. Did it occur to you that Horn might have been murdered for some foolish reason of the *murderer's,* a reason that had nothing to do with Calder?"

"No. I mean, yes, that did occur to me, but that doesn't explain something else, something you don't know about. I'm pretty sure Horn wasn't the last person to break into Calder's office."

"Oh?" It sounded as if I'd finally said something that interested him. "How do you know that?"

"It's a long story," I said.

"I have time. Let's hear it."

"The brother of a friend of mine died," I told him. "In January. He was murdered. He was a skilled computer programmer. So was Horn, as I told you the last time we talked. He was recruited by the same person who recruited Horn, and he broke into Calder's office, too.''

Marty shook his head. His eyes stayed interested, curious. "How do you know this?"

"It doesn't matter. But it's true, I'm sure of it. Both Horn and Michael Parrish—my friend's brother—were involved with the same woman. I think she's the one who wanted something from Calder's office, and she used them to try to get it. You caught Horn before he could get what he'd come for. She couldn't use him again, so she sent the other man in, Parrish. He came in on Christmas Eve, when Calder was away, when everybody was away from campus.''

"Why?"

"Why what?"

"Why did this mysterious woman send these men into Lucas' office? He's never done research that anybody'd want to steal. Christ, he doesn't do research anymore—"

"I know that," I replied. "I think Calder's using *his* access to the supercomputers to break into *other* scientists' supercomputer files, scientists who are working for the defense contractors in the area. He steals their research and sells it to the Russians, or anybody who's willing to pay for it.''

Marty stared at me. "I think you're nuts, Peggy."

I was getting tired of hearing him call me that, but I swallowed my anger and kept on. "That explains why he was so anxious to get the Supercomputer Corporation, even though he couldn't care less about supercomputers as far as his own research goes—which you say is non-existent anyway.''

"He's always been a strong advocate of research, Peggy. He's always supported it even if he doesn't do it himself anymore. That's the explanation for his interest in the supercomputers. You're going to have to come up with something better than that.''

"Does the name Eric Fridell mean anything to you?" I asked him.

He blinked, said, "Lucas is working with him on his

book. Eric's doing the computer part of it. What about him?''

"You know him?"

"Just to say hello to. I've met him at a few of Lucas' parties. What's he got to do with all this?"

I didn't say anything for a moment, just sat there listening to the voice inside me telling me to stop now, not to give away the secret of the two Customs men. It was a very small voice and it died of exhaustion.

I said, "Fridell works for a company—Educational Technology—that smuggles American technology into countries that our government doesn't want to have it. The small stuff, like microchips, manuals for new computers. It's called 'techno-banditry.' ''

"I know what it's called," Marty said.

"But that's not all Ed. Tech does," I went on. "I think Calder is stealing research the Russians, and probably other countries, too, will pay for, and Fridell and Ed. Tech smuggle it out of the country disguised as educational software—'Mickey Mouse Teaches Fractions,' things like that.''

"How do you know this—about Fridell and Ed. Tech?"

"It doesn't matter, it's true."

"Well, so what if it is? That doesn't mean Lucas is involved or knows anything about it. Ed. Tech may be doing what you say it is, but it's also a legitimate company. Fridell's writing an educational software program for Lucas. You're saying Lucas is stealing secrets from local scientists—most of whom are his friends, by the way—and that he's involved in two murders. I don't believe it. How does murder fit into your theory?" There was the slightest pause between "your" and "theory," just enough to fit "harebrained" or "stupid" or, of course, "nutty."

"I think Ann-Marie's blackmailing Calder," I said. I started to go on but Marty interrupted me.

"Who?"

I was very tired. I didn't realize I hadn't mentioned Ann-Marie's name before. "A woman named Ann-Marie Ekdahl. She's Fridell's lover, or she was. They broke up."
And Fridell killed her, I should have added, but I didn't

want to get into that: two murders were enough for Marty for one night—more than enough, considering what I was going to ask him to do.

Marty dug slots into the rim of his coffee cup with a fingernail while he gazed at me thoughtfully. I returned his stare, waited for him to say something.

He laughed suddenly. "You're saying Lucas Calder *murdered* two people?"

"Of course I don't think he killed anybody himself," I snapped. "That must have been Fridell."

"Because this woman is blackmailing them?"

"Yes."

"And now they're home free, they've got whatever it was she had over them?"

"No. I think they're still looking and they're desperate."

"Desperate. You know so much, Peggy, I'll bet you even know where Ekdahl's hidden whatever she's got on them. Right?" Light from the food and drink machines seemed to dance in his eyes, but it was hard to see the expression on his face in the darkness of the lounge.

"No," I said. "If I knew that, I wouldn't need you to help me."

"Help you? How?"

"You could do what I think Horn and Parrish did, except you wouldn't have to do it from Calder's office. You could get into Calder's supercomputer files and look for the proof that he's created a way—a program—to gain access to the research of off-campus scientists. There's no way he could catch you—not if you just do it once."

The look of disbelief grew as he listened to me. *"Me* do what you think those two guys did? I'm flattered to be in such distinguished company, Peggy! Dead company, too."

I said: "If you don't help me, Marty, the police will. They'll get a search warrant, and get somebody who knows computers to do what I'm asking you to do. If it becomes a police matter, it'll get out to the media and there'll be a big uproar. If Calder's innocent, you'll be doing him a favor by helping me, even though he'll never know it. He was your father's friend, Marty, your mentor.''

There was a pause that stretched out a mile. Then: "If I could get into Lucas' computer files," he asked quietly, "what would I be looking for?"

"According to Dr. Swanson, all a person with access to the supercomputers needs, to get from his own computer to somebody else's files, would be the other person's password. He'd also need his departmental budget number, of course, but those are easy to get."

"How does he get their passwords?"

"That would be easy for Calder. You told me yourself he's on a first-name basis with just about every scientist in the area. My guess is that it's just a natural consequence of being a part of the Old Boys' network. Calder invites people whose research he wants access to to his parties, or takes them to lunch or dinner, he stuffs them with expensive food and booze, and then he turns the conversation to the supercomputers and the research they're doing on them. Most scholars use easily remembered names for their passwords—their wives', their kids', their lovers'. You must know that. Calder wouldn't have any problem getting them. Then he just has to come into his office, close the door behind him, and start dialing into their files."

"That's pretty good, Peggy" Marty said. "But there are a couple of problems with it, problems that might prove fatal."

"Not fatal, I hope. I know the problems you mean."

"You tell me then."

I recited from Dr. Swanson. "People using the University's supercomputers have to change their passwords every two months. The supercomputers tell them to. You're going to tell me that Calder can't keep going back and asking people for their passwords every two months." I shook my head. "But that's no good. According to one of the articles I read, once a skilled programmer gets into your program, he *owns* you. That means he could probably make his own password, then create a kind of private entrance through which to enter your program. You might have to change *your* password once every couple of months to get access to your files, Marty, but if Calder ever got access to your program, I'll bet *he* wouldn't have to, because he'd be coming through a door you and the super-computer don't even know is there.''

He didn't say anything for a moment, just appeared to be thinking about what I'd told him. ''You've done your homework, Peggy,'' he said finally. ''You ought to take up computers yourself.''

''Am I right?''

He shrugged. ''I suppose so. I've never given it any thought.''

''The other problem you're thinking of is the time one,'' I went on. ''Dr. Swanson told me that people are billed for the time they use the supercomputers and the super-computer keeps a record of it. Sooner or later the scientist whose files Calder is strolling through is going to notice that he's being charged for time he hasn't used. But that problem's solved by the same virus—because that's what it's called, isn't it, a virus?—that lets Calder in the back door. The time is being stolen, but the supercomputer isn't being told to bill it to anybody. It's not even recorded. It's no time at all.''

Marty was watching me closely. Finally he nodded, said, ''And that's what you want me to look for, the virus you think Lucas is using to access the research of other scientists?''

''Yes. I think that's what Jason Horn went into Calder's office hunting for, and Mike Parrish after him.''

''What makes you think I have Lucas' password?''

''You could get it easily enough.''

''Yes,'' he laughed. ''I suppose I could. And if I find what you're looking for, you'll have motive, and then everything else falls into place including murder.''

''Yes.''

''And if I'm caught, and you're right about Lucas, I'll have more to worry about than just losing my job, won't I? I'll have to worry about losing my life.''

''You won't get caught. Not doing it from your office.''

''No, I don't suppose I will.'' He didn't say anything

for almost a minute, just tilted back in his chair, finished destroying his coffee cup, and dropped the pieces on the table between us, his eyes never leaving mine. "I'll think about it," he said finally. "You realize that if Lucas is innocent and this gets back to him, we'll both be facing lawsuits and ruin. So we'll keep it to ourselves, Peggy, for now, won't we?" He got up.

"Okay." I got up, too. "How long do you think it'll take you?"

"If I do it at all, not long. If it's there, hidden somewhere in his files, I should be able to find it, if one of your two dead friends did." We walked out into the hall, bright after the darkness of the lounge. "Out here in the light," he added, "it sounds crazy."

He followed me to the door and we stood and talked for a few moments outside. The cold air felt good.

"Do you remember the last time we stood here like this?" he asked me suddenly.

"I was thinking about that, too," I answered. "We'd just eaten at that Cambodian restaurant. That's also when I saw Eric Fridell for the first time. With Calder. I didn't know who he was then, Fridell, I mean. He came here afterwards, I saw him from the bridge."

"That wasn't what I meant," Marty said. "Don't you ever have anything on your mind except business? I was remembering that we agreed to go to a hockey game, instead of a Marx Brothers movie you wanted to see. That cost me, didn't it?"

"You didn't know him, either," I blurted out.

"What?"

"Nothing." I shook my head, to clear it. "What were you saying, Marty?"

"I didn't know who, Peggy?"

Eric Fridell. In the restaurant, I'd caught him staring at me. I'd asked Marty who he was and he'd said he didn't know. But tonight he said he knew Fridell well enough to say hello to, had seen him at a few of Calder's parties. And he'd called him Eric, too.

Fridell had come here, to the Science Tower, from the restaurant, alone. I'd assumed he'd come to see Calder, but why, since he'd just left Calder? He could as well have come to see somebody else.

"Peggy?" It was Marty's voice. I looked at him. He gave me a tentative smile, a smile that had once reminded me of Al's. "What's wrong?"

"I just drifted off," I said. "It's been a long night. Good night, Marty. I need to walk, or I'll fall asleep. Call me when you've got something for me, will you?"

I didn't punch his arm this time as I turned and walked away. I wonder if it's really true that you can feel eyes on your back.

Twenty-seven

I had no trouble making it through the rest of the night without falling asleep. The trouble I had was not drawing my revolver at every shadow that moved. I kept telling myself it wasn't possible, it couldn't be Marty instead of Calder. Sure, Marty—with his supercomputer access—could do anything Calder could do, and he was in the Science Tower most nights. But Jason Horn had broken into Calder's office, not Marty's, and it had been Marty who'd caught him there and called the campus police. If Marty was doing what I thought Calder was, he wouldn't have done that.

I was back on the Old Campus at 6:30. I walked to police headquarters, checked in, and changed into my street clothes. I stayed for a few minutes to warm up and drink a cup of coffee with some of the morning watch cops, and then drove home.

My phone was ringing as I opened the door. I thought it would be Carol, calling to tell me she was okay.

"Guess what?" It was Al. "I've decided you're too old to get married, you wouldn't know what to do with someone if he was living with you, underfoot your whole life long. I've also figured out you don't like those words, 'your whole life long'—they echo in your funny ears like a death sentence. So, if that's the way it is, fine. I can learn to—"

"What do you want?"

"How about dinner tonight?"

"Sure," I snarled. "How about Mexican?"

There was a pause while he worked that one out. Then he said, "I saw you with some guy a couple of weeks ago, in a white BMW."

"Touché," I said.

"That's not what I meant. What I was about to say was, you kicked me out because you thought you might be lusting after somebody else, didn't you? And you couldn't handle the stress. You're sequentially monogamous."

"Stop psychologizing me," I said, "I'm not one of your damned animals." It really was time for bed. "Besides, I didn't kick you out and anyway, why'd you go so easily? You never did before. It was because you thought you wanted to get married—even if it meant marrying Deirdre and having to eat Mexican food the rest of your life!"

"Apropos of nothing, I've been considering getting a BMW. But not a white one. I'm thinking of—"

"You're not getting a BMW, Al. You can't load large, sick animals into BMWs, and you wouldn't be the same without your van, anyway."

"This guy of yours must be a lawyer. I didn't think you liked lawyers. You have any idea what BMWs cost?"

"No." It occurred to me suddenly that it would be easier to find out where Marty's money came from than Calder's.

"Can I come over for a few minutes?" Al asked.

"You mean now?"

"Yeah. I know you're pooped, but—"

"I'm beyond pooped, honest. But dinner tonight, if I manage to wake up, okay?"

"Okay. It sounds like you've been burning the candle—"

"There's somebody at the door, Al. I'll see you tonight."

Still standing by the phone, still thinking about Al, I glanced over at the door to make sure I'd put the chain on when I'd rushed in. I walked over, peered through the window, and saw Carol on the porch. She was staring at the door and she looked so awful that I hurried to unlock and open it. Maybe if Al hadn't still been stumbling around in my weary head, I wouldn't have done that so quickly.

She just stood there looking at me and trying to get words out. None came.

Eric Fridell, a knife in his hand, stepped up beside her and pushed her at me, so we both stumbled into the house. Behind Fridell was Marty Reid and he was holding a pistol.

Twenty-eight

"Who lives upstairs?" Marty asked me.

"My landlady," I told him, "an elderly woman."

"Then we'll have to be very quiet," he said. "Unless you think it would be better if I sent Eric up there?"

"Better for whom?"

"That's the spirit, Peggy, keep up the banter."

Fridell must have appreciated it, too. He'd tied Carol to one of my kitchen chairs and now he was finishing work on me. He gave the ropes an unnecessarily hard tug and I said "Ouch!" quite loudly. I couldn't help it.

"Huh-unh, Peggy," Marty said. "Don't do that again."

I wasn't planning to do it again, but not out of any concern for Mrs. Hammer, who was in Florida for the winter. It was 9:30 in the morning in the Keys, the temperature was in the 80s, and she was undoubtedly sitting under an umbrella on white sand, drinking Campari on ice with a dash of bitters and writing postcards to her less fortunate friends, me among them.

"I've worked hard to get where I am, Marty," I told him. "Now that I've arrived, how about telling me about it?" I was feeling remarkably calm. I hadn't been shocked at all to see him behind Fridell in my doorway. It seemed obvious, somehow—once the answer hit me in the face.

"You just knew too much, Peggy," he said. "You knew the whole story—the what, where, when, and why. You just had the 'who' wrong. It was eerie, listening to a story I knew so well, but with somebody else playing the villain. Lucas Calder!"

186

He tucked his pistol in his jacket, pulled a chair over in front of me, straddled it, and hung over the back of it as he talked. "I received a letter, you see," he went on, "in early January. It came as quite a shock. It explained that *they* knew what I was doing and how I was doing it, and *they* wanted money from me if I expected to continue doing it. I was desperate, Peggy! I had to play at being a detective, just the way you've done—except that I was luckier than you. I had to find out who was behind the blackmail attempt and, naturally, I thought of Jason Horn. After all, I'd caught him in Lucas' office a few months before. He was the only lead I had."

"You caught him," I said, "and yet you called the police. Why?"

"How could I have known what he was doing in Lucas' office?" he asked, throwing his hands out in a gesture of helplessness. He looked so boyish, so innocent, with his curly hair going gray at the sides, Tom Sawyer as aging matinee idol. "I assumed he was in there just in his role as troublemaker. So I played it straight and called the cops. That's what you get when you play it straight!" he concluded in a voice of mock indignation.

And because he'd played it straight, I hadn't been suspicious of him and I'd spun my suspicions around an innocent man. I recalled a professor once, warning his class against what he called "the tyranny of the original idea." I was beginning to understand what he meant.

"Eric and I agreed that Eric should visit Horn," Marty continued. "The result, from what I've read in the newspaper, was a little messy. Unnecessarily so, perhaps. Eric is a very excitable guy."

"I got what we wanted from him," Fridell said, "and that's all that matters. I couldn't have gotten it any other way."

"Maybe not, Eric," Marty said, as if soothing a baby. "It must have come as quite a surprise to Eric," he continued, "to learn from Horn that his mistress was behind it all—or ex-mistress, the woman scorned. Because it was Ann-Marie Ekdahl, of course, a woman I hardly knew— Eric and I rarely saw each other in public, and usually only at Calder's social gatherings. There was no 'they' behind the blackmail plot, there was only Ann-Marie.''

"I'm still not sure I get it," I said. "Ann-Marie sent Horn into Calder's office to get evidence with which to blackmail *you?*''

"No, Peggy. She only knew that somebody at the University was feeding Eric classified research for sale abroad. Eric let that slip—during one of their passionate little couplings, I imagine. Ann-Marie apparently had the ability to make weak men babble.''

"Shut up," Fridell said.

"You should be able to take a little ribbing," Marty said pleasantly, "considering how your babbling nearly ruined us. In any case," he went on, "Ann-Marie assumed Calder was Eric's source at the U, since Calder was working with Eric on the astronomy project. But she'd also seen me with Eric a few times, and when Horn told her he hadn't found anything in Calder's computer, she decided to try mine.''

"She sent Mike Parrish in," I said, "at Christmas.''

"I suppose so. Somebody, anyway. She couldn't have done it herself.''

"We were farther along than we'd been before," he went on, "but not much better off. Ann-Marie was upset over Horn's disappearance, of course, and she feared the worst for him. But she still thought she had the upper hand. After all, if anything happened to her, the evidence she had against me would go to the police.''

"What did she have against you?" I asked.

"A floppy disk," Marty replied.

"Floppy disk!" I repeated the words with a disgusted laugh.

"A floppy disk containing a copy of the program I created to take over supercomputer files I'm interested in. You were right about that, Peggy, you were right about a lot of things. The tricky part, you see, isn't breaking into somebody else's computer files—any hacker can do that. The tricky part's creating a program that allows you to breech the supercomputer's security without leaving any traces.

"Until Ann-Marie came along, I kept the program I'd created stored in my computer, just like any other program. Why not? I wasn't suspected of anything, I had no idea anybody would do something . . . well, so underhanded as to break into *my* computer!" He grinned, not at me but at how amusing he found himself. "That's what she stole from my office—or rather, what you say your friend's brother stole from my office at Christmas. He found my control program and simply copied it onto a disk. He also copied the names and passwords of the scientists whose work I've been 'appropriating.' So that's what we're looking for," he concluded, "one common, garden-variety floppy disk."

What a stupid name for something for which three people, so far, had died. It somehow lacked the resonance of "Kohinoor Diamond" or "Maltese Falcon," I thought.

"He had to have been good to find the program in your computer," Carol said.

Marty looked over at her, as if surprised to learn somebody else was in the room with us. "Oh yes," he said to her. "He had to be good." Marty and I both waited for Carol to say something else.

When she didn't, I asked him: "Why didn't you just close up shop when you got the blackmail letter? Erase all the evidence from your computer, or whatever it is you do? Then it would be just her word against yours."

"You don't know what you're saying!" he replied. He got up, began wandering around in my living room. "I've only just gotten started, Peggy. After more than a year of patient, painstaking work, I've managed to get the passwords to the files of engineers, physicists, chemists working for defense contractors all over the state. As you guessed, I get some of the passwords from Lucas—he loves to gossip about his important friends, he's a child that way—but most of them I get directly from the researchers themselves. It isn't hard to get people to discuss their work and get them to tell me their supercomputer passwords—especially after they've spent an evening enjoying Lucas' food and drink. I might start by mentioning that I know somebody whose password is 'Kimberly,' because that's his girlfriend's name, and he'll tell me his password is 'You bitch'—one man's is, as a matter of fact. I've discovered that, since passwords are just between the researcher and the supercomputer, the researchers tend to indulge their fantasies, especially the men.

"Once I have their passwords," Marty went on, "I own them, as you so aptly put it." He picked up a black pottery bowl from New Mexico that my landlady had given me and pretended to look at it, turning it in his hand. "I can log onto their computers," he said, "and modify their programs so that I can access them with passwords of my own invention. And then, whatever's in their files is mine. It's like having access to *all* the forbidden fruit in the Garden of Eden, Peggy, except that God himself doesn't know I'm there. I'm talking about research the Russians, the Israelis, the South Africans—you name it—are willing to pay for. And I'm right in the middle of it! And you're saying that, on account of some fucking female—"

His own dubious achievement and Ann-Marie's threat to it were carrying him away. "Whoa," I said, "you'll bring Mrs. Hammer down here, hollering stuff like that. She's death on sexist losers, Marty, so lower your voice."

"I'm not a loser, Peggy," he said, and put the bowl back where he'd found it. For some reason, the fact that I was tied to a chair, and he wasn't, negated my opinion. "Of course," he went on, "I suspended my operation temporarily, and erased all evidence of it from my computer's memory. When I started up again, I used a copy of my program on a floppy disk, and I take it home with me when I'm finished for the night. Alas, I've learned the hard way not to trust anyone! So if somebody were to look into my files, the way you wanted me to look into Calder's, they'd no longer find any evidence against me."

"So Ann-Marie's floppy disk *is* worthless," I said.

"No, more's the pity. Because while her accusations alone wouldn't convict me, I'd still never be able to do what I'm doing again. And if she produced my control program and the passwords, it would convince a lot of people of my guilt. I'd be ruined.''

''It would certainly cramp your style,'' I agreed. ''It might also pique the FBI's interest enough that they'd take a look into your financial records, maybe ask embarrassing questions about where you get your money. It sounds like Ann-Marie had you stalemated.''

''She did. So we met to discuss it. She was very reasonable—and personable, too. I can almost see why Jason Horn and Michael Parrish fell for her and let her use them. I can even—barely—understand why Eric here might have been careless around her.''

Fridell didn't like being talked about; he stirred uneasily. He was sitting in the well of one of my front windows, a piece of Lake Eleanor's frozen surface just visible in the distance behind him.

''She told me all she wanted was to go back to Sweden to live,'' Marty went on, ''back to her parents' farm. Away from all this mess, she said, tearfully and dramatically— as if she hadn't created the mess herself! She wanted three hundred thousand dollars for her floppy disk.''

''That's *all* she wanted?''

''Yeah. She'd come down in price by the time we talked, you see. She wanted out badly and, I think, she was worried that maybe she'd gotten a tiger by the tail.'' He looked at Fridell. ''I'm surprised she didn't realize that before she started, after having spent so much time in Eric's company. However, I had no intention of paying her anything and then leaving her alive to turn me in anyway, if she took it into her pretty head to do that. Or to come back for more money someday.''

''Let me guess what happened next,'' I said.

''Sure.'' He waited, his chin resting on his arm, watching me.

I thought of being cute and describing what I'd seen at the abandoned house yesterday afternoon, but decided to keep that to myself. They didn't know I'd been in that attic, and it was nice to have something they didn't know about.

''Eric volunteered to torture the whereabouts of the

floppy disk out of her and then kill her, as he'd done with Jason Horn.''

"Yes."

"But it didn't work," I said. I stared at Fridell. "That's right, isn't it? It didn't work." He returned my look without blinking. I wondered if he had eyelids.

"We are hoping that, in spite of Ann-Marie's intransigence, it did work," Marty said.

"Meaning what?"

Fridell broke in suddenly: "Meaning she told me that your friend there knows where Ann-Marie hid it." He pushed away from the window and came over and stared down at Carol.

"Me!" Carol exclaimed.

"Let's hurry this along," Fridell said, turning suddenly to Marty. "I don't want to stay here all day, listening to you tell them how clever you are." He brought something out of a jacket pocket that turned into a knife in his right hand. I'd seen the work it was capable of doing twice before.

"I was about to send Eric to talk to Carol," Marty explained, not letting Eric rush him, "when I met you in the Science Tower lounge. After you'd left, it occurred to me that Carol might be more cooperative if you were there, too. And that way I could get you out of my hair, as well. Especially since I'd seen the expression on your face at something I'd said as we were saying goodbye. What was it that made you begin to suspect me all of a sudden, Peggy?"

"It doesn't matter now, Marty," I said bitterly.

"No, I guess it doesn't. Suspicion is the one thing I don't need, in my line of work, so I suppose I'm glad it's turned out the way it has. Maybe Carol can endure pain, but I doubt that she'll enjoy watching you getting hurt."

"You're wrong," Carol said. "Nothing you can do is going to force me to help you." She said it calmly, as if she really meant it. Oh, good.

"Why do you think Carol knows where Ann-Marie hid the floppy disk?" I asked Marty.

"Ann-Marie told Eric that Carol had it," he replied,

"and she also told him that it would be in the hands of the authorities by spring—the end of April at the latest. According to Eric, her words were 'Carol has it, you see, Carol has it.' She laughed at Eric when she said that. Perhaps, by taunting him, she hoped to goad him into giving her a quicker death."

She'd achieved more than that—if she'd achieved that. By telling him that Carol knew where she'd hidden the evidence against Marty, she was keeping the pendulum swinging, the pendulum of murder she'd helped start herself.

"Did it work?" I asked Fridell. "Did she goad you into killing her?"

He didn't answer that. He said: "I went to her house"— he nodded down at Carol—"and searched it thoroughly, but I found nothing. When I returned to Ann-Marie, she was dead."

Carol started to say something, but I said her name and she stopped and turned to look at me. I shook my head and she kept her mouth shut.

Fridell had just told two lies. One of them was that he'd searched Carol's apartment thoroughly. He hadn't, he'd just taken the picture of the troll, Ann-Marie's Christmas present to Mike. That was what Carol was going to point out before I interrupted her. The other lie was that Ann-Marie had died while he was off getting the picture at Carol's. I didn't think that was true either, because I'd seen the knife wound that killed her. Unless he'd stabbed her in the heart after she was already dead, he was lying. Why?

There wasn't any point in Fridell lying to Carol or me, which meant he was lying to Marty. Knowing that was the only advantage we had.

Ann-Marie, I thought, realizing she was going to die anyway, had teased Fridell, told him something that made him break into Carol's apartment and steal the picture of the troll. And he was lying about it now—not just to us, but to Marty.

" 'Carol has it, you see.' " Fridell repeated the words,

squatting and saying them into Carol's face. "That seems straightforward enough, doesn't it?"

Carol looked at me. I kept my face blank. "No," she answered. "I don't know what she could have meant. I don't have anything you want!"

"Perhaps you have it," Marty said, "and don't know you do."

"Even if I did, I wouldn't tell you. You murdered my brother. I'm not telling you anything."

"Oh dear," Marty said. The tame words were said ironically, but there was real distress on his face.

Eric straightened up, looked at Marty, and Marty nodded. Eric came over to me. Marty turned his back on all of us, appeared to be looking for someplace to hide where he wouldn't have to watch Eric at work.

"Not to worry, Marty," I said, "I know where it is." I said it in a sort of awed voice. Marty turned, a smile of relief appearing on his face. On the other hand, Fridell was looking worried.

I realized then that Fridell knew where Ann-Marie had hidden the floppy disk too, but I wasn't ready to taunt him with that yet. I needed time to consider what that meant and how I could use it. He started toward me again, his knife in his hand.

"What do you think you're doing, Eric?" Marty asked him, puzzled, and that stopped him. Marty said to me, "Something seems to have occurred to you, Peggy. How about telling us what it is?"

"I can do better than that," I told him, "I'll show you. You'll never find it on your own." I turned to Fridell and said, "I don't think even Eric could find it on his own—even though he might think he could." Fridell looked at me as if he were wondering what would happen if he stepped on me, then turned away.

"Peggy," Carol begged, "if you know, don't tell! They're going to kill us anyway. If we don't tell them, we'll ruin their plans. We'll ruin Reid. That's the important thing, isn't it, ruining him? Don't tell them!"

"I'm sorry, Carol," I said, "but I don't like pain. Let's

let them have their freedom for as long as it lasts. That's a punishment, too, for men like these."

"Just tell us," Fridell said, standing close to me, "and save the sermon."

"No." I suddenly felt the laughter bubbling in me, because I'd solved another part of the puzzle, and maybe I was hysterical, too. To Marty I said, "Carol's brother broke into your office, found your wonderful control program, copied it, and brought it up to Ann-Marie at Carol's parents' farm. I was there. That's where she hid it. It's up north, a hundred miles or so. And don't imagine that Carol's parents know where it is, they don't. I'm the only one who knows. It's beautifully hidden, and you'll never find it on your own. And it *will* come out of hiding—I'd say no later than the first of May. Don't you think so, Carol?"

Then I could see on her face that Carol knew, too. She didn't say anything, just stared at me. She must have heard something in my voice—the confidence, whatever. As Fridell turned, reluctantly, to Marty, I met her gaze and winked.

Marty saw that. "I hope this isn't some sort of joke," he said. "If it is, if you're wasting our time, Peggy, I promise you, I'll *feed* you to Eric." The skin around his mouth was white. Why hadn't I noticed the muscles around his mouth before, and how large his teeth were? It's hard to kick yourself when you're tied to a chair. "How long will it take to drive there?" he asked.

"Two, two and a half hours," I said. "It depends on the roads."

Marty looked at the other man, thinking, trying to make up his mind.

"I can handle this," Fridell said. "I can make her talk, just as I made Jason Horn talk." He was almost pleading with Marty.

"You'd like that, Fridell, wouldn't you?" I said. "To be alone with us, the only one to hear what we have to say. To report back to Marty what you want him to *think* we told you, and with us no longer there to contradict you. The way it was with Ann-Marie."

Even though he wasn't moving at the time, he froze,

visibly, like Eskimos think the damned do in hell. Marty looked from me to him. "What does she mean by that, Eric?" he asked.

"Ask her," Fridell said, "I don't know." He was looking frightened and, at the same time, looking like the sort of man you don't want to frighten often.

I had nothing to gain by telling Marty what I'd meant. He'd put his pistol back into his jacket and I doubted he could get it out fast enough, if Fridell attacked him with his knife. And no matter which of them won in a fight like that, Carol and I would still be tied to chairs and we'd still die.

"Do you want me to show you where Ann-Marie hid her evidence or not?" I asked him.

He didn't answer for a few moments. Then he said, "My car's out front. I'll drive."

Twenty-nine

Fridell untied us from the chairs and retied our hands behind our backs, then draped our jackets over us. Each man took one of us by the arm and led us out of the house to Marty's BMW.

Marty held the back door and I got in. To anybody watching, we were two women on our way to breakfast with rich men. It was a dark morning, sleet mixed with snow was falling, heavy and wet.

I scooted awkwardly over to the middle and Carol got in after me. We stayed close together, our shoulders touching through our jackets.

Marty pulled away from the curb and, as he did, Fridell let us see his knife.

"I have this in my lap," he said.

Carol said, "Great! So much for my plan to take over the car. Let's just relax, Peggy, and enjoy the ride."

"Okay by me." I smiled at her and hoped she'd look at me and see it.

Marty drove slowly, his wipers making easy work of the wet ice and snow. When he'd turned onto the freeway and picked up speed, I asked him why he was doing all this. "You've got a good future as a teacher and scientist," I said. "Are you so greedy that you need to earn money like this—or is it ideological?"

"Ideological—me? Don't be silly, Peggy, it's just business. I'm very fond of money, and this seems to me to be a nearly foolproof way to make lots of it. As you say, I've got a 'good' future as a scientist. But not a great future.

I'm not my father, may he rest in peace—I'm not even Lucas Calder. I just have Calder's tastes."

" 'They name buildings after the Calders of the world, not the Reids,' " I said, quoting him.

He laughed. "Exactly. I have to make the best of my situation. I found myself in a scientific field that's virtually innocuous, in terms of research that's useful to national defense—but I do have access to the supercomputers, which other people whose work isn't so innocent use. It occurred to me one day that I was surrounded by research that would be worth a great deal of money, if I could get my hands on it. And I suspected that wouldn't be very hard to do. It seemed to me to be both an interesting challenge and a great business opportunity. I don't know which of those had the greater appeal for me."

"You're committing espionage," I said.

"Industrial espionage. There's a difference. I'm not a traitor, giving away military secrets like codes and troop movements, the names of our spies abroad. I'm just a businessman, Peggy."

"Businessmen don't murder people," Carol said.

Fridell laughed. Marty said, "We could discuss that, I suppose. It would serve nicely to pass the time."

"You murdered my brother," she said.

"No," Marty said, "I didn't. He must have been Ann-Marie's problem, not mine, and she didn't share him with me. She never told me the name of the man she conned into breaking into my office after Jason Horn. Did she tell you, Eric? Did you know about this?"

"No," Fridell replied, not appearing to be very interested in the question.

"Perhaps Ann-Marie killed him herself," Marty said.

Mike Parrish's death seemed to have happened a long time ago, and almost in another world. It no longer seemed very interesting to me either. At least Eric Fridell and I had that in common. But it did seem odd that, if they'd killed Mike, they wouldn't admit it now. After all, Carol and I weren't getting out of this alive, and they'd already admitted committing two murders.

The sleet turned into light snow and then, after about

an hour, stopped entirely, but the sky stayed overcast. There was a lot of traffic, people on their way to do normal things, unlike us. Marty turned on the radio and the car was suddenly flooded with music, one of Schubert's impromptus. I was afraid he'd switch to a rock station, but he mercifully left the dial where it was. I was moving my wrists in the ropes, slowly, so as not to rub the skin off, but enough to keep the blood flowing. Carol, I noticed, was doing that, too. Once she tried to move her hands over to where I could reach them with my fingers, but there was no way to do that without twisting our bodies, and Marty or Fridell would have seen that.

Fridell put a cigarette in his mouth and lit it.

"Slimeball!" Carol hissed. "I don't suppose it would occur to you that some people are allergic to cigarette smoke."

"I don't like the smell of cigarettes either, Eric," Marty said. "Put it out."

Fridell took a deep drag, exhaled, and then started to roll down the window.

"Not out the window!" Marty said. There are laws against that. Marty wasn't taking any chances on getting stopped.

"I wasn't planning to throw it out the window," Fridell explained. "I was just cracking the window a little to let out the smoke."

"I said put the cigarette out, Eric," Marty repeated. "Use the ashtray."

Fridell continued to smoke, found something outside his window to stare at.

They were a happy pair of conspirators.

The freeway became a four-lane highway, the strip malls began to give way to farmland. There was still a lot of snow on the ground; there'd been no major thaws up here.

The Schubert ended and a voice that sounded as if it had been dipped in Vaseline announced the next piece, a Mozart piano concerto. I was glad that one of the last pieces of music I would hear in my life would probably be Mozart. The thought of how silly that thought was made me giggle.

"What's the joke, Peggy?" Marty wanted to know.

"She's hysterical," Fridell said, his voice suggesting that that's just about what you'd expect of a woman on her way to a painful death.

Carol leaned into me, but she looked at me with a half smile, as if asking me to let her in on the joke. It looked as if she'd forgotten she was mad at me, at least for now.

"If you are playing some kind of trick on me," Marty said, "either of you, you will regret it very much."

"Why don't bad guys ever contract words when they're making threats?" I asked him. " 'You will regret it very much,' " I repeated, in as deep a voice as I had. "And besides, Carol and I aren't playing tricks on you. Somebody in this car is, but it's not us."

"You seem to be full of little arch hints about Eric," Marty asked. "Are you trying to make me nervous?"

"Yes."

Carol told Marty where to turn off the state highway onto a paved county road. We drove west for about twenty minutes, retracing the route we'd taken at Christmas. I should have been exhausted and fighting sleep in the warm car, but I wasn't; I'd never been more awake in my life. I looked occasionally in the sideview mirror next to Marty, to see if anybody was following us, but as we drove deeper into the country, the roads got emptier. The sides of the roads were walls of snow in places, and beyond them the fields were billowing seas of white. We were driving back into winter.

Carol continued to give Marty directions. She sounded resentful about it, but she did it anyway. I was glad of that because I was lost, as I'd been at Christmas. If she refused to give them directions, I wouldn't be able to.

I felt depressed suddenly, not because I was going to die soon, but because I'd gotten Carol and myself into this mess through my own stupidity. Because Ann-Marie had sent Horn into the wrong office, I'd jumped to the conclusion that Calder was the man I was after. That wasn't all of it, of course; I'd had some pretty good reasons to suspect Calder, but it was still my fault. Oddly enough, it was Marty who brought me out of it.

"Don't blame yourself, Peggy," he said, and smiled at me in the rearview mirror. "It's all Ann-Marie's fault."

He was feeling pretty good about himself, he could afford to be generous. After all, he had one woman, now dead, to blame for his problem, and two more trouble-making women, soon to be dead, about to get him out of it. Who wouldn't feel upbeat, in his situation? It occurred to me that a woman who'd tried, however ineffectually and misguidedly, to cut Marty Reid and Eric Fridell down to size, couldn't be all bad.

But if I was going to finish the job Ann-Marie'd started, I was going to have to get busy.

"How much farther is it?' Fridell asked.

I got busy. "What's your hurry, Eric?" I said. "There's nothing left for you back in town."

He turned and looked at me with his cold eyes.

I was feeling just as cold, in spite of the fact that it was warm in the car. For some reason, I thought of my father—the con-man, hustler—who played bad hands just about every day of his life, and even managed to win with them sometimes. I was his daughter, and I asked for his help.

"When you burned the old house down yesterday," I said to Fridell, "I was there, in the attic with Ann-Marie."

"You—" he said, and then shut up. He watched me, waited for me to go on.

"Me, yes. I followed you there from Terry Rhodes' place. And after I escaped from the fire, I went to a Homicide detective, a friend of mine, and told him all about you and what I'd seen of what you'd done. When I turn up missing, he's going to know who to look for."

"Why aren't they looking for me now? Why haven't they arrested me yet?" It took him two tries to get the questions out.

"They want to be sure first. Get an identification on Ann-Marie's body."

Marty said, "If you're the only witness, Peggy, I don't think they're going to have much of a case against Eric."

"They'll have enough. Enough, at least, to wreck Eric's stay in this country. They'll find people in Ed. Tech who'll testify that Eric and Ann-Marie were lovers and that Eric lied about her having gone out of the country on business. Maybe Eric'll beat a murder rap. He'll spend a lot of time and money doing it, though, and he'll be finished in his particular line of work—whether *you* survive or not, Marty.'' I paused a moment to let all that sink in, and then I said, ''You're not going to have much use for Eric after today. What's Eric going to do for a living now?''

Fridell managed a laugh. ''She's trying to cause trouble between us, Marty.''

''I can see that, Eric.''

''Wouldn't dream of it,'' I assured them both, then said: ''Whoever owns the floppy disk we're going after, owns the research, present and future, of all the scientists whose names and passwords are on it.''

''What of it?'' Marty asked.

Fridell stirred in his jacket. When Marty's eyes came up to look at me in the rearview mirror, I met them with a wink.

''Give that a little thought,'' I told him and added, trying to imitate his voice, ''it will serve nicely to pass the time.''

A minute later we drove by Carol's parents' farm. Neither man seemed to attach any particular significance to it; they both seemed deep in other thoughts. Carol's father was walking toward one of the outbuildings, away from us.

I looked at Carol. When she felt my eyes on her, she turned and gave me a sudden smile. I leaned into her, put my head on the shoulder of her jacket, and her fine hair tickled my cheek and nose.

She was watching for the turn-off that led down to the lake. I'd been hoping she'd take us to the cabin by way of the road this time, since if the car went through the ice, Carol and I wouldn't have a chance to get out, but she didn't. ''Slow now,'' she told Marty, and, a moment later, ''Turn there,'' and Marty braked and turned and we bumped our way down to the lake and across its frozen surface.

Thirty

"This is the place?" Marty asked, as he turned off his engine on the shore beneath the cabin. "Help them out, Eric."

"No," I said. "We're not getting out until you've untied us."

Fridell laughed.

"Come on now, Peggy," Marty said, "what're you trying to do now? You don't have anything to bargain with."

"Yes, we do. We're not getting out with our hands tied behind our backs."

Fridell put the point of his knife close to my right eye. The knife was trembling slightly, perhaps because Fridell was cold.

I didn't flinch away. "I don't want to be hurt," I told him, staring cross-eyed down the blade to his fingers, "and I don't want to be blind. Every day of my life, I'm learning to see a little better, and I want to continue my progress. If you blind me in even one eye, Fridell, if you hurt me at all, I won't tell you what you want to know—just as Ann-Marie didn't. And Carol won't either, you know that. So go ahead and waste this chance you think you have. Get blood all over Marty's big, expensive car. Why not? Without my help, Marty won't be keeping it long anyway. I'm not getting out with my hands tied behind my back." It was a long speech and I delivered it well.

Marty brought his revolver out of his jacket. "Untie them, Eric. Cut the ropes. Do you have a gun?"

"No." I wasn't sure what Eric was saying no to. I tried

203

to breathe normally until I found out. He looked at me. The deadness behind his pale eyes seemed to harden, if that's possible, but nothing changed on his face. "All right," he said. "I want to get this over with, too. But don't try to be clever. There are good ways to die and bad ways."

"You know all about that, don't you?" I turned my back to him, held out my arms. He cut the ropes—why not, since he wasn't planning to use them again?—shoved my face roughly down into Carol's lap so he could saw off her ropes, and then backed out of the car and let us crawl out, too. Marty stood a little distance away, covering us with his pistol.

The lake was empty and silent, a white surface stretching to the shore we'd come from a quarter of a mile away, its flatness broken by the crazy silhouette of the fishing village against the leaden sky.

I stood there massaging my wrists, then put my hands in my pockets. I wanted them to be warm and functioning, in case I had some further use for them.

"What are you waiting for?" Fridell demanded. "Let's get this over with. I don't like being cold."

"Do you have a key," Marty asked Carol, "or do we break in?"

"We don't need to go inside," I said. "Just follow me."

I didn't wait to see what they would do, I just started up the wooden steps that led from the lake to the cabin. I stopped at the top, in front of the cabin, and waited for them to catch up. In the side yard, I could see the snowman we'd made at Christmas, just visible against the brush and trees. Snow that had fallen since we'd been there at Christmas covered its head and shoulders, blurring its outline, but the face was still an evil thing, the nose larger and more hooked than before beneath the massive brows and above the twisted driftwood grin.

I pointed to it. "Look over there, Eric. What do you see?"

He looked where I was pointing.

"I don't see anything." He started over toward it, uncertainly.

I waited until he was almost there. Then, *"Carol's troll,"* I said in a harsh whisper, trying to imitate the way I'd remembered Ann-Marie saying it at Christmas: *"Carol's troll!"*

He spun around as if he'd heard a ghost, I jumped back, tripped, and fell into the snow. He started toward me and I shouted at Marty to stop him, scrambling to my feet.

"Eric!" Marty's voice cracked like a whip and Fridell stopped abruptly and turned to look at him.

"Ann-Marie didn't tell Eric *only* that Carol had the evidence," I said to Marty. "She told him it was hidden in Carol's troll. You saw his reaction when I said those words."

"It's a lie, Marty," Fridell shouted. "Don't you see what she's trying to do?" He was still shaken from having heard again Ann-Marie's dying words, mocking him as he stood over her. The knife trembled in his hand.

"How do you know that, Peggy?" Marty asked, moving closer to us, keeping his gun moving among the three of us.

Carol said, "Because he didn't search my apartment the way he told you he did. He told you he'd searched it *thoroughly,* but all he did was take one thing—a picture that Ann-Marie gave my brother, a picture of a troll. He thought that's what she'd meant when she said she'd hidden the evidence in my troll."

"I found the picture in the attic of the house where Fridell tortured and killed Ann-Marie," I went on. "The frame, anyway, and the glass. Next to her body, smashed to bits. God, how she must have laughed!"

"They're making this all up, Marty," Fridell said. He switched his knife from his right to his left hand, dropped his right hand into his jacket pocket. He grinned, a buddy's grin.

"I wouldn't put it past Peggy to make up something like that," Marty said mildly. "But didn't you notice how the two girls take turns telling the story? When did they have time to make it up and rehearse their lines, Eric?"

I said: "Eric knew Ed. Tech's days were numbered. Eric was going to have to head back to Europe—empty-handed, just the way he'd come here. Emigrants never like doing that—do they, Eric? But you figured that, with Ann-Marie's floppy disk, you could go on being Marty's partner in crime, even if he decided he no longer needed you. You killed Ann-Marie in a rage when you discovered the disk wasn't in the picture—and because she was laughing at you. You planned to go to work on Carol on your own then, make her tell you what Ann-Marie'd meant by 'Carol's troll.' Unfortunately, this time Marty wanted to make a party out of it." I turned to Marty. "Ann-Marie's dead now, Marty, but what good's that going to do you with Eric alive?"

"Eric," Marty said, his revolver no longer moving, "please take your hand out of your pockets, slowly." And when Eric was slow to obey him, he went on, as if coaxing a child. "We'll get the package. We'll take care of the girls, then we'll go back to town where we can be warm and discuss all this. I realize that we have lots to discuss."

As Fridell started to bring his hand out of his pocket, a figure burst out from behind the cabin. It was Terry Rhodes. One moment he wasn't there—nobody was—and the next he was stumbling through the snow at Fridell, his arms flailing, screaming, "You killed Ann-Marie!" It was as if the troll had come to life and was going on a rampage.

When Fridell's hand finished the gesture of coming out of his jacket, there was a gun in it.

Marty shot him.

Fridell staggered back, regained his balance and fell onto one knee as Marty's second shot missed. Holding his pistol with both hands, Fridell aimed and fired at Marty. Marty fired again and Fridell fell back as if hit by a train.

Marty sat down in the snow. He tried to twist his body around toward us, but then Carol was there. She reached down and took the gun before it could fall out of his dying hand and stood up and pointed it at Rhodes.

Rhodes was trying to dig Fridell's gun out of the snow.

"Who are you?" she called to him. She didn't raise her

voice, but she didn't have to. Sound carries well when it's cold.

"I'm Ann-Marie's husband," he said.

"Terry Rhodes." She nodded. "I thought you might be. There's something I want you to tell me, Terry. But first, stop looking for the gun."

Still bent over, he looked up at her. She was pointing Marty's pistol at him with both hands, arms outstretched. Like her brother, she'd grown up with guns. She knew how to use them and wasn't afraid to.

"It's over now, isn't it?" he said. "They're dead. I'm free of all of them now, Ann-Marie, too!" He started crying. "Ann-Marie, too."

"I'm going to shoot you, Terry," Carol said.

"No, you're not!" He straightened up, put his hands in the air. You don't shoot people whose hands are in the air.

"I want you to tell me how you found your way up here," she told him.

"I saved your lives! I followed them to your apartment. I wanted to find out what Eric'd done with Ann-Marie. Then I followed you to hers"—he pointed to me. "And then I followed you up here."

"No," Carol said. "I looked in the sideview mirror a lot, hoping somebody was following us. You might have followed us from town, but once we got on the county roads, I'd have seen you. Reid would have seen you, too. You didn't follow us, Terry, you knew the way. You've been up here before."

"No!"

Carol fired. The shot went over his head and hit the snow troll's driftwood smile, made it disappear.

"You came up here and killed Mike," she went on. "You followed Ann-Marie's directions."

"I didn't kill him," he shouted, "she did!" He fell onto his hands and knees in the snow.

"Why?"

"She talked your brother into breaking into Reid's office, to get whatever it was she wanted. I never knew what it was, it wasn't my business. When he got it, he brought it up here at Christmas. Then Jason Horn disappeared.

Your brother figured out what that meant. He got scared, he was intending to go to the cops, thought he wouldn't go to jail if he confessed. He wanted her to confess, too. He was going to go away for a while, to think things over, he said, before he did anything, and he came up here to get his skis. She came with him, and I came up after them. I just thought we were going to try to scare him, that's all. When I got here, she killed him. I drove her back to town.''

"You said Mike found out about Ann-Marie's connection with Jason Horn," Carol said. "How?"

He hadn't expected that question. Neither had I. His mouth opened, but no words came out.

"How?"

"I loved her," he said softly.

"Right," Carol replied, not much moved by that. "*You* told Mike about Horn's relationship with Ann-Marie."

Rhodes licked his lips, looked around for help. Nothing looked very promising.

"That's why he decided to go to the police," she continued. "Not because he was scared, Terry, but because, thanks to you, he knew she'd made a chump out of him."

"He let her come up here with him anyway," Rhodes said, as if that were an extenuating circumstance.

"You set him up to die," she said.

"I wanted her back, you see."

I stood off to one side, watched and waited. There was just Carol with her pistol dipping toward the snow as if measuring the decrease in her anger and Rhodes on all fours, his face resembling a dog's I'd once seen, its back broken, in the street when I was a child.

For a long time there was only the silence and the breathing, the two of them and the two bodies, and then I realized Carol wasn't going to kill Rhodes, and I was glad about that. He wasn't worth an execution, and she was too good for the job.

"Make yourself—" she said, and had to stop and clear her throat and start over. "Make yourself useful. Go get what we've both lost so much for, you and I."

Rhodes didn't seem to understand the words at first, just

stared at her, his mouth open. And then he realized she wasn't going to kill him. He lowered his head into the snow, as if to hide his face.

When he brought it up again, he was the troll. His eyes were burning, he had Fridell's pistol in his hand, and it was coming up at Carol.

She fired once and he went back into the snow.

Thirty-one

We found what all the killing was about wrapped in Ann-Marie's bright red scarf, the one she'd brought from Sweden that she was so proud of. We found it where a troll's heart would be, if trolls had hearts. Maybe that was just coincidence, maybe it was another one of Ann-Marie's jokes.

Carol's father would have found the scarf in late spring, in the grass, where the troll had been.

Wrapped inside was a padded manilla envelope. It contained a blue soft plastic case that held one floppy disk. The disk looked like a 45 RPM record, but square and not at all floppy. There was also a letter.

As we stood next to the demolished snow troll and the three dead men, I read the letter aloud to Carol. It sounded like an elaborate explanation of a series of events nobody could remember.

It started to snow.

"Where'd he come from?" I asked, looking down at Terry Rhodes.

"Back there." She gestured at the trees behind the troll. "Where the road is that we use in the summer. That must be how he came up here the last time, too. So nobody on the lake would see him, or see him drive off with Ann-Marie, after—" She stopped, cleared her throat. "Funny, he got here just in time to mess up your plan and die," she added.

I just looked at her.

"I mean," she explained, trying to smile through her

210

tears, "you had it all worked out so Reid and Fridell were going to shoot each other, right? Rhodes' arrival messed up the symmetry of it."

I wasn't so sure the end would have been that symmetrical.

"If he hadn't shown up," I said, "you'd probably never have learned how Mike died, and why—or even who did it, for sure."

"I still don't know who did it for sure," she said. "Rhodes might've been lying, he might have done it himself. Anyway, what difference does it make now?"

We went down to Marty's car and Carol drove us back to town. The trip across the lake didn't bother me this time; I was too preoccupied with trying to figure out how to clear up the mess at the Parrishes' summer place with a minimum of fuss.

When we got to my apartment, I called Customs and asked for G.B. or George. I didn't remember their last names. I heard some mumbling, as whoever answered called out something with his hand covering the mouthpiece. It sounded like "Tweedledee" or "Tweedledum," and then the man spoke to me again, said he'd have one of them return my call. I told him it was urgent, gave him my phone number, and Carol and I sat in my living room eating toast and drinking coffee.

G. B. and George didn't call first, they just came over.

I explained what had happened since the last time I'd seen them. Their faces grew longer as they listened.

"You really queered our scheme," George said when I'd finished, uncharacteristically blunt.

"No," I said, "spring did. The threat of spring. Ann-Marie told Marty Reid that if she died, her evidence against him would be in the hands of the authorities by spring—by the end of April. That's why the people at Ed. Tech panicked, why Fridell tortured Ann-Marie and then killed her and came after Carol, and why Ed. Tech's owner took off for South Africa, too. It had nothing to do with me."

"And Ann-Marie was right," Carol said, rubbing it in.

"My dad would've found her scarf when he went to open the cabin up, as soon as the ice is gone from the lake."

"I warned you," I added, "that Ann-Marie was a loose wire in your scheme. You should have listened to me."

"*C'est la guerre!*" G. B. said bravely.

"You win some, you lose some," George translated.

"You didn't know about Martin Reid and Fridell," I said.

"We might have," George replied.

"No," G. B. admitted, "we didn't."

"I didn't think so. You were so happy to be using Ed. Tech. to play tricks on the Russians that you didn't notice what Reid and Fridell were doing right under your noses."

"It wasn't our scheme anyway," George said, getting defensive about it. "Some friends of ours thought it up. They just put us in charge of keeping it running smoothly."

"It'll work again," G. B. said with conviction. "There are lots of companies out there anxious to earn the dishonest buck smuggling technology out of the country, and there's new technology being created every day, as the old becomes obsolete. There's always been smuggling, there always will be, and right now we're living in a golden age for smugglers." He seemed very pleased by that, as well he might, since, after all, it paid his bills.

"As things stand," I said, "nobody but us knows what you—or your friends—were using Ed. Tech. for. It'll be hard to work that little con again, if your scheme gets out."

"It won't get out," George said.

"What's your point?" G. B. asked, giving me a narrow look.

"It's going to be hard—to put it mildly—for Carol and me, or Carol's parents, to explain the stiffs scattered around up there in front of the cabin."

"Stiffs!" George repeated, shocked.

"We'll probably have to explain the entire business, from A to Z, including what you and your friends were doing, and what Reid and Fridell were doing that you didn't know about. If necessary—"

"You wouldn't do that," George said. "That would be—"

"You won't have to," G. B. said, getting up, shifting quickly into action mode. "We'll take care of it. It was snowing up there when you left, you say? Great! It's a weekday too, the lake'll be deserted on a weekday." He headed for the door, trailed by George. "By spring," G. B. called back, "there won't be anything up there but trees in leaf and birds making nests in them and singing and crapping and laying eggs."

They left, on their never-ending quest for national security. Carol and I sat drinking coffee for a few minutes in silence. Then she asked me: "What do you suppose she wanted out of it?"

"Who?" I asked.

"Ann-Marie, of course! I mean, do you think she wanted Fridell, but he dropped her, or just wanted a share of the profits?"

"I don't know." I suddenly recalled the image Betty Hall had given me, of Ann-Marie looking up at a man who was talking down to her. Something about Ann-Marie had appealed to Betty then.

"I hate her," Carol said, "even though she wasn't a whole lot worse than Mike—and I don't hate him. But I know so many good things about him. I don't know anything good about her."

I'd disliked—well, let's be honest, hated—her, too. "I create myself, sometimes as I go along," she'd said to me. And she'd suggested I try it—unless I liked the role I was playing, she'd added, smiling.

I thought of the last time I'd seen her smile.

Carol saw me shudder, asked what it meant.

"Nothing." I began straightening up my living room. "I'd like to visit the cabin in the summer," I told her. It was really a question. I was asking whether she'd ever go up there again.

"That Customs man was right about how it is in the

spring,'' she said. ''But it's even more beautiful in the summer, when the wild flowers are in bloom.''

My phone rang then. I assumed it was either Buck checking up on me, or Al wanting to know about dinner. I went to answer it.

ELLIOTT ROOSEVELT'S
DELIGHTFUL MYSTERY SERIES

MURDER IN THE OVAL OFFICE
70528-1/$4.50US/$5.50Can

An Alabama congressman is dead...shot to death in the Oval Office. The evidence points to suicide, but the First Lady decides to investigate the matter herself.

*Don't miss these other mysteries
featuring Fird Lady Eleanor Roosevelt*

MURDER AND THE FIRST LADY
69937-0/$3.95US/$4.95Can

THE HYDE PARK MURDER
70058-1/$3.95US/$4.95Can

MURDER AT HOBCAW BARONY
70021-2/$3.95US/$4.95Can

THE WHITE HOUSE PANTRY MURDER
70404-8/$3.95US/$4.95Can

MURDER AT THE PALACE
70405-6/$3.95 US/$4.95Can